Copyright © 2

The right of Peter Jay Black to be
been asserted in accordance with the Copyright, Design and Patents Act
1988.

All rights reserved. No part of this book may be reproduced, stored in or transmitted into any retrieval system, in any form on, or by any means (electronic, mechanical, photocopying, recording or otherwise) without permission in writing from the publisher, except by a reviewer who may quote brief passages in a review. Any person who does any unauthorised act in relation to this publication may be liable to criminal prosecution and civil claims for damages.

This is a work of fiction. Names, characters, businesses, brands, titles, places, events, locales, and incidents are either the products of the author's imagination or used in a fictitious manner. Any resemblance to actual persons, living or dead, or actual events is purely coincidental.

1 2 3 4 5 6 7 8 9 10

OAKBRIDGE
K150724
ISBN 9781739549657 (paperback)
ISBN 9781739549664 (eBook)
A CIP catalogue record for this book is available from the British Library

Black, Peter Jay
Murder on the Finsbury Flyer / Peter Jay Black

London

Note to the reader
This work is a mid-Atlantic edit.
A considered style choice of both British and American spelling, grammar, and terms usage.

Visit peterjayblack.com and join the free VIP list to be notified of future releases in the series.

*Also grab a **FREE** copy of*
DEATH IN BROOKLYN
A Short Story set in the Fast-Paced
Emma & Nightshade Crime Thriller Series

IMPORTANT

Please remember to check your spam folder for any emails. You must confirm your sign-up before being added to the email list.

Ruth Morgan Investigates...

PETER JAY BLACK

1

Ruth Morgan, her teenage grandson Greg, and a perplexed Scottish car park attendant found themselves in a peculiar standoff. They stared up at a steel bar swathed in yellow and black tape, several feet above their heads.

Ruth cleared her throat and tried not to allow desperation to edge her voice. "You're absolutely positively sure there's no way to raise it?" She waved a hand at the bar in a dramatic fashion. "This height-restriction thing. You can't make an exception for us?" Ruth had a sneaking suspicion batting her eyelids wouldn't help.

Indeed, the car park attendant gawped at her as though she'd informed him aliens had landed in Scotland nine hundred years ago and built Edinburgh Castle using nothing but space rays and stardust.

Ruth sighed and looked from the unyielding bar to the rooftop of her motorhome. The former was two inches lower, so zero chance her beloved tin palace would slide underneath. Plus, it was already evening, so they didn't have time for this nonsense.

Her narrowed eyes swept the car park on the other side of the barrier. It sat there all flat and concrete-y, taunting her with its smug, featureless expanse. To add insult to injury, her client had reserved ten spaces in the far corner. Ample room, but no way to reach it.

Ruth growled. "Just blinkin' typical."

They were on their way to her first paying food-consultancy gig in almost a month. A vital job she hoped would get things back on track since the disaster on board the *Ocean Odyssey*. It promised to be a high-profile affair too, with plenty of future clients to impress, so Ruth did not want to be late.

"So near, and yet so far," she said through clenched teeth.

For a fleeting moment, Ruth considered abandoning Greg with the motorhome and forging ahead on foot. But deserting her grandson was unthinkable. Well, almost. Besides, Greg was far nimbler than Ruth, and even with the element of surprise in her favour, he would catch up to her in a few paces.

The three of them flinched at the blast of a car horn.

Greg peered round the side of the motorhome. "There's like fifteen cars waiting behind us now."

"What do they expect me to do?" Ruth pulled her long black coat tight, and adjusted her bright pink beanie and scarf. "It's not as if I can reverse out of here now, is it?"

They'd followed a narrow lane between buildings to reach the current predicament, and Edinburgh's mazelike roads weren't renowned for their motorhome-accommodating girth.

Another car horn blared, this one more incessant and higher pitched.

Greg's cheeks flushed scarlet. "So embarrassing."

"Nonsense. It's not our fault." Ruth eyed the car park attendant.

He blinked at her. "I didnae set the height restriction. It's nae my fault either." His gaze shifted to the motorhome.

Ruth let out another long breath. "Nothing else for it, then." She motioned to Greg. "Go on, before I change my mind."

His brow furrowed. "Huh?"

Ruth pointed at the bar high above their heads. "Climb up there."

Greg gaped at her. "And do what, exactly?"

"See if you can unbolt it."

"The bar? How?" Greg flinched at another blasting car horn.

"We must have tools in the motorhome. I'm pretty sure there's a screwdriver in the bottom of the utility cupboard. Try that."

Greg shook his head with a look of pained exasperation. "It's got a broken handle."

Ruth faced the car park attendant. "Do you have an adjustable spanner?"

"No."

"Pliers?"

"No."

"Anything at all that may help?"

He glanced up at the bar. "It's welded in place."

"A saw, then?"

"Yer nae removin' it," the car park attendant snapped. "Boss would kill me."

Ruth threw her hands in the air. "Well, that leaves us with only one alternative." She couldn't believe how thoroughly unhelpful the men were being.

"What are you going to do?" Greg asked in a hushed

voice, as though fearing her actions would set off a chain reaction of bad karma.

Ruth inclined her head. "I thought I'd play upbeat calypso songs and ask my giant motorhome to kindly limbo under the nasty bar."

Greg snorted. "That's your plan?"

"Would be if I could find a big enough grass skirt at such short notice." Ruth smirked. "It still is my plan, in a manner of speaking. Sans the music and the Caribbean attire." She tapped her chin. "Although now you mention it, I do fancy a trip to Trinidad and Tobago." Ruth looked up at Scotland's overcast sky and shivered.

Yet another car horn blared.

Ruth poked her tongue out at her grandson, marched around the motorhome, waved at the not-so-patient drivers, and knelt by a rear tyre. She removed the dust cap and pressed a key into the valve.

Air hissed.

Greg rushed over to her. "What are you doing?"

"Solving a problem with a bad idea." Ruth then muttered, "Story of my life." She nodded to the other side. "Do that one."

Together, Ruth and Greg released pressure from the motorhome's tyres at the back and then moved to the front. As the wheeled metal mansion dipped, Ruth peered up at the bar.

The car park attendant looked at her as though she were mad. Or a genius. It was hard to tell.

Once they were done, Ruth straightened. "Come on, Gregory." She stepped on board the motorhome with a supreme level of confidence this would do the trick, and she slid into the driver's seat.

Greg dropped into the passenger side, looking nervous.

He stared up at the height-restriction bar through the windscreen. "This will never work."

"Have a little faith." Ruth rubbed the exposed backside of the ornamental gnome on her dashboard, said a silent prayer to the wheeled-home gods, and turned the ignition key. The engine rattled to life. "Here we go." She edged the metal beast forward, and the tyres made a horrible *thrup, thrup, thrup*.

Both Ruth and Greg gazed up at the bar, as did the car park attendant, who'd retreated to the relative safety of his hut.

Coward.

The front of the motorhome passed under the bar by a hair's width.

"See?" Ruth said. "'O ye of little faith.'" She winced at a scraping sound. "Okay, so the roof might need a little repainting here and there." Ruth would send her grandson up with a spray can. *No big deal.*

Greg turned in his seat and stared at the ceiling. "It'll hit the skylights."

"It will be fine," Ruth said. "The back of the motorhome is quite a bit lower than the fron—"

There came a loud grinding, followed by metal tearing, and then a deep clunk as something expensive and important broke free.

"Front skylight's gone."

"Yes, thank you, Gregory." Ruth kept her foot on the accelerator. "No need for a running commentar—"

Another ear-splitting crunch intercepted her words, followed by more metal tearing, and then a repeat of the familiar clunk.

"Other skylight's gone."

"Awesome." Ruth gritted her teeth. "That means there's

nothing else to—" She winced at a rapid staccato, and yet another grinding, this one accompanied by a high-pitched screech. "What's that?"

Greg faced forward and crossed his arms. "TV antenna."

"Well, that doesn't matter." Ruth gripped the steering wheel so hard her knuckles stretched white. "Stupid thing never worked anyway."

The shrill scraping continued for a few seconds and then cut off, leaving nothing but an ear-ringing silence.

Ruth sighed. "There you go. Easy-peasy, Morgan-squeezy." She drove in a straight line across the concrete expanse, but had a little more trouble when she turned the wheel. The motorhome took a wide, metal-grinding arc, and she finally managed to pull into the allotted spaces. Ruth turned off the engine, and climbed from the motorhome with Greg.

Outside, the pair of them stared at the carnage they'd left behind.

Lying beneath the height-restricted bar of doom were two skylights, a TV antenna, several strips of plastic trim, and around a billion flakes of white paint that danced in the Scottish breeze.

The car park attendant glared at them from his hut.

"He looks like he's in the world's worst snow globe." Ruth swallowed. "Be a good lad and fetch all that stuff."

Greg muttered a few swear words as he marched back to the entrance, along with something about dying of embarrassment.

So dramatic.

Ruth gave the car park attendant a thumbs-up and climbed into her motorhome. "Merlin?"

There came a raspy meow from his oak box.

Ruth looked inside. "Hey. There you are, sweetie pie."

Merlin sat pressed against the rear wall, back arched, his midnight fur on end.

"Oh, come on," Ruth said. "It wasn't that bad. All fine now. No one was hurt."

Merlin glowered at her.

"Well, if you're going to be like that, feel free to let me know the moment you grow opposable thumbs and can take over driving duties." Ruth huffed. "Until that day, stop giving me accusatory looks." She fetched a cat treat, placed it on his cushion by way of an apology, and then padded to her bedroom.

On Ruth's bed sat an open suitcase, already packed with essentials: wash bag, several sets of clothes, her night things, and, most importantly of all, *Mrs Beeton's Book of Household Management*. That last item tripled the weight, but no way would she go anywhere without it.

After double-checking she had everything she needed for a couple of days away, Ruth zipped up the suitcase. Her agile grandson could do the heavy lifting.

Speaking of whom, he called, "Grandma?"

Ruth opened the window and peered out.

He'd leaned both skylights against the side of the motorhome. "What shall I do with these?"

"Put them back."

He scratched his head. "They're broken."

"Only at the hinges, from what I can see." Although Ruth wasn't an expert when it came to anything mechanical. "We can't leave gaping holes in the ceiling, Gregory. This is Scotland. What if it rains?"

He sighed. "Fine. But you'll have to pass them up to me."

"Would love to. It will be the highlight of my day." And that was the truth. Ruth closed the window and rushed outside.

Greg scaled the ladder on the back of the motorhome—now Ruth understood what it was for: so you could get up there and reattach parts to the roof—and with a lot of huffing, puffing, and effort, she handed up both skylights. Greg rested them in position, covering the gaping holes, and went to climb down, but Ruth held up the twisted remains of the TV antenna.

"I think that's deceased, Grandma," he said with a forlorn look.

He had a point. The wire had snapped and frayed.

Greg returned to terra firma and grabbed the suitcases from the motorhome, while Ruth placed several pots and pans under the skylights, just in case. Then she made sure Merlin was safely inside his box. He'd eaten his treat while she was away—a good sign all was forgiven.

A few minutes later, Ruth carried Merlin's box in one hand, her handbag slung over the opposite shoulder, while Greg waddled along with the suitcases. The pair of them headed from the car park, and down a narrow lane flanked by grey and sandstone buildings.

"You still haven't told me where we're going," Greg said as he swayed from side to side with a suitcase in each hand.

Ruth had given up trying to convince him to use the pull handles and wheels. Besides, the scrawny teen could do with putting on some muscle. At present, one strong gust and he'd likely snap in half.

Greg gazed up at the ancient stone structures as they passed by. "You know, over seventy-five percent of Edinburgh's buildings are listed."

"Is that right?" Ruth exchanged smiles and nods with an elderly couple walking arm in arm in the opposite direction.

Greg shifted his grip on the suitcases. "Some of the oldest ones are over five hundred years old."

Ruth wondered if her motorhome would be around for so long. Somehow, she doubted it would make it through the next five years, let alone five hundred.

Her grandson was a boffin when it came to history or archaeology, and he was off to Oxford University later in the year to expand that knowledge. He loved everything from the ancient times until the early nineteen hundreds, and had accumulated a billion books back at Morgan Manor.

As far as Ruth was concerned, her chosen vocation meant she got to travel and experience some wonderful places around Britain. And this next destination was no exception, which was why she'd kept it from him.

They followed another narrow road flanked by more stone buildings and shop fronts.

Greg gazed into a baker's window. "I'm hungry."

"You're always hungry."

"What does that tell you?"

Ruth glanced at him. "That your stomach's a bottomless pit that constantly demands empty calories?"

"I must still be growing," Greg murmured as he navigated round a couple with a pushchair and a thousand bags of groceries.

At the end of the high street, they hung a left and strode into a courtyard with an apple tree in the middle, surrounded by a stone wall.

Ruth stopped outside a narrow brick building with a slate roof, leaded windows, and a black front door with brass fittings. Gas lamps hung from wrought iron brackets.

A sign above the entrance, with orange lettering on a black background, read,

Kat's Kitty Hotel

Greg gawped up at it, doing a good impression of the car park attendant. "A hotel for cats?" His shoulders slumped. "You cannot be serious."

Ruth looked at him askance. "Can't very well take Merlin with us."

Greg's expression darkened. "Where. Are. We. Going?"

"As far as you're concerned, it will be a nice, relaxing holiday. You'll love it."

"Whenever you say that, I never do . . . *love it*." Greg set the suitcases down and flexed his fingers. "It's always the opposite."

"Not always," Ruth said.

"Every single time."

"Then this will be the exception to the rule." Ruth opened the door and stepped into a reception area.

Cat portraits lined the walls from floor to ceiling, a vast array of every imaginable breed: from Persians to Pixie-bobs, from a glorious Siberian cat to a Sphynx, and everything in between.

Ruth studied the image of a Bengal with its magnificent golden leopard spots and beautiful green eyes.

She sighed. "Stunning."

Greg brought the suitcases in. "No way Merlin would let you have one of those. He'd chase it off or try to kill it. Probably both."

"Your mother has talked about breeding Bengals," Ruth said with more than a spoonful of wistfulness.

Her only daughter, Sara, ran the family business: a professional cat-breeding facility. Ruth had kept it going after her husband's death, but when Sara had taken over, it had really flourished. Not only did Sara produce some of the healthiest and purest cat breeds in Britain, she'd also expanded into ethically sourced pet food and animal supplies.

A door at the back of the reception area opened, and a woman with purple hair, wearing a headband complete with cat ears, strode through. To contrast her look, she also wore a bright orange dress and matching shoes.

"Welcome to Kat's Kitty Hotel." She beamed at Ruth and Greg. "I'm Kat." She indicated her name badge, and then bent to peer through the side vent of the oak box. "And this glorious young man must be Merlin?"

He replied with a raspy meow, tinged with a hiss.

Kat straightened and nodded at Greg. "You can leave those cases here. They're perfectly safe." Kat pointed at a CCTV camera in the top corner of the reception. She then opened the rear door and gestured them through. "Kitties first."

Ruth walked into a vast space with a high ceiling and a fenced-off area with faux grass and a jungle gym. Cats of all shapes and sizes played under the watchful eye of several assistants.

In the corner sat an infrared heat lamp, with several more cats curled up asleep under it.

A feline paradise.

Down both sides of the main area were rows of colourful doors, and windows next to each.

"Anything with a green light above is currently available." Kat indicated the nearest one.

Ruth looked into a 1950s-themed room with a single bed covered in floral blankets, a mini mustard-yellow sofa, a smoky glass coffee table, and pictures of Clark Gable, James Dean, Doris Day, and Marilyn Monroe adorning the walls.

"Cute," she said. "But not quite Merlin's style."

"Got anything with a coffin and knives?" Greg asked Kat with a deadpan expression.

"No. But I'll make a note of it for future additions."

She had styled the next vacant room with yellow carpet, blue walls plastered with plastic seagulls, and deck chairs.

Merlin had never seen a beach, let alone developed a fondness for them, so it was another hard *no*.

There were twenty themed rooms in all, half of which were currently unoccupied, and Ruth peered through the windows as she made her way along.

Greg looked into a room based on Camelot, with cut-out castles and jousting knights. "These are bigger than my bedroom in the motorhome. Way cooler too."

Ruth faced Kat. "Do you take wayward teenagers?"

She smirked. "Not recently."

Greg's phone rang, and he answered. "Hey. I was just thinking about you."

"Hi, Mia," Ruth said in a sickly sweet voice.

Greg frowned at her. "Mia says hi back."

"How are you?" Ruth asked.

"She says she's fine."

"And your brother?"

"Scott's fine too."

"Recovering from his ordeal?"

"Grandma, seriously." Greg turned away.

Ruth grinned at Kat. "His new girlfriend. Long-distance."

"That must be tough on them."

"They'll work out great." And Ruth meant it. She liked Mia, and it was clear the two of them got on fantastically well.

Ruth headed to a log cabin–themed room in Kat's Kitty

Hotel, complete with a comfy armchair covered in blankets, and a stone fireplace. "This looks good."

Kat opened the door, and the two of them walked inside. "I'm sure Merlin will love it."

Ruth set his box on the floor. She hinged the front aside. Merlin glared at her. "Don't look at me like that. Kat says you'll love it." She straightened and took several steps back.

After a minute, Merlin stuck his head out, looked around the room, and then disappeared into the box again.

Greg appeared in the doorway and chortled. "Fussy git."

"Don't worry," Kat said. "He'll settle in just fine." She pulled a card from her pocket, jotted down log-in details, and handed it to Ruth. "That's the web address and password for this room." She indicated a CCTV camera above the door. "You can check on him whenever you like."

"Probably every five minutes, then," Greg said.

"Thank you." Ruth took the card.

After a few more reassurances that she'd make sure Merlin settled in and had all the attention he needed, Kat saw Ruth and Greg out.

As they headed down a hill, Greg asked, "How far is this place?"

"It should be right about . . ." Ruth indicated a narrow alleyway. "Here."

At the end stood a red door.

Greg frowned and looked about. "Are you sure?"

Ruth marched down the alleyway and opened the door. "After you."

Greg's eyes went wide.

"I knew you'd like it." Ruth grinned. "Grandma knows best."

2

Ruth and Greg stepped into a cavernous foyer with a marble floor partly covered by Persian rugs, leather wingback chairs, and a walnut reception desk. Immense pillars held up a coffered ceiling with gold filigree and ornate architraves. An enormous crystal chandelier, as big as a car, commanded attention.

Ruth wasn't sure what she'd expected, but certainly hadn't pictured something so grand.

Adding to the opulence, oil paintings hung on the walls, landscapes depicting the Scottish Highlands, Coldingham Bay, the Isle of Skye, and, of course, Edinburgh Castle in all its imposing glory. Ruth hoped they'd have time to visit after her work was done.

In the middle of the grand space, beneath the chandelier, stood a marble statue of a man wrapped in a fishing net, while an angel helped break it open.

"This is a copy of a work called *Release from Deception*." Greg stared up at it with reverence. "I can't remember the sculptor's name, but the net symbolizes sin, and the angel is setting him free." He turned on the spot, eyes wide, taking it all in. "This place is amazing. Looks Victorian." He eyed an orange clay vase on a plinth, with an image painted in black that depicted a man with a spear, with others behind assisting him thrusting it into a giant cyclops' eye. "Odysseus blinding Polyphemus."

"You know your Greek mythology." A slender man with silver hair slicked back, wearing a fine black suit, glided across the foyer.

A gold name badge on his lapel read:

HUGO FINSBURY
OWNER

He held his arms wide. "Ruth. It's been too long."

They embraced.

Ruth smiled and stepped back. "Greg, this is Hugo, an old acquaintance of your grandfather's, and mine, of course." She chuckled at fond memories of the three of them sitting up late, drinking far too much red wine, and making far too much noise in a royal household. "Hugo, this is my grandson, Gregory Shaw."

"Pleased to meet you, Gregory." Hugo had a posh British accent, mixed with a splash of local Scottish dialect. He extended a hand, and they shook. "You remind me of your late grandfather. Same eyes, and the shape of your jaw."

"I owe Hugo everything," Ruth said.

"Come now. You don't owe me a thing. I'm glad to have you here." He glanced at the reception desk. "I settled your invoice and transferred the funds to your account an hour ago."

Ruth shook her head. "I'm happy to help where I can, and I still say I would've done it for free."

"Nonsense. I won't hear of it." Hugo sighed. "In for a penny, in for a pound, I say." His eyes glazed.

"You've invested a lot?" Judging by their current location, Ruth wouldn't be surprised. Hugo had spared no expense with the lavish interior, and this wasn't the most important part.

"Everything I had is gone. All this is now owned by the bank. Including our house." Hugo cleared his throat at Ruth's inquisitive expression. "My business partner passed away before we completed this latest venture." He motioned around them. "Unfortunately, his wife wasn't keen to continue. The long and short of it is, I had to buy out her fifty percent stake, or it could've turned nasty. The bank refused to loan me any more, but I found another way forward." Hugo offered a tremulous smile. "And so, here I am, with everything on the line. Quite literally."

"I'm sure it will be a roaring success." Ruth hoped for his sake it was.

"Oh, there's no doubt it has to be perfect. The friendly people at the bank are poised to sell everything if it's not." Hugo tugged at his cuffs. "Which is why I've asked you here, Ruth. I'm only sorry we couldn't have you sooner, but it's all been a bit of a last-minute rush, you understand." His expression relaxed. "I am so very pleased you're here now. When you said you were visiting your sister in Scotland, I knew it had to be divine providence."

"Well, for what it's worth, I like your hotel," Greg said. "A lot. It's impressive."

Hugo's eyebrows arched. "You haven't told him, Ruth?"

"I've been keeping it as a surprise."

"In that case, let's get you under way." Hugo motioned to a porter, and then headed toward a set of double doors. "Follow me, if you please."

The porter hurried over, retracted the suitcase handles, and the four of them crossed the foyer.

Greg leaned in to Ruth, hushed. "What does he mean, under way?"

She winked. Ruth loved keeping this from him until the very last moment. Besides, if Greg knew what was about to happen, he'd likely back out.

They continued along a short corridor into an oval room with a door on the left, another on the right, and a third straight ahead.

Above the left-hand door was a silhouette of a woman in a dress, and the one on the right had a gentleman in a suit.

Hugo gestured Greg to a velvet sofa. "Please wait here. I'll be back momentarily." He linked arms with Ruth.

After Greg sat down and the porter disappeared through the unmarked door with their suitcases, Hugo steered Ruth through the left-hand door, into a large Victorian dress shop.

It stood two storeys high, and racks of clothes jammed every available inch, along with mannequin displays on plinths.

There were formal ball gowns, skirts and blouses, petticoats and bustles, bonnets, scarfs, and parasols matched with lace gloves. All in a Victorian style.

Ruth stared at it all. "This is incredible." It was as though she'd stepped through a portal and emerged a hundred and fifty years prior.

Hugo beamed. "All replicas, of course, but based on the finest examples, copied from the originals with the utmost attention to detail. Spared no expense."

"You've outdone yourself." Ruth examined a bone corset.

A woman in her midthirties with dark hair cut into a neat bob, pulled back a curtain and stepped from a changing room. She wore a black dress, and reminded Ruth of Queen Victoria when she'd mourned the loss of her husband, Albert. The lady moved with grace and poise. She also wore a magnificent diamond necklace with an oversized emerald, and a pair of sunglasses—each lens D-shaped and with side panels, in keeping with the era.

A blonde girl in a deep blue dress rushed forward, took her arm, and placed a white cane in the woman's other hand.

"How do I look?" the blind lady asked.

"Beautiful."

A shop assistant cooed as she escorted them through a golden archway and a set of double doors at the back of the shop.

Another shop assistant in a plain black skirt and striped red and white blouse moved into Ruth's field of view. "Welcome."

Hugo bowed his head. "I will see you out there. Take all the time you need." He lifted Ruth's hand, kissed the back of it, then strode across the shop and into the vestibule. "Right then, Greg. This way."

Ruth watched him go with a slight tingle in her stomach. Hugo had certainly aged well. Although he had always been rather debonair, in her humble opinion.

"Anything particular you fancy?"

"Tempting." Ruth shook herself. "Sorry? What?"

A wry smile played on the assistant's lips. "To wear, madame."

Ruth exhaled and peered around the shop. "I don't know where to start." It was all rather overwhelming.

"Let me help." The assistant gestured for Ruth to follow her. "The porter took your suitcases ahead, but we ask you to wear era-appropriate clothing when dining or mixing with fellow passengers." She stopped at a display with a mannequin wearing a skirt of deepest maroon, and a matching long-sleeved blouse. "We suggest you select an appropriate evening dress, and a second more casual outfit for day wear." The shop assistant motioned to a rack of skirts. "You're more than welcome to pick any style. We are at your service." She indicated more racks on the other side of the room with various trousers. "If you prefer?"

"Dresses will be fine." Besides, Ruth couldn't recall the last time she'd worn anything other than her usual black skirt or trousers and shirt combo. The change would be a rare treat.

"Any particular colour?" the assistant asked.

Ruth gazed round at the tremendous variety, and forced herself to say anything other than black. "How about green? Something in a dark green?" She'd never been one for colour, other than her vibrant pink hat, scarf, and gloves, all of which accented her black attire.

"I have just the thing." The assistant guided her to a rack, selected Ruth's size, and lifted out a marvellous dress with ruffles.

Ruth sighed. "Incredible."

Ten minutes later, Ruth stood in front of a full-length ornate mirror, wearing the green dress.

"I don't know what magic enchantments are on this"—she swished the fabric from side to side—"but I feel a-ma-zing."

The assistant then had Ruth pick out a more casual

dress for day wear, and once that was boxed, she led Ruth to the golden archway. "We'll make sure the porter places it in your compartment with your other belongings."

Ruth stopped short. "Hold on." She hurried back to the dressing room, scooped up her phone and handbag, and returned to the assistant.

The assistant eyed the phone. "We kindly ask you to leave any mobile phones with your belongings, in your compartment."

"Right you are," Ruth said. "No modern items that may detract from the experience?"

The assistant smiled. "I can make sure the porter collects your bag. It's perfectly safe."

Ruth placed her handbag on the nearest counter, but while the assistant's back was turned, she slipped the phone into the sleeve of her dress. It was on silent, after all.

The door to the vestibule burst open, and a man with messy white hair stomped into the room. He clutched a leather holdall to his chest. "Where is he?" His face was red and blotchy, and sweat glistened on his forehead.

Another assistant rushed over to him. "Sir. This is the ladies—"

"I know perfectly well where I am," he snapped. "Seeing as most of this was my damned idea." He waved her off and looked about with mad eyes. "Well? Where's Hugo?"

"Sorry, sir. I don't—"

"Hugo?" the white-haired man shouted. "Get out here."

Ruth considered helping the poor shop assistant to calm the gentleman, but before she'd taken a step the door behind the man opened, and another man with short-cropped red hair rushed into the room.

A gold name badge like Hugo's on his lapel read:

WAYLON ELLIS
Owner's Assistant

Waylon made a beeline for the white-haired man. "Miles."

"Where is he?" Miles shoved him away. "I demand to see him."

Waylon staggered back. "Hugo is dealing with the other passengers," he said in a level tone. "Can I—"

The door burst open again, and this time a security guard dressed in a Victorian police officer's uniform—dark blue trousers and jacket, polished black shoes, a helmet, and whistle—marched into the room. "You cannot be in here, sir." He reached for Miles' arm.

Miles pulled back and glared at the men. "I have every right." He snarled and turned his back on them. "Hugo?" he shouted. "You can't hide forever."

The security guard gripped Miles' shoulder. "Sir. I must ask you to leave."

"Get your hands off me." Miles yanked himself free, and glared at the guard as though he were about to strike him. His gaze met Ruth's for a moment, and then he shoved past Waylon and stormed from the room.

The security guard followed hard on his heels. "Sir?"

Waylon threw the shop assistants an apologetic look and traipsed after the two men.

"I'm so sorry about that, madame," Ruth's assistant said.

"Who was he?" Ruth's curiosity alarm was going off full tilt in her head.

"I'm afraid I don't know." The assistant motioned to the golden archway.

Despite not being convinced by her answer, and wanting

to run after the man to see what he did next, Ruth instead followed the girl through the double doors, and along a hallway lined with portraits of kings and queens, both Scottish and English monarchy stretching back hundreds of years.

At the end, the shop assistant stepped to one side, bowed, and motioned to a set of doors with wrought iron filigree and stained glass. "I hope you enjoy your time with us."

"Thank you. I'm sure we will." The doors swung open, and a gasp escaped Ruth's lips.

She staggered onto a platform, complete with a ticket office. On the tracks stood a magnificent green train. Smoke and steam issued from its funnel, and a hand-painted sign on its side declared it to be the Finsbury Flyer.

Ruth gaped.

Behind the steam engine sat ten carriages, each painted in matching green with their windows accented in gold.

Passengers boarded, all in Victorian outfits, while porters loaded their luggage from trolleys.

The blind lady and her blonde assistant stood by an open carriage door.

"I hear you were a detective," a deep voice remarked, drawing the attention of all those gathered.

A man with dark hair and a handlebar moustache stood arm in arm with a tall woman in a navy dress. They both appeared to be in their late fifties and clearly looked after their appearances. The woman had tied her hair into a neat bun that pulled her face into a constant look of upper-class astonishment.

Ruth forced a smile at them. "A police officer. And that was a long time ago. How did you know?"

"Hugo told us all about you." The man offered his hand.

"Lord Hamilton. And this is my wife, Lady Hilary Hamilton."

Ruth shook their hands in turn. She recognised their names, but couldn't immediately place them.

"If you'll excuse us." Lord Hamilton assisted his wife on board, following a porter to their compartment.

A brunette lady in her late twenties, wearing an elegant white lace dress, glided along the platform, flanked by two burly protection officers—one blond, the other with dark hair, both short cropped.

Ruth's breath caught as she recognised the regal young lady in the lead, but raised voices drew her attention to the nearby ticket office.

Unable to help herself, she edged over to it.

The first voice was Hugo's.

"I beg you to calm down, Miles. We've been over this. Since Grant's untimely passing, and the bank's refusal to loan me any more money, I've had no choice but to—"

"Don't give me another one of your excuses," a second man growled.

Trying her best to look casual, Ruth sauntered closer to the ticket office and risked a peek through the window.

Hugo stood next to the counter, and Miles squared up to him, fists balled. "I won't have it, Hugo. You hear me? It's dangerous. You're making a gigantic mistake."

Hugo raised his hands. "I would be angry if I were in your shoes, but you have my word you will be handsomely reimbursed once finances start flowing." He leaned in to Miles and murmured, "What did you do with the last payment I gave you? Gambled it away, I suppose."

Miles erupted, shoving Hugo back, and snarled, "How dare you."

Hugo bowed his head. "I apologise. I won't back out of our deal. You have my word. I only request some time."

"I don't care about money," Miles retorted. "But the way you secured financing to finish the Flyer was a disgrace, Hugo. The new contractors cut corners."

"That's all in the past."

Miles held up the leather holdall. "Why won't you look at these?"

Hugo sighed. "How about you come with us?"

Miles glared at him. "What?"

"Come with us," Hugo repeated. "This is our maiden voyage, after all. You were a part of this, so come along. You'll have a good time, see us make a success of it, and realise your fears are misplaced."

"They're not misplaced." Miles stepped toward him, lip curled. "They are far from misplaced."

"I promise to make time to hear you out." Hugo nodded at the leather bag. "You'll have my undivided attention. How does that sound?" He inclined his head. "Come on. What do you say, old man?"

Miles grumbled, "You'd better listen."

Hugo guided him to the door at the back of the ticket office. "Quickly get changed. We leave soon. Can't miss our time slot, or it'll be over before we've begun."

Ruth had to hand it to Hugo for dealing with Miles so calmly. However, with him on the train with them, it would take all her willpower not to ask Hugo about what had Miles so angry and—

"You know it's rude to eavesdrop."

Ruth started, spun round, and clutched her chest. "Greg." She let out a sigh of relief, but when she laid eyes on her grandson properly, Ruth did a double take. "Goodness me."

Greg wore a fine Victorian gentleman's suit: a knee-length charcoal grey herringbone frock coat, black trousers, a matching vest with a gold pocket watch chain strung across, a crisp white dress shirt, and a red and silver patterned cravat.

Ruth gawped at him, stunned into silence.

"Yeah," Greg murmured. "Don't make a thing of it." To complete his look, he also wore a top hat, and held on to a silver-handled walking cane.

Ruth unstuck her tongue. "Excuse me, sir," she whispered. "Have you seen my grandson? I'm supposed to meet him here."

Greg fiddled with his collar. "Very funny."

"I'm serious," Ruth said. "He can be a scruffy oik, so I'm worried he'll stand out like a sore thumb."

"I'm not scruffy."

Ruth gasped. "Gregory Shaw, as I live and breathe." She squinted. "Can that really be you?"

"I'm taking this off." Greg turned to leave.

Ruth grabbed his arm. "Wait." She swallowed a lump of pride. "Greg, you look incredible. Seriously. I should take a picture." She glanced about to make sure no one watched them, then reached for her phone inside her dress, but a deep voice interrupted.

"We have that covered." Hugo stood behind them, tugging at his shirt cuffs.

Ruth's gaze moved to the ticket office. The white-haired man, Miles, had gone. She lowered her voice. "Everything okay?" Ruth was acutely aware she owed Hugo everything, and wanted to help where she could, no matter what the situation.

However, Hugo let out a small breath. "All fine." He motioned along the platform, to an alcove where a photographer stood behind a box camera on a tripod. "To commemorate the day. Waylon?"

His red-haired assistant, Waylon, hurried over, escorted them to the front of the train, and positioned Ruth and Greg in front of the bellows camera.

The photographer adjusted the brass lens and ducked under a black curtain at the back. "Say cheese."

Greg removed his top hat, revealing slicked-back hair, and lifted his chin as though he were Victorian aristocracy.

Ruth grinned. "Cheese."

The photographer held aloft a flash lamp on a rod, and a snap of light assaulted Ruth's eyes.

"Excellent. Thank you."

"No smoke," Greg said. "Real ones had powder."

"Digital camera," Hugo said. "Disguised as a George Hare whole plate."

Waylon then escorted a middle-aged couple to the train, trailed by a porter.

"Gregory likes everything historical." Ruth blinked away red blotches that floated across her vision. "Which is why he hangs out with his dear old grandmother. I'm an antique."

"You're only in your sixties," Greg said. "You're far from an antique, Grandma."

"Aw. Thank you, dear. That's so sweet of you to say."

"I think most people would class you as a slightly worn-out classic," Greg said. "Vintage?"

Ruth tilted her head. "Nice to see you've picked up some of your Aunty Margaret's acid tongue."

"And how is your sister?" Hugo asked.

"Same as always."

"Oh dear." Hugo chuckled, then motioned. "Let's get you settled on board."

As they made their way along the platform, following

Hugo, Ruth leaned in to Greg and murmured, "You'll never guess who's on the train already."

Greg shrugged.

Ruth cleared her throat. "Princess Mary. Tenth in line to the throne, or thereabouts."

Greg snorted. "Yeah, right."

Hugo stopped and faced them. "We're honoured to have her on this maiden journey." His expression turned grave. "It's imperative we make a good impression."

Greg's face dropped, and his attention moved to the train. "Is it an experience only for the rich and famous?" He tugged at his shirt collar, clearly uncomfortable at the notion of over-the-top indulgence.

"Not at all," Hugo said. "Quite the contrary. But it will be at first, while we recover our initial outlay. Then we'll lower ticket prices. Who knows? Perhaps we will have family coupon days."

Greg looked back at him. "Where are we going, exactly? What's our destination?"

"I'll explain everything once we're underway." Hugo offered a hand to Ruth and helped her on board.

Greg remained at the platform's edge.

"Of course," Hugo said. "I almost forgot." He fished in his coat pocket and retrieved a metal canister an inch long with a screw top. "Ruth told me about your motion sickness. I hope you don't mind, but I took the liberty." He unscrewed the lid and tipped out two tablets into Greg's hand. "Meclizine. I find they work for me. Besides, I think you'll be pleased to discover it will be a smooth journey."

After an encouraging look from his grandmother, Greg muttered, "Thanks," and swallowed the tablets.

The train whistle shrieked, and a guard shouted, "All aboard."

The white-haired man, Miles, marched down the platform, now wearing a suit, his leather holdall tucked under his arm as he did up a tie. He glared at Hugo and stepped onto a carriage farther down.

Butterflies danced in Ruth's stomach.

No doubt about it, they were in for a fun couple of days.

3

Hugo showed Greg to his first-class single compartment, and then led Ruth through a connecting gangway into the carriage next to it—with first-class double sleepers.

"You needn't have gone to all this trouble for us," she said as Hugo stopped outside an open door to compartment 3A. "Could have put us in economy. We would've been more than happy."

"Nonsense. I wouldn't hear of it," Hugo said. "Besides, those carriages are unoccupied for this inaugural journey. We have everyone in the two first-class carriages. Including you and your grandson, twelve passengers in total, and now Miles. However, for most of the journey, I want you to experience everything as a guest."

"How many people can the train take at full capacity?" Ruth asked.

"One hundred and eight passengers in total, along with twenty-four crew members on rotation. We currently have twelve crew, plus Waylon and me."

"Twelve crew to only eleven passengers?" Ruth said,

surprised. "Doing everything possible to ensure excellent reports?" Not that she could blame him with so much at stake.

Hugo glanced about and whispered, "As you've realised, we have some extraordinary VIPs on board. It's essential they enjoy themselves and recommend us to all their friends. That's why you're here too, Ruth. To make sure the dining is exquisite. I want no complaints."

"I'll do my best." Although Ruth had a firm grasp of fine dining, she was a meat-and-two-veg kind of a gal. Hugo had invited her to work with the kitchen staff and offer advice where needed.

"Chef is anticipating your input with great gusto." Hugo's expression softened. "But for tonight, you're our guest. Let us know what you think from that point of view, and then we'll arrange for you to spend part of tomorrow with Chef in the kitchen. How does that sound?"

"Perfect."

A free trip on board a luxury train? What's not to enjoy?

Hugo motioned to her compartment. "I'll see you in the salon." He bowed and left.

Ruth stepped inside to find a room six feet by seven, with wood-panelled walls, a narrow mahogany desk with a brass lamp bolted to it, a small chair, and an ornate mirror on the wall. A bed sat opposite, and heavy curtains hung to either side of the window. Finally, a door stood open to a compact, private en suite bathroom.

Ruth let out a little squeal of delight.

She was definitely going to enjoy this trip. *A lot.*

A porter had placed her handbag and suitcase in the closet, unpacked, and hung her clothes.

"Wow. Talk about service."

Speaking of which, a male porter appeared at Ruth's door. "Everything to your liking, madam?"

"Fantastic," she said. "Thank you."

He'd also set the hefty tome of *Mrs Beeton's book of Household Management* on the desk.

The porter stepped inside and closed the wardrobe door. "Should you require further fresh towels, please let me know." He edged back. "Would you like me to show you how to operate the television?"

Ruth looked about. "Where is it?"

The porter flipped open a panel on the wall to reveal a hidden compartment. Inside was a remote control. He aimed it at the mirror. A screen flickered to life, replacing the mirrored surface with a view outside, looking down the track from the train's point of view.

Ruth gaped at it.

"We have a selection of onboard movies, series, and documentaries. The guide is on channel zero." The porter switched off the TV and returned the remote to its hiding place. He then backed out of the room and almost bumped into the blind woman's blonde assistant. "Sorry, miss."

"This is my compartment." She looked over his shoulder at Ruth and held up a ticket. "I'm supposed to be 3A because it's next to 2A." She pointed to the right. "But you've put me in 4A."

The porter pulled a list from his back pocket and unfolded it. "Your name?"

"Hunter. Zoey Hunter. I'm here to assist Victoria Wallace."

The porter scanned the names.

Victoria was the blind lady, so it would make sense to have them in rooms next to each other.

"I can move," Ruth said.

The porter frowned at the sheet. "I'm not sure what's happened. This is correct." He looked up. "Ruth Morgan?" She nodded. The porter showed Zoey the list. "Victoria Wallace, 2A; Ruth Morgan, 3A; Zoey Hunter, 4A."

"I'm telling you it's wrong," Zoey said in an exasperated tone. "I'm supposed to be next door to—"

"I can swap." Ruth went to pick up her Mrs Beeton's book.

"It's fine, Zoey." The blind woman, Victoria, appeared in the hallway. "Leave it be."

"But—"

"I said let it go."

"Are you sure?" Ruth asked Victoria. "It's no bother. My name is Ruth Morgan, by the way."

"Nice to meet you, and we'll be fine. Thank you for offering."

"I love your necklace," Ruth said as it glinted in the light.

Victoria touched the jewels at her neck. "My great-grandmother's." She smiled. "If you'll excuse us. Zoey?"

Zoey hesitated, glanced at Ruth and the porter, and then headed into her mistress' compartment. They closed the door behind them.

Ruth forced a smile at the porter. "I was happy to move."

He bowed, and left.

Ruth closed the door and squeezed into the bathroom to freshen up.

Five minutes later, she slipped from her compartment.

To her right, at the far end of the carriage, was a door marked "Royal Carriage."

"He really has spent a lot," Ruth murmured.

She headed left, through the connecting gangway, and continued along the first-class single-sleeper carriage. At the end, she passed through another door and stepped into an impressive salon with armchairs, tables, a plush carpet, and a bar with brass fittings that matched the lights.

People chatted among themselves in twos and threes.

Princess Mary, her brunette hair pinned up with a pretty butterfly comb, sat in a high-backed chair at the far end of the carriage, flanked by her two protection officers.

Both looked ready to jump into action.

Miles waved a finger in a slender middle-aged lady's face. "You're wrong." His cheeks flushed with anger. "You know this was all my idea."

"What's going on?" Hugo asked as he stepped through the door.

The slender lady retreated to another middle-aged man who looked ready to punch Miles.

Waylon, Hugo's red-haired assistant, hurried over to Miles, wearing a painted smile. "Now is not the time."

Nearby, Lord and Lady Hamilton snickered.

"Not a laughing matter," Miles snapped at them. "Serious business." His expression darkened as he looked Hugo up and down. "Very serious business."

"And like all business"—Hugo guided Miles to an armchair next to the bar—"we should conduct it behind closed doors."

Miles sneered at him.

Greg appeared at Ruth's side. "He seems nice."

"Delightful," she muttered.

Greg handed Ruth a flute of champagne.

"Thank you. All settled in?"

"This train is amazing." His expression lit up. "Hugo has made it so authentic to the Victorian era. Well, cosmetically, at least. Have you seen the TV?"

"Is yours in the mirror too?"

"Can we get them for the motorhome?"

"Let me think on that." Ruth tapped her chin. "Hmm . . . no."

Greg's shoulders slumped. "Why not?"

"We don't have a television antenna, remember?" Ruth's gaze scanned her fellow passengers and then followed Miles as he stood again, joined Lord and Lady Hamilton, and muttered what sounded like obscenities.

By their faces, they now regretted their snickers.

Princess Mary watched on with a bemused expression.

Waylon reached for the last flute of champagne held out on a tray by a server, but Miles beat him to it and downed it. Waylon glared at him.

"What?" Miles snapped. "Oh for goodness' sake." He turned to the bar and grabbed another full champagne flute from next to the blind lady and her assistant. "Plenty to go around. Here."

Zoey started to protest, but he shoved it into Waylon's hands.

Hugo seemed about ready to throw Miles from the train, and they'd not yet left the station. Instead, he lifted his chin, and spoke in a loud, clear voice. "Welcome, one and all." The chatter died down. "I'm honoured to have you on board the Finsbury Flyer."

This was greeted by a ripple of applause.

Hugo glanced between them all with fondness. "As no doubt some of you have already worked out . . ." He nodded to Greg. "This is not a steam train, but fully electric and modern in every way possible."

"How did you know?" Ruth asked Greg. Apart from the TV, it had seemed old and original to her.

"The tender has no coal in it," he said. "It's not a container, but a sealed box with doors at both ends. None of the furniture or mouldings are original. Only done in a Victorian style."

"Right," Ruth said, not quite understanding. "I'll take your word for it."

Hugo continued, "As you may also know, it's been a grand vision of mine to replicate the travel of bygone years." He moved between the guests as he spoke. "To recapture that magical era."

Miles glared at him, but kept his lips pressed together.

"This is a sleeper train," Hugo said. "And as such, we'll be travelling overnight from Edinburgh to Penzance." He bowed his head to Princess Mary. "And to better imitate the feel of the golden age of steam, we'll be moving at a leisurely forty miles an hour. Which means"—he held up a finger—"we'll arrive in Cornwall at seven tomorrow morning. There'll be no stops, and we have a big surprise for you waiting at the other end." Hugo did an about-face. "After spending half the day there, we'll then take another leisurely ride back, returning to Edinburgh tomorrow night."

"Is that all?" The middle-aged slender lady looked disappointed. "Two days?"

"Lest we forget." Hugo's lips twitched. "Our country is only a small one in comparison to Europe and America."

This resulted in muffled laughter.

"However, I'm confident this trip will go well," Hugo said. "And we'll not only be granted future permission to use other tracks around the country, but I have plenty of ideas on how to extend our journeys to the continent." He cleared his throat. "For now, I promise you'll be more than satisfied." Hugo looked at his watch.

Ruth's attention shifted to a clock on the wall above the bar. As soon as the second hand hit the twelve, indicating it was precisely eight o'clock in the evening, the train whistle blared, and the Finsbury Flyer pulled from the station.

Hugo lifted his glass. "Bon voyage, everyone."

They all raised their glasses and said "Cheers" in unison.

Greg took a pretend sip. "Hate champagne." He set his glass on a nearby table.

Ruth knocked hers back, then poured Greg's into her flute and gulped that too.

He frowned at her. "Thirsty?"

"Waste not, want not. That's the first rule of Grandma Club."

Greg smirked. "What's the second rule?"

"Fill all biscuit tins with nothing but assorted buttons." She winked. "Eternally disappointing grandchildren the world over."

"Now," Hugo said. "Chef has prepared a special meal for your enjoyment in the dining carriage. Follow me, if you please." He offered an arm to Princess Mary. "May I escort you there, Your Highness?"

"You may." She rose from the chair, took Hugo's arm, and the pair of them swept from the salon.

As Waylon ushered the rest of the guests out, Ruth leaned in to her grandson. "How about you charm the princess with some of your rugged Gregness."

"My what?"

"Impress her, and then marry her. I want to be Queen of England." She pictured herself in a royal carriage, waving at her subjects. "Ooh, I could put my sister in the Tower of London."

"I don't think that's how it works," Greg said.

"You're right. Margaret would be better suited in the dungeon." Ruth's eyes narrowed. "I'm thinking either the rack or iron maiden."

Greg pinched the bridge of his nose. "I meant I don't think that's how royal succession works." He sighed. "Anyway, I have a girlfriend, remember?"

Ruth's shoulders slumped. "Spoilsport."

"And you like Mia," Greg added.

"I suppose so." Ruth turned her head and muttered, "Darn it." The images of a royal carriage evaporated, along with the palaces, crown jewels, and the handsome footmen...

The Finsbury Flyer's dining car was as opulent as the rest of the carriages, with accents of gold, crystal light fixtures, and wall-to-wall mahogany. Place cards in silver holders rested on each table.

Princess Mary sat at the head table, dripping in jewels, and flanked by her protection officers.

Hugo's assistant, Waylon, showed Ruth and Greg to their allotted places opposite Lord and Lady Hamilton.

Ruth leaned across the table. "I must ask, are you the same lord and lady who own the big red castle with the moat? The one we passed on the way into Edinburgh?"

Greg's jaw dropped. After all, he'd been regaling Ruth with its links to Andrew Moray and the First Scottish War of Independence.

Lady Hamilton nodded politely. She wore a pink lace dress and diamond earrings in the shape of daisies, which sparkled, sending points of light dancing across the table.

Ruth sat back and motioned to Greg. "My grandson: Sir Gregory of No Fixed Abode."

Greg wore a pained expression, and murmured, "Nice to meet you."

"Likewise," Lord Hamilton said.

Lady Hamilton blinked at Greg, her already perpetually

surprised features turning to a look of astonishment. "You're homeless?"

"Not exactly."

Ruth examined the fine details of the silver cutlery. "Our current house roams around the countryside like a wayward vagabond, and we cling on for dear life."

"Ah." Lord Hamilton brushed his moustache. "You're travellers? How exciting. What a life that must be." He sounded genuinely intrigued, and Ruth didn't have the heart to set him straight.

Lady Hamilton opened her mouth with what would no doubt be a loaded question but closed it again when a server wheeled a cart to their table.

He placed bowls of chicken soup with couscous in front of them.

Scents of thyme, rosemary, and a hint of garlic wadted from the dish.

"Heavenly." Ruth looked over at the table next to theirs.

Miles sat there, arms folded, glaring at the middle-aged couple opposite as the slender lady complained to their server about requiring vegetarian alternatives.

"Have some bloody consideration," Miles griped.

"Jane Minchent and her husband, Robert," Lady Hamilton whispered to Ruth. "They own a chain of coffee shops."

"Minties Coffee," Lord Hamilton said. "Not bad. Not bad at all. Nice selection."

"We've been in one before," Greg said to Ruth, wide-eyed. "It was just outside Basingstoke, remember?"

"Right," Ruth said. "Yes. A coffee shop combined with a boutique." She recalled the mismatched tables and chairs, along with the reclaimed-wood walls.

"That's them." Lord Hamilton glanced at Miles and

leaned forward. "There's a long history of animosity between those three. I'm surprised Hugo seated them together. Asking for trouble."

"His assistant organised the seating arrangements." Lady Hamilton's gaze followed Waylon across the dining carriage. "Clearly doesn't know about their past."

Ruth looked between the Hamiltons, eager for gossip. "What's their past?"

"Miles had a contract with Jane and Robert," Lady Hamilton said.

Lord Hamilton nodded. "Some interior design work for their shops. It all ended in tears."

"My humble apologies." Hugo glided to the Minchents' table. "Chef has made alternative dishes." He lifted their bowls away and set them back on the cart. "We have a delightful cauliflower velouté you're sure to enjoy."

The server hurried off.

Hugo frowned at Miles and was about to leave when Waylon spoke in his ear, hushed, but loud enough for Ruth to still make out.

"Sir, I'm not feeling so well."

He did look a little green around the gills.

Waylon rubbed his stomach. "It came on suddenly."

"I can take care of this," Hugo said. "Go and have a lie down. I'll check in on you later." As he watched his assistant leave, Hugo's jaw flexed.

Ruth made a mental note to force a brandy or two down his throat after dinner. Hugo was wound so tight that a few more turns would see him snap.

Her gaze wandered around the other diners and came to rest on a bald man with dark brown eyes, seated at a table on his own. "Who's that?"

"Never seen the fellow before," Lord Hamilton said. "Must be an acquaintance of Hugo's we've not met."

Ruth refocussed on the Hamiltons. "You've known Hugo long?"

"Oh, yes," Lady Hamilton said. "We're friends with Princess Mary's father, and have been acquainted with dear Hugo for a very long time." She smiled. "We're ever so fond of him."

"When Hugo told us he was leaving Balmoral to start this new venture, we pledged our undying support," Lord Hamilton said. "Wanted to be the first to experience it." He adjusted his cuff links. "Took the poor fellow a few more years than expected, of course, but he got there in the end."

Lady Hamilton sipped a glass of water and set it back on the table. "No one deserves success more than Hugo. We're ever so proud."

Greg tucked a napkin into his collar. "Bon appetit." He slurped his soup. "Mmm."

Ruth smirked at Lord and Lady Hamilton's attempts to ignore the uncouth teenager.

∼

Two hours later—belly bulging with four courses of delightfulness, head light, cat-print pyjamas on—Ruth sat in bed with her hefty 1901 edition of *Mrs Beeton's Book of Household Management*.

She studied a particularly odd recipe for curried celery fritters, and had reached the part about tossing them in thick béchamel sauce when a door opening and closing drew her attention from the page.

Ruth stared down at the vent in her compartment door as a shadow moved past, from left to right. There came a soft knock, then a squeal of a hinge, followed by whispers. Then the door closed again with another screech.

Ruth shuddered and returned to her recipe.

Mrs Beeton suggested once you'd cooked the celery fritters, it was best to sprinkle them with salt, plus extra helpings of curry powder, and then dish them up on a folded napkin immediately.

Ruth assumed this was to ensure the spicy bombs reached their victim before they exploded.

Footfalls passed her door again.

Ruth looked up from her book.

Then there came a knock on a door to the right of her compartment.

Unable to help herself, Ruth set Mrs Beeton aside, slipped out of bed, and pulled on a dressing gown.

She opened her compartment door and peered out.

Hugo stood at the door to the royal carriage.

It opened to reveal the dark-haired protection officer. He held a polished walnut box, twelve inches by eight, and a few deep.

"The safe is in the luggage carriage at the end of the train." Hugo reached for the box, but the officer pulled back.

"I promised her I'd see to it myself."

Hugo cleared his throat. "Very well. Follow me."

Ruth retreated into her compartment, and the two men marched down the corridor.

Why is the princess locking her valuables away?

Ruth closed her door and slipped back into bed.

She'd just opened Mrs Beeton's hefty volume again when another squeal of the door hinge drew her gaze back to the air vent. "What now?"

Shadows moved across, right to left, a door opened and closed, and then a single shadow returned in the opposite direction. This was followed by the loud squeak, and all fell silent.

Ruth yawned. "I give up." She set Mrs Beeton and her bohemian ideas aside, and then lay down.

A few minutes later Ruth drifted off to a land of celery forests, where it rained curry powder.

∼

A banging of fists on a hard surface awoke Ruth with a start. She sat up in bed and looked at the time on her phone: 4:32 a.m.

Ruth groaned.

The banging came again, more insistent, from the front end of the train carriage.

"What on earth is going on?" Hugo's boomed.

"He's got my watch," another man slurred in reply. "I know he took it. Bloody thief."

Ruth swung her legs out of bed, pulled on her nightrobe and slippers, and padded to her compartment door.

She opened it and peered, bleary-eyed, into the hallway.

The window blinds were down, and the lights dimmed.

The bald man stood outside the door to 1A. His bloodshot eyes met Ruth's for a fraction of a second, and he wobbled on his feet before waving to the other end of the carriage. "We played cards. I took off my watch, and now it's gone." He thrust a shaking finger at the door. "He took it. I know he did."

"Who?" Ruth asked.

The bald man hiccupped. "Miles."

Hugo moved him aside and knocked. "Miles? Are you awake?"

"Of course he's bloody awake." The bald man leaned

against the wall to steady himself. "I inherited that Rolex from my great-grandfather."

He'd been seated alone at the table in the dining carriage, but Ruth couldn't recall him wearing a watch, let alone such an expensive one.

Hugo knocked again, and when he received no answer, he opened the door. "Miles?" Hugo leaned in to the compartment, flipped on a light switch, and froze.

The bald man stared too, and then clapped a hand over his mouth, as though he were about to throw up.

Tense, Ruth shuffled along the corridor, and then peered into the compartment.

Miles lay on the floor, facedown. Blood soaked the carpet around his head like a gruesome halo.

4

Ruth stared at Miles' lifeless form on the floor of the compartment, while several more doors in the first-class carriage opened and people stuck their heads out.

"What on earth is going on?" Lord Hamilton yawned.

Ruth's mind reeled, and the first person she thought of was Greg. "Excuse me." She rushed to her compartment, snatched her phone from the desk, and texted him, praying he'd not left his mobile on silent.

A few seconds later, Ruth's phone vibrated, and the message from Greg read:

I AM ASLEEP!!

She let out a breath. Greg always wrote in all caps when he was being dramatic, so he was fine.

Ruth told him to remain in his compartment, with the door bolted, then she slipped her phone into her dressing gown pocket and returned to the corridor.

The voice of Lady Hilary Hamilton came from inside

their compartment. "Well, Tobias? What is it? What's going on out there? Do they know what time it is?"

Lord Hamilton looked back at his wife. "No idea what they're playing at, darling. People standing about the place. None of them speaking." He shook his head. "All very odd, if you ask me."

Jane Minchent stood in the doorway to their compartment with her mousy blonde hair jutting out at odd angles. She addressed Hugo. "Don't tell me that horrid man has gone and done something ghastly?"

Ruth edged her way back to Miles' compartment, trying to get another glimpse, but before she could check out the crime scene, Hugo closed the door.

"Zoey?" a muffled voice called from their right.

Ruth's brow furrowed. That had come from 4A, but she thought Zoey was in that compartment. It sounded like the blind lady, Victoria.

Hugo knocked on the next door down: 2A.

Has something terrible happened to Zoey too?

Hugo knocked again, louder this time.

"I'm coming. Hold on." Zoey opened the door, and it let out a squeak in protest.

Hugo frowned at it.

Zoey blinked at them all with confusion, and then she pulled out a pair of earphones that blasted heavy metal music. "What's wrong?"

"Waylon assigned Victoria to this compartment," Hugo said.

Zoey tightened the belt of her bathrobe. "We swapped. Victoria didn't want to be next to him." She tipped her head in the direction of Miles' compartment and looked between them all. "What is going on?"

Ruth peered over Zoey's shoulder, but nothing seemed out of the ordinary.

"Zoey?" Victoria's muffled voice came again, more urgent.

Zoey hurried along the corridor and opened the door to 4A. "I'm here. It's okay." She slipped inside.

Lord Hamilton scratched his head. "I'm going back to bed."

Hugo caught the door before it closed. "Get changed." He scowled at the others. "That goes for all of you. We'll meet in the salon in five minutes."

Jane Minchent stared at him with incredulity. "You can't be serious, Hugo. It's quarter to five."

"I'm deadly serious." Hugo turned to Ruth. "Please do the same." He then marched back along the corridor and through the door to the royal carriage.

People mumbled under their breath, but did as he asked, and the bald guy stumbled back to his compartment.

As soon as Ruth closed the door behind her, she called Greg.

He answered on the fourth ring. "Grandma," he croaked. "This had really—"

"Someone's been murdered."

A few seconds of silence greeted this declaration.

"Who?"

Ruth sat on the edge of her bed. "Miles. The white-haired guy we saw at dinner. He sat opposite the Minchents."

"I— I don't know what to say."

Ruth recalled her grandson opening the first door in the single-sleeper carriage, right after they'd left the salon the previous evening. "You're in 18A, right?"

"Yeah," he said in a solemn tone. "I'll get changed and come find you."

"No." Ruth kept her voice low. "Bolt your door and stay where you are. Don't open it for anyone other than me. Understood?"

"Do you know who did it?"

"Not a clue." Ruth balled her fist. "But I'll find out."

Greg let out a low groan. "I knew you'd say that."

"Keep your phone always on you. It may come in handy." Ruth hung up and quickly changed clothes, removing her cat-print pyjamas, and pulling on her normal attire: black shirt, black trousers with a pink belt, and pink trainers. The Victorian era could take a back seat.

She stopped in front of the mirror, pulled in a few deep breaths, trying to clear the fogginess of sleep, and then stepped back into the corridor.

Hugo had returned, and he ushered weary guests toward the salon. "Princess Mary will stay in the royal carriage," he said to Ruth. "Along with her officers. She's perfectly safe there. I saw to it with the design." He tapped the side of his nose. "One of the primary features that convinced her protection detail to agree to this trip."

"Where are we?" Ruth stepped to a window, but couldn't figure out how to roll up the blind.

"They're automatic." Hugo took a breath. "I'll scoop up any stragglers on my way back." He gestured. "After you."

Ruth looked at the closed door to room 1A and pictured Miles' lifeless form sprawled facedown on the floor.

"Please," Hugo said through tight lips.

"We only have a few suspects on board," Ruth whispered. "If I can get a good look inside—"

Hugo shook his head. "I'll call the police."

"I understand." Ruth's expression softened. "But we could—"

"Absolutely not." Hugo then let out a juddering breath. "Thank you, Ruth. I appreciate the proposal, and I know you were an outstanding police officer during your time on the force, but I can't let you do that." He motioned to the end of the carriage again. "If you please."

Admitting temporary defeat and fighting the urge to run past him and investigate the crime scene anyway, Ruth trudged along the corridor.

Once she'd stepped foot into the gangway connecting the carriages, Hugo closed the door between them and pressed a phone to his ear.

Ruth peered at him through the window for a moment.

Is there some other way to convince him to let me look at the crime scene?

Someone cleared their throat.

Startled, Ruth spun toward an alcove by the door.

In it sat a night porter.

"Sorry to frighten you, madam." He tipped his cap.

Ruth forced a tremulous smile. "Quite all right." She turned to leave, hesitated, and faced him again. "See anyone go past in the last few hours?"

"Mr Finsbury only asked me that a few moments ago." He nodded. "Around ten minutes ago. Him from 14A."

Ruth glanced at the compartment door. "Who?"

"Mr Price."

"The bald gentleman?"

"That's him. Looked a bit worse for wear. Staggering about the place. I offered to see him back to his compartment, but he wouldn't hear of it."

"Interesting." Ruth rubbed her chin. Although the bald guy could've killed Miles in those few minutes, she felt it unlikely given his condition. "No one else? Any strange noises?"

"Only someone snoring." He pointed farther down the single-sleeper carriage.

I bet I know who that was, Ruth thought.

"Thank you." She hurried to Greg's compartment and knocked.

"Who is it?" came his muffled reply.

"It's me."

"Me who?"

Ruth ground her teeth. "Now is not the time for games."

The door opened.

Greg had dressed in his normal clothes too: jeans and a hoodie "Is it bad?"

"Yes, Gregory. Murder is generally pretty bad." Perhaps Ruth could hide in his compartment, and once Hugo had headed to the salon, she could slip past and ...

"I mean." Greg lowered his voice. "Is it gruesome? The body?" He screwed his face up. "What happened to him?"

Ruth snapped out of her thoughts. "At a guess, blunt force trauma to the back of the head."

Greg winced. "Sick."

Ruth stepped aside. "Come on. Hurry."

Other people filed behind them as they left the carriage and traipsed into the salon.

They each had pale faces and shocked expressions.

Clearly word had got round as to what had occurred.

However, none of them were as pale as Hugo's assistant. Waylon sat at the bar, head in his hands.

The bald guy, Mr Price, slumped at the other end with a glass of Alka-Seltzer.

Both men looked as though someone had run them over with a truck ... and then a tank.

Ruth and Greg sat in chairs nearest the door.

Bleary-eyed servers handed out drinks, some passengers nursing brandy, others requesting only water.

Ruth swept the room with her gaze, studying everyone's faces, searching for hints among their reactions.

Excluding herself and Greg, there were many suspects on board the Finsbury Flyer: Mr Price at the bar; Waylon; the blind lady, Victoria, and her assistant, Zoey; Lord and Lady Hamilton; Jane and Robert Minchent; the rest of the train staff; and Hugo Finsbury himself.

Unless it was some grand conspiracy, Ruth couldn't imagine Princess Mary sneaking past her protection officers and committing the dastardly deed. Nor could she picture those highly trained officers killing Miles either. Although, she could not rule out anything, seeing as he'd ruffled so many feathers the previous evening.

Had the victim angered someone enough to warrant murder?

He'd certainly had an abrasive attitude.

Lord and Lady Hamilton's status amid high society would be something they'd eagerly protect, but that could also give them the perfect cover to commit the unspeakable crime.

Then there were the unassuming Jane and Robert Minchent: wealthy owners of a chain of coffee shop boutiques. Ruth remembered the disgust Miles had fired their way at dinner because of their dietary choices.

As far as Ruth was aware, they'd eaten in silence from then on. *But did Miles say something else to justify his untimely demise? Push them too far this time? What happened after I went to bed? Did their long history of bad blood finally catch up with them? Had they finally seized the opportunity for retribution?*

Ruth's gaze moved to the loner, Mr Price, at the bar. He was a mystery to her. She'd have to remedy that.

Her attention then shifted to the remaining passengers.

Along with Ruth, Victoria and Zoey slept in the compartments closest to Miles. However, she couldn't imagine how Victoria could've murdered him, and Zoey's door let out an awful squeak when opened, which would have awakened the whole carriage.

Waylon had been poorly and in his compartment.

Unwell enough to keep him from killing Miles?

Ruth hated to admit it, but right now Hugo seemed the most likely culprit. He also had a history and a definite beef with the victim. However, she also couldn't imagine her old acquaintance would risk the negative publicity that would surely follow.

On the other hand, it was certainly a way to ensure the Finsbury Flyer would gain notoriety. Some people were attracted to that kind of thing.

Hugo entered the salon and held up his hands for silence. "If I could have everyone's attention, please." He looked between the gathered passengers with a mournful expression. "As you may know, there's been an accident."

"A murder," Ruth murmured.

Greg nudged her.

"It appears as though poor Miles, a longtime and dear friend of mine," Hugo continued, "slipped and hit his head."

Ruth opened her mouth to argue, but Greg nudged her again. She huffed out a breath and folded her arms.

"Naturally, I've informed the police," Hugo said. "We are to meet them at our destination in Penzance." He looked at his watch. "We will arrive in two hours and five minutes. For now, everyone is to remain in this carriage."

"Why don't we stop at the next available station?" Robert Minchent asked.

"This train only has a permit to travel on a particular

route, and at precise times, with no stops," Hugo said. "Penzance is our destination, and that's where they'll meet us." He studied the confused faces staring back at him. "Suffice to say, it took me a little over three years to get the final approval. We're on a track which normally accommodates much faster trains. If we slow or stop, we could cause problems, even an accident." His gaze rested on Waylon. "As you can appreciate, we cannot risk that happening."

"Can't we speed up?" Jane Minchent asked in a shrill voice. "Get there sooner?" She wrung a handkerchief between her fingers.

"Again, we're not permitted to do so." Hugo walked to the bar and sat on a stool at the opposite end to Mr Price, who paid him no mind. "We'll wait it out."

Jane looked at Ruth. "But you think he was murdered? I heard you say so just now."

This resulted in several gasps and mutterings.

"I'm not sure," Ruth said with a furtive glance in Hugo's direction. However, she took the opportunity to scan the gathered faces, watching their reactions.

"One of us is a killer?" Jane asked in a small voice.

"Preposterous." Lord Hamilton jumped to his feet, almost spilling his brandy. "I will not remain here when such unfounded accusations are thrown about." He gulped down his drink and slammed it on the table. "Come on, Hilary."

"And where exactly will you go?" Mr Price asked, rubbing his temples and still not making eye contact with anyone. "Are you about to jump from a moving train?"

"I say." Lord Hamilton balled his fists. "How dare you, sir."

Waylon watched both men with an anxious expression.

Hugo held up his hands. "There is nothing to indicate it

was a murder. Please, stop this bickering and remain calm. I assure you we are handling the situation by following police instructions. I must ask for your patience." He shot Ruth a look.

She mouthed, "Sorry."

"If there really is a killer among us," Victoria said, "it's precisely why we all must stay together." She leaned sideways, found her assistant's arm, and squeezed it.

Zoey tapped her hand. "She's right."

"Agreed." Robert Minchent shuffled his chair closer to his wife's. "This way we can all keep an eye on one another." He winced. "Sorry. I mean no offence, Victoria."

She smiled and held her white cane with her free hand. "None taken."

Lord Hamilton glared at Mr Price, then dropped back to his seat. He folded his arms and eyed the servers. "How do we know it wasn't a member of staff who offed the poor fellow? Goodness knows you have enough of them wandering about the place."

Ruth couldn't rule out that possibility either, especially if Miles had worked with any of them leading up to that moment. Perhaps he'd rubbed one of them the wrong way.

Hugo let out an exasperated breath. "It was an accident."

Ruth was convinced otherwise, and as soon as the opportunity arose to sneak out, she'd prove it by investigating the crime scene.

Greg noticed the determined look in her eyes, and his shoulders slumped.

5

Ruth could understand why Hugo wished Miles' death to be a mishap—after all, Hugo's entire business was on the line—but she'd experienced such errors in judgement before.

During only her second month on the force, serving as a metropolitan police officer, Ruth had made two such mistakes in quick succession.

The first had come when some guy had fallen from a sixth-floor balcony to his death. When Ruth had checked the railing, she'd found it pulled away from the wall, and therefore assumed it had been an unfortunate accident.

She had taken the girlfriend's statement, wherein she'd told Ruth the victim had gone onto the balcony for a smoke. When he hadn't returned, she'd checked on him, and discovered the awful truth.

The evidence fit with her version of events, but it turned out the girlfriend had lied.

A witness later came forward, having seen the pair in a physical altercation. The girlfriend had pushed him, he'd toppled back, and the railing had given way.

With Ruth still reeling from that basic oversight, the second error in judgement had come a week later when Ruth had received a call to attend an incident in Portobello Road, Notting Hill.

She'd arrived to find a car had smashed through the front of an electrical shop.

The driver had subsequently climbed from the vehicle, leaned against the back, and waited as though he didn't have a care in the world.

To make matters worse, the car had driven into the corner of the shop, and the entire front of the building was now in danger of collapse. Sparks also flew from various smashed televisions and video recorders.

By the time her colleagues arrived, Ruth had evacuated the shop, as well as several others on either side, plus the flats and offices above. They'd then cordoned off the entire area and called out an electrical engineer to turn off the power to the street.

This had resulted in a lot of arguments and pushback from the residents, but Ruth couldn't afford to have anyone electrocuted while they waited for professionals to assess the damage.

The driver had seemed nonchalant about the chaos, as if he'd simply bumped the kerb, and not caused thousands of pounds' worth of damage.

That should have been red flag number one.

Overlooked red flag number two had come in the form of the accident itself. Traffic moved slowly along Portobello Road, with plenty of pedestrians milling about.

Witnesses recalled the vehicle coming to a stop for several seconds, and then the engine revving and the car racing forward, threading between parked cars and smashing into the shop.

However, the driver had explained he wasn't used to a manual, his foot had slipped off the clutch, and he'd panicked. He'd then managed to swerve around the parked vehicles and narrowly missed pedestrians, only to hit the shop.

In hindsight, all of that should have been cause for immediate arrest.

With the area now cordoned off, Ruth had gone home for some well-earned sleep.

She'd woken to a storm. Metaphorically speaking.

A woman with a fake ID had rented the car, who'd then loaned it to the driver Ruth had interviewed, who'd also used fake ID.

In the small hours of the morning, with an oblivious officer out front, a team of robbers had broken through the back of the shop next door. With the power out, the alarm deactivated, they'd helped themselves to designer gear, leaving the shop and storeroom bare.

From that day on, Ruth chose to not take everything at face value, to dig deeper, and to make darned sure nothing nefarious was going on.

One silly mistake is forgivable, but two are an embarrassment, and Ruth was determined not to make a third.

She waved Hugo over and whispered to him, "With your permission, I'd like to check out Miles' compartment now. While everyone's safely in here."

Hugo's face screwed up. "We've been over this."

"Maybe I can figure out how he slipped and what he hit his head on. You know, to stop any speculation," Ruth persisted in what she hoped came across as a calm yet compassionate voice. "We have a couple of hours, and all I need is a few minutes to—"

"No," Hugo snapped, and backed it up with a vehement

shake of his head. "I see what you're trying to do. It's a police matter. They'll find it was an accident, and nothing more. We can then put this ugly misfortune behind us."

"Hugo, please."

He waggled a finger. "I will allow nothing to jeopardise this business. Do you understand me, Ruth? Please stop interfering." Hugo straightened and adjusted his tie. "That's the end of the matter."

As he headed back to the bar, no doubt to check on Waylon's well-being, a giant wave of frustration surged through Ruth, and only increased with every wasted minute.

Although she empathised with Hugo's point of view, a mystery, two carriages away, lay begging for her to examine it. She itched to check out the compartment more closely. "I need you to cause a distraction," she whispered.

"What?" Greg recoiled. "How?"

"I don't know yet. Let me think." Ruth ground her teeth. "You could do a jig."

Greg frowned. "A what?"

"You know, a jig. A dance." Ruth pumped her arms up and down, swung her head from side to side, and jiggled her feet.

This caught Lord Hamilton's attention.

She smiled at him, and he looked away.

Greg shook his head and spoke through the corner of his mouth. "I'm not doing that, Grandma."

"Please. I must take a closer look at Miles' compartment. You and I both know it wasn't an accident." Images of the broken balcony railing, and the girlfriend's innocent expression all those years ago, flashed through her thoughts. "Definitely not an accident," she murmured. "It can't be." Ruth spotted the night porter at the far end of the carriage.

Greg stared at the carpet. "Don't you think it's a little dangerous to be going off on your own?"

"Why?" Ruth turned in her seat. "Now is the safest time." She jerked her head. "The killer is in here with us."

"You heard Hugo." Greg gripped the arms of his chair and continued to stare at the floor. "It's a job for the police. It is *always* a job for the police. Keep your nose out."

Ruth's eyebrows arched. "I'm police."

"Ex-police."

"Forever police."

"And they fired you."

Ruth huffed and folded her arms.

"Don't go," Greg said. "You'll get into trouble. There's been enough trouble to last us a lifetime."

An idea struck Ruth, and she contained a smile. "How about I buy you a giant bag of junk food when we get to Penzance?"

Greg looked at her. "How big?"

Ruth placed her hands a foot apart.

"Better make sure it's crammed full," Greg said. "No tricks. Filled to the very top with every item of my choosing." He was practically salivating.

Ruth beamed at him. "Grandma loves you very much."

"Whatever. But I'm not dancing." Greg glanced uneasily around the carriage, then got to his feet and sauntered over to the bar, clearly trying to look casual, but looking anything but.

Ruth's whole body tensed with anticipation.

As Hugo talked to the Minchents, Greg stepped beside Waylon, leaned across the bar, and then deliberately knocked a bottle of brandy to the floor.

Waylon jumped.

"Oh, I'm so sorry," Greg said in a loud voice, drawing all eyes. "I'm really clumsy."

With everyone's attention on her grandson, Ruth got to her feet and slipped out of the carriage.

She fetched her gloves—pink woollen ones, because that was the only pair she had—and then pulled them on as she stopped outside the door to compartment 1A.

Holding her breath, Ruth strained to hear over the rhythmic *cla-clat, cla-clat, cla-clat* of the train wheels on the track, but could not make out any other movement.

The automatic blinds were still down, and the lights dimmed.

Everyone, save for the princess and her protection officers, was in the salon carriage or farther back along the train.

Ruth was alone.

She let the breath out, preparing to focus on the job at hand. She needed to move with swift efficiency, and then sneak back to the salon before anyone noticed her absence.

With both excitement and nervousness coursing through her veins, Ruth opened the door to Miles' compartment, leaned inside, and flicked on the light switch.

Poor Miles lay undisturbed on his front, legs crumpled at odd angles, head to one side, eyes cold and staring at the floor with frozen astonishment.

Ruth scanned the area around the body, the bed, and the desk, examining every inch, but she found no stray fibres from the assailant, nor an obvious murder weapon. Which meant the killer had taken it with them.

Ruth examined the compartment again but could see nowhere Miles may have struck his head—the only thing that could've done the job was a brass desk lamp, but it was bolted down—which ruled out an accident.

Ruth stepped into the compartment fully, careful where she placed her feet, and made sure not to touch anything. Then she squatted to get a better look at the body.

The blood on the back of Miles' head stood in stark contrast to his white hair. The impact point was the crown, toward the top, indicating a blow from behind and above, consistent with someone swinging down with a heavy object.

A red line also ran across his left cheek, from the corner of his eye to the earlobe. The mark looked fresh.

What could it be from?

Ruth drew a blank, so she scooted to one side for a better look at his legs. Judging by how they'd folded as he'd fallen forward, this pointed to two conclusions: firstly, Miles had known his assailant and felt comfortable enough to turn his back on them; and secondly, he'd been kneeling or bending over.

So what was he doing?

Miles' phone lay beside him, face up, with the torch illuminated. Clearly, he'd answered the door in the dark.

Ruth's gaze rose to the desk. The drawer sat open by half an inch, as though Miles had been in the process of fetching something when his assailant had struck with such ferocity.

So did the killer ask for an item, Miles turned to retrieve it, and then ... whack?

What about the Rolex?

Did Miles really steal it? Did Mr Price then return for the watch and kill him? But if that was the case, why then come back later to bang on the door and wake everyone up?

Ruth pursed her lips.

Might Mr Price have done that to then feign innocence? After all, why would any guilty person return to the crime scene, drawing attention to it and themselves?

He was the only passenger she so far knew absolutely nothing about. Other than he liked a tipple. *Why is he here? Why has Hugo invited him?*

Ruth edged her way over to the desk.

She slipped her phone from her pocket, and took a picture of the open drawer. Zoomed in, the resulting image showed the corner of something white farther inside.

Ruth activated the torch function, leaned down, and angled the light into the drawer. Sure enough, a rectangular white piece of paper lay in there, along with a silver object glinting toward the back, and . . . a stack of money.

She straightened and frowned.

Her gaze moved to the door, to the drawer, the door, and back again. Ruth muttered, "Really shouldn't do this." She stretched out a gloved hand toward the drawer but hesitated. "Bad idea, Morgan." Ruth pulled back, shook her head, and sighed. "Oh, nuts to it." Making a mental note of how far Miles had pulled the drawer open, Ruth grabbed the bottom and slid it out some more.

She stared down with incredulity.

Inside was indeed a stack of bills: ten- and twenty-pound notes. During her time on the force, whenever Ruth had bagged evidence, she had always found it hard to gauge amounts of money. However, there had to be at least a few hundred pounds.

Along with those notes were several handfuls of coins.

She glanced at Miles. "Why do you have all this cash?"

The Finsbury Flyer was an all-inclusive experience, after all.

Reaching past the money, Ruth carefully lifted out the rectangular paper and flipped it over.

It was half a torn cheque.

She looked in the drawer again, found the other half, and placed them on the desk together.

The amount was made out to Miles for the sum of fifty thousand pounds, and signed by...

"Hugo," Ruth breathed. "I thought you didn't have any money left?"

Or did Miles know this would bounce, and that's why he tore it up?

She stared at it for a few seconds before gathering herself, taking a picture, and returning the cheque to the drawer, exactly how she'd found it.

Ruth's attention then moved to the next set of objects inside: a pair of diamond earrings, shaped like daisies.

"Lady Hamilton's." She looked down at Miles, and her brow furrowed. "Why do you have these?"

And, more importantly, how did he come by them?

"You appear to be quite the thief." Ruth envisaged him picking the pockets of fellow passengers, sliding a watch from the drunk Mr Price's wrist, emptying a few wallets and purses... *But taking Lady Hamilton's earrings off, right in front of her?* That was a whole other level.

"No Rolex, though." Ruth slid the drawer back to its previous state, leaving it open by half an inch, and then after another careful look around the cabin, she peeked into the bathroom.

A shaving kit, shower gel, toothbrush, and toothpaste, plus a small selection of eau de toilette bottles, sat in a neat line along the back of the sink.

Damp towels on the floor.

Ruth checked the wardrobe.

Inside was the jacket Miles had worn to dinner, along with a pair of jeans and a grey shirt, which he'd worn when he arrived in Edinburgh.

Ruth checked the jeans. The back pocket held a note typewritten in all caps, like an old-fashioned telegram. It read:

> COME TO STATION IMMEDIATELY.
> HUGO IS LYING.

The note had no salutation, nor was it signed by anyone.

Ruth examined the paper under the light, but it had no watermarks and seemed unremarkable. As did the typeface and ink used. Someone could well have written this on a computer and then printed it out.

She sniffed the paper but detected no unusual scents.

Ruth took a photo of the note with her phone, then returned it to the jeans pocket, and closed the wardrobe.

After one more look around the compartment, she backed into the corridor and shut the door, more determined than ever to unmask the killer.

6

Ruth raced to her compartment and stood inside for a couple of minutes, staring at the wall, trying to understand what the limited evidence suggested, and piece together the clues.

Someone had sent Miles a note, telling him to come to the station, which meant that person had already been there, knew him, and that person was likely on the train right now. Also, that same person accused Hugo of lying. *Something to do with money? The train? Someone on board?* Perhaps the note-writer would have insider knowledge, which could mean they were a member of staff.

"Hmm." Ruth scratched her chin. "His assistant, Waylon?"

Next was the cheque, torn in two. A sizeable sum of money to dismiss, but Miles had made it clear to Hugo back at the station ticket office that his grievance wasn't about finances.

Ruth pictured the leather holdall Miles had clutched, wanting Hugo to look at whatever was inside. However, the holdall wasn't in Miles' compartment.

Where's it gone? Has the killer taken it? Is that what they came for, and murdered poor Miles in the process? Does it hold some kind of evidence Hugo wished no one to see?

Ruth wanted to confront him about the cheque and the holdall, but that would mean confessing she'd snuck into Miles' compartment.

What about the Rolex? Where's that?

She paced her compartment.

If Miles took it? When? And why?

He'd made it clear money wasn't an issue, but then there were the diamond earrings and stack of cash in his desk drawer.

No doubt about it, Ruth needed to speak to Mr Price first, and see what light he could shed, particularly on the circumstances surrounding his watch. The only question was how she could get him alone or somewhere the others could not overhear. Especially Hugo.

Ruth then returned to the idea that Mr Price had already visited Miles earlier that night. She pictured him in Miles' compartment, waving a fist and swaying while he demanded his watch back. *Had he then struck Miles in a fit of rage? Stolen his holdall?* Perhaps, panicked by what he'd done, and in a drunk stupor, Mr Price had abandoned the crime scene.

He could've returned to his compartment, trying to sober up and clear his head, when reality sank in. Maybe the idea to return later, and therefore feign innocence, had struck him. Making a big show of banging on Miles' door.

It was certainly one theory.

Not a solid one, but a place to start, and Mr Price could be the primary suspect.

However, a gap in her theory popped into Ruth's thoughts: if Miles had turned to retrieve the watch, Mr Price had no reason to kill him.

Also, the Minchents had a bad history with Miles, so both of them may have had motive to kill him. Not to mention Miles had been rude to them at dinner, but Ruth couldn't see that alone warranted murder. Not unless he'd said something else she'd not caught.

As for Lord and Lady Hamilton, she didn't know their history with Miles. Something she'd have to remedy.

What with the four previous people being couples, it would've been harder for one of them to have snuck out and done the deed. Unless they were both in on it.

Ruth sighed, stepped back into the hallway, and looked to either side of her door.

To the right stood 2A, the room occupied by Zoey—the blind lady's assistant and another suspect. However, if she was the killer, Ruth couldn't immediately figure out how she could've left her cabin without setting off the squeaky hinge.

With Ruth being a light sleeper, that noise would've woken her in an instant. If Zoey was innocent, and it wasn't for the fact she had worn earphones blasting music, she might have heard a commotion and Miles' body hit the floor.

Ruth needed to question everyone in turn, including Victoria, hoping one would give the game away. No way could Ruth rule anyone out at this stage.

To the left of compartment 1A was the door that led to the royal carriage, with the princess, plus her highly trained and vetted protection officers. Ruth still could not discount them entirely, but also couldn't immediately picture any of them being the murderer.

Ruth could definitely exclude herself as a killer. Well, unless she'd sleepwalked, but she'd never done that in her life. Night-time excursions were Greg's thing.

Ruth rejected him as a killer too, because not only did

Greg bolt his door to limit his sleepwalking, but he also had a weak stomach for violence.

Victoria stayed in compartment 4A; 5A was the Minchents; while the Hamiltons were in 6A. As far as Ruth knew, 7A was vacant, and there was Hugo in the last compartment: 8A.

Ruth hated to admit it, but he still sat squarely at the top of her list of suspects. He knew Miles, they'd worked together, and had argued on at least one occasion, but she struggled to accept he could be capable of murder.

The staff way back in the crew carriage were an unknown. Ruth couldn't see any of them risking their jobs, plus the palace would've vetted them closely—checked for criminal backgrounds—but Miles may have said something to push one of them over the edge.

Ruth thought back to dinner the previous evening.

She and Greg had gone to their compartments straight after their dessert and coffee, but several people retired to the salon. It was more than possible Miles had insulted someone during that time.

The person in the note seemed familiar with the Hugo vs Miles situation.

But who?

The night porter said no one other than Mr Price had passed him during the last few hours. Ruth couldn't imagine he'd lied. Not unless he was the guilty party.

"Hugo," Ruth murmured, and her gaze shifted to his compartment door. "I can't believe you could have done it. There's no way you'd risk everything you've built over an argument." She'd taken a step when the creak of another door opening in the other first-class carriage's connecting gangway made her freeze.

Ruth peered through the window, and her heart leapt into her throat at movement in the corridor.

Someone was coming.

She scrambled into her compartment and shut the door. Panting, Ruth turned an ear to it. Footfalls marched along the corridor. Ruth held her breath, ready for the capture, but sighed in relief as they continued past her room. She opened her door a crack and peered out.

Hugo knocked on the door to the royal carriage. It opened, and one of the protection officers greeted him. They exchanged a few words, then Hugo did an about-face and returned the way he'd come.

Once clear, Ruth slipped back into the corridor and stared at the door to the royal carriage.

The protection officers—with certainly more than a decade of experience each—were among the least likely suspects on board. However, they may have heard or seen something. The force trained officers to observe and report, especially at their calibre.

Ruth jogged to the royal carriage door. She raised a fist to knock but hesitated. "This is a bad idea."

The officers carried Glock pistols. If they saw her as a threat, an uninvited guest, she could land herself in a lot of hot water.

Or worse.

However, a wave of curiosity washed through her. She had to find out if they'd noticed anything suspicious. Perhaps they could help shorten the list of suspects.

Ruth removed her gloves, slipped them into her pocket, and tried to look as nonthreatening as possible.

She then held her breath and knocked.

The door opened, and a burly officer greeted her. He had short-cropped dark hair, and day-old stubble.

He frowned. "What can I do for you?"

Ruth swallowed and forced a smile. "I— I suppose you've heard about what's happened?"

The officer nodded.

"I'm Ruth Morgan." She extended a hand.

The dark-haired officer didn't take it. "The shamed ex–Met sergeant. I know who you are."

Ruth baulked. "Erm. Well, yes. I suppose. You've done your homework." Her brow furrowed. "Although, *shamed* is a bit harsh. I was sacked, it's true." She lifted her chin. "For investigating my husband's murder."

The officer stared down at her, unblinking.

Ruth glanced past him, taking in the opulent interior with its red and gold upholstered furniture, walls lined in walnut, crystal chandeliers and light fittings, and the finest Persian rugs.

Halfway down the carriage, a door to a room on the right was closed. This must lead to the royal bedroom suite. Ruth imagined the princess inside, isolated from the commoners, and twiddling her thumbs.

Running alongside the bedroom suite was a narrow hallway, which led to another closed door at the far end of the carriage. Ruth's gaze shifted to her right. Lastly, next to the door she stood at was an enclosed office, six by six, with a single cot and desk inside.

The blond protection officer stepped out and smiled at her. "Morning."

She smiled back.

The dark-haired officer moved into Ruth's line of sight.

The smile slipped from her face. "I wondered if you'd heard or seen anything suspicious?"

He folded his arms. "Other than now?"

"Yes." Ruth nodded. "Precisely. Other than now."

"We were in here. Doing our jobs."

"You work shifts?" Ruth asked.

"Only through the night."

"And who was awake in the last few hours?"

"Me."

"You didn't hear or see anything?"

"I've already told you."

Deciding not to push her luck any further, Ruth backed away. "Thank you for your time."

The door closed, and Ruth's jaw firmed. She would not give up until she uncovered the murderer's identity. After all, and if nothing else, doing so would impress her fellow passengers, and guarantee they'd talk about the famous food consultant to their friends.

She'd have jobs lined up for years to come.

Ruth hurried along the first-class double-sleeper carriage with a sense of determination, through the connecting gangway and into the single sleeper. She was about to go through to the salon, when a thought struck her, and Ruth stopped dead in her tracks.

If she could find the murder weapon, that would help uncover the killer's identity, and the mystery would be hers to solve; over before they reached their destination.

Surely that would go some way to repaying Hugo from all those years ago.

She faced the door to Mr Price's compartment: 14A. "Let's see what you've got." Ruth opened it, flicked on the light, and stepped into a room identical to hers, apart from a couple of feet narrower width and a smaller bed.

She scanned every inch, from floor to ceiling, even behind the drapes, but nothing stood out as the murder weapon. Ruth then checked the bathroom and the wardrobe for good measure but found nothing there either.

"That would've been too easy, huh?" She stepped back into the hallway and closed the door.

Ruth eyed the door at the end, back to the connecting gangway and the double sleeper beyond, and her stomach tightened.

Hugo had worked as a butler at Balmoral Castle for several decades. That was how he knew Princess Mary. He'd known her since she was a baby and had been a trusted, well-loved, and respected employee.

Not long before Ruth had met her husband, John, he'd been on one of his infamous archaeological crusades. This time, in Bonnie Scotland.

John had been on the trail of a supposed relic linked to William Wallace, dredging part of the River Dee, hunting beneath the rocks, when he'd slipped, hit his head, and fallen into the water.

Hugo Finsbury, fly fishing on his day off and farther down the river on the Balmoral estate, had spotted an unconscious John floating past him face up, at quite some speed. Hugo had then leapt into action, and risked his own safety to venture into the river, grab John, and drag him ashore, where he'd called for medical attention.

If it hadn't been for Hugo, Ruth would have never met her husband, and their daughter would not have been born, nor Greg and his twin sister.

Ruth owed Hugo a lot, which was why she felt terrible for even considering what she was about to do.

But maybe I can rule him out of Miles' murder completely?

Ruth jogged back through the gangway, into the double-sleeper carriage, and stopped outside 8A. She reached for the door handle to Hugo's compartment but pulled back. "I can't do this. It's stupid. Hugo is not involved. He can't be."

She turned to leave, and the note from Miles' pocket drifted into her thoughts:

HUGO IS LYING.

Lying about what?

Ruth swore under her breath, opened the door, flicked on the light, and slipped inside the compartment.

She shut the door behind her, and pressed her back against it as she took in the sparse interior.

On the desk sat a picture of Hugo during his time at Balmoral, with several members of the royal family, including a young Princess Mary smiling cheekily at the camera.

Ruth's stomach did a backflip, and she felt terrible for being in here but pressed on regardless. The sooner she got this over with, the quicker she could leave.

She checked the desk drawer. It was empty. Ruth stepped into the bathroom, but that had nothing of interest either. She then opened the wardrobe door, and her breath caught.

"Oh no. Hugo."

In the bottom, beneath hanging suits, sat a canvas tool bag. It was open, and inside lay various implements of the handyman's trade, but on the top, in the most prominent position, was a hammer.

Ruth knelt and used the torch on her phone to examine it, looking for any stray white hairs or signs of dried blood.

Trying to get a grip of herself, thinking it through calmly, with an ounce of rationality, Ruth then doubted the murderer would be stupid enough to replace the murder weapon in a tool bag. Whoever had killed Miles, it would have been easy for them to throw it from the train.

Right?

Mind you, she mused, far stranger and ridiculous things had happened during her time on the force. People did odd things in the heat of the moment.

Forensics and an autopsy would uncover the instrument of death used for the deed, and the police would send search teams to scour along the train tracks, if needed.

Ruth stared at the hammer. "Although. This is very suspicious." She contemplated hiding it somewhere.

The cabin door opened.

Ruth leapt to her feet, staggered back, and almost toppled over the chair.

Hugo loomed large in the doorway.

His face twisted with anger. "What the hell are you doing?" Veins bulged from his neck and forehead, and he seemed about ready to explode.

Ruth opened her mouth to explain, to quell the impending storm, but no words formed. All she could do was stare at him, thoughts numbed.

And then an image of Greg's smug face swam into view, with an expression as if to say, "I told you so, Grandma. I said you'd get caught. Didn't I say you'd get caught? Now look at what trouble you're in. You wait until I tell Mum what you did."

7

In his compartment, Hugo's eyes darted to the tool bag in the bottom of his wardrobe, and then, as though he sensed pending accusations, he thrust a finger at the hammer. "You don't for one moment think I used that to stave Miles' head in?"

Ruth cringed at the crude comment and unstuck her tongue. "Of course I don't, but you've got to admit how bad it could look, Hugo. I— I mean . . ." She eyed the hammer, and her chest tightened. "Seriously bad, no?" Ruth pulled in a juddering breath and tried to calm her racing heart. "Tell me you didn't do it." And then she instantly regretted her words.

Hugo's lips quivered with rage, and Ruth was all too aware of how trapped she was, in this compact space, with him blocking her only viable means of escape. For a second, Ruth considered locking herself in the bathroom, but her cleithrophobia glued her feet to the floor.

Hugo glared at her with defiance, and then he spoke slowly and deliberately through clenched teeth. "I brought the tool bag from the luggage carriage last night." He raised a hand, and Ruth flinched. "Not to kill anyone, but to fix the squeaky hinge on 2A's door." Hugo stepped forward. "I intended to see to that this morning. But, well . . ." He swallowed. "I didn't get the chance." He eyed Ruth for several seconds, perhaps wondering if she believed him, and moved aside.

Ruth mumbled an apology and slipped past him. She then stopped in the corridor and faced Hugo as he left his compartment. "Can I ask what you were arguing about?"

Hugo looked taken aback. "Excuse me?"

"At the station in Edinburgh," Ruth said, unable to help herself. "I overheard you and Miles arguing. He seemed angry." She left out what little details she knew, hoping Hugo would elaborate.

He folded his arms.

Ruth mumbled another apology, hung her head, and traipsed along the corridor. "Can you at least tell me what was in that box Princess Mary's protection officer had last night?" Ruth opened the door to the connecting gangway and looked back at Hugo.

"How do you know about that?"

Ruth half shrugged.

Hugo's lip curled. "Not that it's any of your damned business, but it's jewellery. What else?" He lifted his chin. "We have a state-of-the-art safe on board. Spared no expense. I can assure you all our passengers' valuables are quite secure. An absolute essential given our current passengers, wouldn't you say?"

Ruth frowned at the rhetorical question and made her way along the first-class single-sleeper carriage. "Why would the jewellery not be better staying with the protection officers?" Princess Mary's jewels had to be somewhere between astronomical and priceless, with a smidge of irreplaceable thrown in, but an armed officer would be better than a safe, no matter how advanced.

Hugo pressing his lips together and continuing to glare at her.

"Forget it," she murmured. "Their priority is the princess, not valuables. Right. Got it."

"Every eventuality has been covered." Hugo adjusted his tie. "Let's just say there are certain allowances in the train's design."

Ruth stopped at the door to the salon and turned back. "Is that what Miles was so worried about? Something in the train's design? A safety concern?"

Hugo's glower intensified. "Let me make this perfectly clear: the safety of our passengers is, and always has been, my number one priority. I would not allow anything to jeopardise that." He shook his head. "Miles' accusations were completely unfounded, and he wouldn't listen to reason. Nonetheless, I assured him I'd investigate, to put his mind at ease, once we get back to Edinburgh."

"Who else has access to the safe?" Something felt off about that too. "Your assistant, Waylon?"

Hugo's expression softened. "Look, Ruth." He lowered his voice and leaned in. "I know your intentions are honourable, and you feel you owe me for John, but I simply must implore you to stay out of this. I cannot afford any more problems. A murder? On our inaugural journey? It's my worst nightmare made manifest. You understand?" He tugged one of his earlobes. "I have no doubt the police will take care of it. They'll figure out what happened, and we can put this sordid mess behind us."

Ruth wanted to ask Hugo a million more questions, but instead she admitted temporary defeat, gave a half-hearted nod, and trudged into the salon.

All eyes followed her as she sat in the armchair next to Greg.

Hugo clapped, drawing everyone's attention to him instead. "Hungry? We'll gladly have Chef prepare breakfast. French toast? Pancakes? Waffles?" He looked to Waylon. "If I'm not mistaken, we have a delightful selection of croissants and iced buns."

Waylon looked about ready to throw up at the mention of food.

"Coffee," Lord Hamilton said.

Greg raised a hand. "A full English, please."

"Of course," Hugo said. "Bacon, sausages, eggs, beans, the lot. Whatever your hearts' desire." He motioned to the servers.

They pulled notepads from their pockets and moved among the passengers, taking drink and food orders.

Greg leaned in to Ruth. "Told you not to go. Didn't I warn you?" He shot an uneasy glance in Hugo's direction. "He realised you'd left. Seemed really irritated. Didn't believe me when I told him I had no clue where you'd gone."

"You could have said I'd left to use the loo."

"I did." Greg motioned to the other end of the salon carriage. "Nearest one is that way. He was only a few minutes before coming back though. Twice as mad as before."

Ruth crossed her arms and thought through the events of the previous night: the opening and closing of doors, the moving about, swapping compartments. Someone must have seen or heard something suspicious during all those shenanigans.

Ruth's gaze wandered to Victoria and her assistant, Zoey. With Hugo's attention on the other passengers, and

Waylon helping the servers, she slinked over to them and sat opposite. "Hi. This is Ruth Morgan."

"The retired detective?" Victoria smirked. "I heard you've been sneaking about without permission." She clucked her tongue.

"I was never a detective," Ruth said. "But I was part of the Metropolitan Police Force." She watched Hugo to make sure he paid her no mind. "And you're right about the lack of permission. Listen." Ruth edged forward in her seat, careful none of the other passengers eavesdropped. "Zoey, you didn't hear anything unusual last night?"

She shook her head. "I can't sleep without my music. Sorry. If I had, I would've alerted the night porter." Her face drooped. "I feel terrible about what happened to that poor man."

Victoria reached out, found her knee, and rested a hand on it. "It's not your fault."

"She's right," Ruth said. "If you'd heard a commotion and gone to investigate, you may have got hurt." She looked round the room. The night porter sat in the corner, talking to another train employee in a dark blue uniform—perhaps a cleaner.

She refocussed on the ladies. "Victoria, you didn't happen to hear anything either, did you? No matter how small or insignificant."

"As a matter of fact, I did." Victoria adjusted her sunglasses, leaned forward in her chair, and the three of them huddled. "Zoey and I were just discussing it."

Ruth looked between them. "Go on."

"Well." Victoria cleared her throat. "The strangest thing. I—"

Zoey touched her arm as Waylon approached.

He held a notepad. "Can I take your breakfast orders?" He still looked unwell.

Ruth sat back. "What's on offer?"

"Other than what Mr Finsbury already mentioned, we have a wide selection of cereals, toast with jam or marmalade..."

"I'll have the full English." Greg dropped into the chair next to Ruth.

"You'll have to forgive my grandson's lack of manners," Ruth said to Victoria and Zoey. "To him, *ladies first* only applies to doorways and settling bills."

"Sorry," Greg muttered. "I'm really hungry."

"I already have your order written down." Waylon's tone could've given a polar bear frostbite.

Ruth checked the time on her phone: 6:05 a.m. "You don't usually eat for another two or three hours."

"I'm used to eating when I wake up," Greg said. "I am awake now. Therefore I am hungry."

Sound logic.

Once Waylon had taken the rest of their orders, with Ruth opting for a bowl of cereal and three cups of milky tea, she refocussed on Victoria. "What were you saying, Victoria?"

"Right. I was telling Zoey about last night, and how I heard people going back and forth past my door."

"Me too," Ruth said. "Can you elaborate?" After all, the people she'd seen and heard were most likely Victoria and Zoey switching compartments. She hadn't noticed anyone else. Well, no one other than Hugo and the black-haired protection officer. Ruth's brow furrowed. Come to think of it, she'd not heard him return to the royal carriage, so she could've missed anything else too.

"First person was a few minutes past one in the morning. Not too long after I'd settled." Victoria screwed up her face as she recalled. "Heavy, determined footfalls. A man. Going from right to left."

Ruth pictured the carriage. Victoria stayed in room 4A, next to her. So, unless someone else had already been in Miles' compartment, 1A, that had to be him because next door was Zoey, and then Ruth. The only other men down that part of the train were the protection officers.

"I heard more footsteps at one twenty-five," Victoria said. "Yes. I'm sure the argument was right after that. A couple of minutes at most."

"Argument?" Ruth sat bolt upright. "What argument?"

"Between two men. They clearly tried to keep their voices down, but I heard them. Not enough to make out what they argued about, though."

"Where was this taking place?" Ruth asked.

"From what I could tell, at the other end of the carriage," Victoria said. "Near the door that leads to the gangway and single sleeper."

That would tally with somewhere near Hugo's compartment.

Ruth had slept through all these goings-on. "Any idea who the men were?"

"No, sorry. They kept their voices down."

"You said earlier one of them could have been Waylon," Zoey said in a low voice, and glanced furtively in his direction.

Victoria shrugged. "Maybe."

Ruth's eyebrows arched.

Waylon was supposed to be sick, and in his compartment, which Ruth assumed was either in the crew quarters or the single sleeper.

"How could you know the time, Victoria?" Ruth asked.

"Voice-over." She pulled a watch from her pocket, held it up, and pressed a button on the side.

"Six-oh-eight a.m.," a softly spoken man's voice said.

Ruth smiled. "He sounds dishy."

Greg pinched the bridge of his nose. "Can you not say stuff like that until I've eaten?"

"Hands off." Victoria waved the watch about. "Adonis is all mine."

"You named him?" Ruth chuckled.

"Of course," Victoria said. "Reminds me of an old college professor." She sighed and returned the talking watch to her pocket.

Zoey looked about and nudged Victoria's arm.

"Oh right. Yes." She ran a hand through her hair. "After the argument—it stopped abruptly, by the way—there came more heavy footsteps, right past my door, so I can say with absolute confidence it was a man. Another door opened and closed, and then more footsteps followed, as if hurrying after the first."

Ruth held her breath. "And then?"

Victoria swallowed and whispered, "A muffled thud. I didn't think much of it at the time, but now . . ." Silence greeted this proclamation, and Victoria's hands trembled. "If I'd known it was a murder, I would've screamed for help. Called for Zoey. But I thought— I thought someone had dropped something heavy. A suitcase toppled over. I never for one moment . . ." Tears streamed down her face.

Zoey squeezed her hand. "It's not your fault."

"Absolutely not your fault," Ruth said with what she hoped came across as unwavering certainty. "Neither of you are to blame."

Greg plucked a napkin from a side table and handed it to Zoey.

"Thank you." She in turn pressed it into Victoria's free hand.

As Victoria mopped her eyes behind her sunglasses, Ruth imagined the killer striking Miles in the back of the head, and it didn't take a genius to figure out the most likely culprits—her primary suspects were now Hugo *and* Waylon.

"You heard someone leave Miles' compartment after, and return to theirs?"

"That's the thing." Victoria sniffed. "I didn't."

Ruth stared at her. "Nothing?"

Victoria shook her head. "I was listening intently by then. I would've heard them open and close a door, even if they'd crept away, wouldn't I?"

"They might have taken their shoes off," Greg said. "Once they, y'know . . ." He mimed swinging. "And I reckon they could've opened and closed a door without you hearing above the noise of the train."

Ruth made a mental note to try that theory out later. "Victoria, is there nothing else you could tell me about their voices?"

She considered for a moment. "Only that one of them had a deeper tone than the other. It carried farther, even though he tried to whisper."

Ruth scratched her chin. That could've been Hugo, Waylon, Lord Hamilton, or . . . Her gaze shifted to Robert Minchent. Miles' voice had been almost shrill at times. At least when he was angry. She looked at Greg, but he shrugged.

"I heard nothing going on from my carriage." He yawned and stretched.

That wasn't a surprise. Greg could sleep through a hurricane.

"At one point, I thought about calling Zoey," Victoria

said. "But it was late, so I let it be. Besides, apart from that drunken fellow banging on the door a few hours later, there was no other movement after that." Her shoulders rolled forward, and her head lilted to one side. "I'm a fool."

Zoey rubbed her arm.

Greg leaned in to Ruth, hushed. "Do you think Hugo did it?"

Ruth vehemently shook her head.

Greg cocked an eyebrow at her. "Seriously? Are you just saying that because he's your friend?"

Ruth's gaze followed Lord Hamilton as he stepped to the bar. "Please excuse me." She hurried over to him.

8

At the salon bar, Lord Hamilton spotted Ruth's approach. "Could you use a brandy?" He took one from a server. "Goodness knows I need one."

"I'm fine." Ruth glanced about to make sure no one eavesdropped. "Did you and Lady Hamilton hear an argument last night?"

"Last night?" Lord Hamilton gulped his brandy.

"After we all went to bed. Around one in the morning." Ruth studied his reaction. After all, the argument had been closer to their compartment than Victoria's. The Hamiltons may have heard what it was about.

However, Lord Hamilton shook his head. "Can't say we did." He finished off the glass, set it on the bar, and motioned for the server to give him a refill. "Forgive me," Lord Hamilton said in response to Ruth's frown. "I don't usually drink this early in the day. Desperate times. You understand?" He raised the glass to his lips, hesitated, and lowered it again. "I have a darned good idea who killed Miles, if you're interested to know."

Ruth gaped at him. "You do?"

Lord Hamilton raised his brandy. "After Hilary retired last night, while on my way back to the salon, I caught Robert pacing the corridor." He knocked back the whole glass and set it down.

"He seemed agitated?" Ruth chanced a peek in the Minchents' direction, but neither of them paid her any mind.

"I'd say a lot more than merely agitated." Lord Hamilton sniffed. "Robert was practically apoplectic."

"What was he angry about?"

"Miles. Who else?" Lord Hamilton lowered his voice. "Apparently, Robert couldn't help himself, and after dinner brought up their past."

"Something to do with their shops?" Ruth asked. "Minties Coffee?"

"Precisely." Lord Hamilton slid the glass aside and turned from the bar. "Miles did their interior design work but had very different ideas. It almost came to blows, apparently. Robert and Jane wanted him to do it a certain way, but Miles deviated from the agreed plan. He then walked out midproject, costing them thousands, and setting the launch back weeks." He shrugged one shoulder. "Although they eventually recovered, Robert seems to have never forgiven him, and Miles apparently showed not even the slightest remorse." He shuddered. "Horrible man."

Based on her brief observations of Miles before, Ruth wasn't surprised by any of this.

"You think Miles said something to Robert that rubbed salt in old wounds?"

"It would appear so."

"Thank you." Ruth looked over at the night porter. He now sat by the window with the cleaner. "Please excuse me."

If Victoria had heard a commotion, he must have too.

After all, he was stationed on the other side of the nearest door, in the connecting gangway between carriages.

As Ruth made a beeline for the night porter at the other end of the salon, several pairs of narrowed eyes followed her.

She supposed, given her recent unsanctioned excursion, Ruth now fell under everyone's suspicion, and she couldn't blame them.

However, she smiled at each one of her fellow passengers as she passed, and then stopped in front of the night porter. "Is this seat taken?" Ruth opted for a sweet-little-lady voice, nonthreatening and disarming.

At least she hoped it came across that way.

Or, judging by the cleaner's face, perhaps it gave off an axe-murderer vibe.

Ruth motioned to a chair opposite.

The cleaner stood and walked away.

"All yours." The night porter got to his feet and went to leave too.

"Wait." Ruth whispered, "Could I have a word? I promise to only take up a minute of your time." She flashed her teeth for good measure.

He hesitated, glanced over at Hugo as he chatted with Lord and Lady Hamilton, and then shrugged.

Once Ruth and the night porter were both seated and comfortable, with no one eavesdropping, Ruth scooted to the very edge of her chair and extended a hand. "I'm Ruth."

He hesitated and then shook it. "Marty."

"Nice to meet you, Marty." She took a breath. "You were situated at the end of the first-class single-sleeper carriage last night, weren't you? Next to the door that leads to the double sleeper?" Of course Ruth knew he had been, but wanted to make sure she was totally clear. "And you say no one other than Mr Price passed you in the few hours prior to Miles' death?"

He nodded.

"Did you leave at any point?"

Marty looked over at Hugo and Waylon, shuffled in his seat, and then shook his head.

"Not even to use the bathroom?"

"No."

"What time did you start your shift?"

"Midnight."

Ruth remembered seeing him at a little after when she'd gone to bed. She sat back. "So the only people you saw were me, Miles, Victoria and Zoey, Mr and Mrs Minchent, Lord and Lady Hamilton. Then no one else after that?"

"No," he said through tight lips, and gave a furtive glance in Hugo and Waylon's direction again.

Ruth detected a lie. She inclined her head.

Marty gripped his knees.

"Who was last into the carriage?"

"Mr Finsbury. There was no one else. No one entered that carriage." Marty went to leave, but Ruth waved him back down.

"I'm sorry," she said. "A couple more questions." Something in his short answers and the cautious glances set Ruth's lie-dar pinging. That was why she often asked the same question several times over—to gauge reactions and convey she knew someone wasn't being truthful. It was an old police interviewing trick: wear the suspect down until only the stub of truth remained. "You saw someone else, didn't you?" Ruth's stomach tensed as she waited for the answer.

Marty gave a small shake of his head, opened his mouth, closed it again, and then nodded.

At last. Progress.

Ruth fought to keep a lid on her eagerness for the details. She had to tread carefully, so as not to frighten him off. "In or out of our carriage?" she asked in a casual tone.

"In."

Ruth's eyebrows lifted, and a rush of excitement coursed through her. "Who was it?"

Marty hesitated for several seconds more, and when he spoke, his lips barely moved. "The dead guy . . . and Mr Finsbury."

Ruth frowned. "Miles? Together with Hugo? Roaming about the carriages in the small hours of the morning? What were they doing?"

"They went inside an empty compartment." Marty waited for Waylon to move by and out of earshot. "Came out a little while later. Ten minutes or so. Not much more than that. Mr Finsbury tried to calm him, but that Miles guy looked madder than ever. I heard them arguing on the other side of the door for a few minutes more, and then it all went quiet."

"What time was that?"

"I'm not sure. A little after one, I guess. Twenty past. Maybe later."

That tallied with the time Victoria also heard raised voices. Now that Ruth had confirmation of who had argued, she sat back. "What were they arguing about?"

The night porter's eyebrows knitted. "Not sure. Couldn't really make it out." Marty then spoke in a rush. "Something about safety? Something not safe? A different design? But Mr Finsbury kept assuring him he'd taken care of it, and there was nothing to worry about. Told Miles he was being irrational. Said he'd prove it when the train arrives at its destination."

Ruth considered him. "Why didn't you speak up earlier?"

He could have saved a whole lot of bother.

Marty looked over at Hugo for the millionth time, and his cheeks grew pale. "Told me to keep my mouth shut. Said it was between him and the police, and no one else's business." His eyes widened as Waylon strode over to the bar and glanced in their direction. "I've said too much. I don't want to get into trouble."

"You won't," Ruth said. "You have my word." She pondered the timings.

As far as she could piece together, most passengers had gone to bed sometime between midnight and one in the morning, but Miles and Hugo had argued later. Hugo and Miles had gone into a vacant compartment, and returned minutes later, still arguing.

Ruth took a breath. "This compartment. Can you show me?"

The night porter stood. "No. Sorry."

Ruth jumped to her feet and blocked his path. "Please. This is very important. Someone has been murdered."

His eyes darkened. "You don't think Mr Finsbury has anything—"

Ruth held up a hand. "I'm only trying to figure out what happened. That's all. No finger-pointing. Facts only."

Marty stared at her, first with an expression of anger, then as though conflicted, and finally his shoulders slumped. "I don't see how Mr Finsbury will let us—"

"Oh, Hu-go?" Ruth called in a singsong voice.

Hugo muttered his apologies to Lord and Lady Hamilton, then hurried over to Ruth. "What do you want now?" He looked between her and the night porter with suspicion.

"This young man has volunteered to escort me," Ruth said in a level tone. "It's very gracious of him."

Hugo's brow furrowed. "What? What do you mean?"

Marty tugged at his shirt collar.

"He's agreed to accompany me while I fetch medication from my compartment." Ruth hated lying to a friend but could see no alternative when he wasn't forthcoming with the truth. "He'll make sure I don't get up to anything I shouldn't be doing." Ruth inclined her head. "Is that okay with you, Hugo? May I get my medication? I promise not to murder anyone on the way."

"Waylon will take you," Hugo said.

Ruth jerked her head in the night porter's direction. "I trust this man only."

"Trust?" Hugo looked as though he was about to argue, but clearly not wanting to cause a scene in front of the other passengers, he growled, "Be quick." He then gave Marty a stern look.

"Yes, sir."

Ruth smiled to herself as she headed back through the salon carriage. She winked at a dumbfounded Greg, and then practically skipped through the connecting doors into the first-class single-sleeper carriage, and then into the connecting gangway.

Ruth stopped by the night porter's alcove and pointed to his chair. "You were here when they argued."

He nodded.

She sat. "You heard Hugo and Miles?" Ruth motioned to the door that led to the first-class double-sleeper carriage. She needed to be perfectly clear about their movements. "Where did they go, exactly?"

Marty pointed through the door's window. "Compartment 7A. It's vacant."

Ruth got to her feet and waved a finger at the far end of the single-sleeper carriage. "My grandson is in 18A. Who are in these others?"

Marty pulled a folded sheet of paper from his pocket and scanned a list. "Mr Price is 14A, and Waylon is in 9A."

Ruth motioned at the compartment closest to the porter's chair. "Hugo's assistant?"

"Yes."

"He was sick, as I recall," Ruth said. "Retired early."

Marty slipped the list back into his pocket. "That's the only passengers staying in this carriage. Three of them. The other compartments are empty."

Ruth opened the door and stepped into the double sleeper. "Wait here." Given the noise of the train wheels on the track, it wasn't surprising the night porter couldn't discern the details of Hugo and Miles' argument. However, to be sure, she closed the door and covered her mouth. "Can you hear me?" Ruth peered through the window at Marty. He didn't react. She raised her voice. "What about now? Can you hear me, Marty?"

He nodded.

Ruth opened the door and beckoned him through. "Raised voices are enough." Her gaze darted to the compartment doors. It was no surprise Victoria had heard an argument but not what it was about. She did however find it odd raised voices hadn't woken the Hamiltons and Minchents.

Ruth moved in front of 7A. "You say they went in here?"

Marty clasped his hands behind his back, and gave a curt nod without meeting her gaze.

Sweat glistened on his forehead, and Ruth couldn't tell if he was nervous about Hugo catching them or something else.

"All right. Stay back." She took a deep breath, grabbed

the handle, glanced at the night porter one more time to make sure he kept his distance and didn't try any funny stuff, and then she opened the door and flicked on the light.

What greeted her was utter chaos.

"What the—?" Ruth staggered inside and tried to make sense of what she was looking at.

Someone, she assumed Miles, had plastered the desk, walls, bed, and even the window with drawings, blueprints, documents, and photographs.

Sure enough, his leather holdall leaned against a desk leg.

The photographs weren't in focus, as if someone had taken them at a distance, or through a dirty window. They showed parts of a train carriage's construction, taken from various vantage points and angles. Miles had circled some sections with red marker and numbered them.

Ruth scanned the nearby blueprints.

She pursed her lips. "What was he trying to say?"

"The fabricators didn't follow his designs."

Ruth jumped and spun around. Marty stood in the doorway, gaping at it all. She'd forgotten he was there.

He nodded at the photographs. "Miles told Mr Finsbury he'd taken those to prove the fabricators had made changes to one of the carriages."

Ruth blinked at him. "How do you know that?" Then it dawned on her. "You listened in, didn't you? Opened the connecting door?"

Clearly realising his mistake, the night porter shook his head and went to leave.

"Wait. I won't tell anyone." Ruth tried to keep her voice level, even though her insides did backflips. "What did Hugo say to that?" She turned back to the room and scanned a document outlining metal part tolerances. It was all techno gobbledegook to her.

"Mr Finsbury said he shouldn't worry about it. Safety inspectors independently checked the carriages and train. They passed with flying colours." Marty pointed to a crumpled photograph on the floor by the bed.

Ruth picked it up and smoothed it out.

The image showed an underside view of a train carriage. "What's this?"

"The last carriage made at the yard," Marty said. "Miles demanded Mr Finsbury look at it, but he refused."

Ruth set the photograph on the desk, along with other paperwork detailing inspection reports and tolerances.

"Do you understand any of this?"

Marty scratched his head. "Not a clue. I used to work in a bakery. Ask me anything about dough and oven temperatures, and I'm your man."

"I wonder if anyone on board does." Ruth knew deep in her bones there was a lot more to uncover. Her attention moved to the far end of the desk and a complicated drawing that seemed to be a wiring diagram of the entire train.

Miles had written and underlined the word: *attack*.

9

Ruth stared down at the wiring diagram, unblinking. "Attack?" she murmured, and leaned in. Another outline showed a complicated CCTV system. "Wait, I didn't know there are security cameras on board."

"Each carriage has two, pointing both ways along the corridors." Marty stepped from the compartment and gestured. "Hidden in the sconces."

Ruth supposed, given the current clientele, cameras were a good idea. An extra level of security and reassurance. "Why doesn't Hugo look at the recordings?" She scratched her chin. "They'd tell him exactly who went into Miles' compartment, unless . . ." She looked back at all the drawings and blueprints.

Hugo and Miles had argued, then Hugo followed him here, to this compartment. Was that *the moment Hugo handed over the cheque? Was it a hush payment, or simply owed for services rendered? Is not mentioning CCTV recordings his way of covering up these facts?*

Clearly Miles had set all this up to demonstrate some

belief in a safety issue with the train, but Hugo had assured him there wasn't anything to worry about.

Determined to confront Hugo and demand a look at the CCTV recordings, Ruth backed out of the compartment, turned off the light, and closed the door. "How long were they in there?"

"Ten minutes at the most," Marty said.

"Who left first?"

"Miles, shortly followed by Mr Finsbury."

"And where did they go next?" Ruth asked, already knowing the answer, but checking his version of events.

The night porter gestured to each end of the corridor. "To their compartments."

Ruth marched toward Hugo's, hoping to find clues she'd previously missed.

"Wait," Marty called after her. Anxiety slipped into his voice. "We need to go back."

"I want to check something." Ruth motioned for him to follow, and then she stopped and spun back. "Hold on. You say no one else passed you after their argument? Not until Mr Price hours later?"

Marty shook his head.

Ruth frowned and muttered, "Which means the killer has to be someone in this carriage." She scratched her chin. "Miles returned to his compartment, 1A." Which tallied with the timings of what Victoria had heard, and she was in 4A. Ruth stayed in 3A . . . Although it was not impossible for Lord and Lady Hamilton in 6A, nor Jane and Robert Minchent in 5A, to have committed the crime.

"What about Waylon?" Ruth asked. "Did he pass you?"

"No."

Ruth wasn't convinced there was no chance Waylon could be involved somehow, but the evidence still came back to Hugo at one end of the carriage in 8A, or . . . Her attention moved back to 2A. "Zoey?" She hurried to Zoey's door, opened it, and the lower hinge let out a loud screech.

Ruth knelt to inspect it more closely.

Someone had jammed an object into it: a piece of metal.

She glanced up at the night porter. "Could you fetch me a pair of pliers? There's a tool bag in Hugo's compartment. In the wardrobe."

Marty hesitated.

"It's okay," Ruth said. "I take full responsibility. Don't touch the hammer, though."

After a couple more seconds of dithering he hurried off and returned a minute later with pliers.

"Thank you." Ruth used them to prise the metal chunk free, and she examined it under the nearest light.

From what she could tell, it was the tip of a nail file.

Which meant someone had deliberately jammed it into the hinge.

Why?

Ruth tried the door. Sure enough, it no longer squeaked.

Perhaps the killer had done that to Zoey's door. What with her being in the next compartment to Miles, it was a surefire way to alert them if she came to investigate any strange noises.

For the moment, Ruth could not fathom any other reason, and felt confident in ruling out Zoey as a potential killer. After all, a murderer would not make their own door squeak and draw attention to themselves.

Ruth returned the metal tip to its original location within the hinge, checked it squeaked again, and then straightened. "That's all for now." Ruth handed the pliers to Marty. Maybe Hugo had used them to break off the tip of the nail file in the first place. "We'd better get back. I don't want you to get into trouble." She followed him along the corridor with deep unease building in her stomach.

Could Hugo really be the one who murdered Miles? If so, why would he? It seems like an awfully big risk to commit murder on your own train, but if not, then who? And, most importantly of all, why?

Marty set the pliers back in the tool bag, and then the two of them headed to the salon.

"What kept you?" Hugo's eyes narrowed as he looked between them. "I was about to come find you."

"My fault," Ruth said with half a painted smile. "I freshened up while I was there." She nodded at Marty. "He was very patient with me." Ruth lowered herself into a chair opposite Greg.

Waylon stared at her from across the salon carriage, and then he continued talking to Robert Minchent in a hushed voice.

Greg stared at Ruth too, and once Hugo and the night porter were out of earshot, he leaned forward and whispered, "Find something interesting?"

Ruth brought him up to speed with everything she'd uncovered so far. Ruth explained what she'd discovered regarding Hugo and Miles' argument, the compartment filled with serial-killer-esque vibes, and what Marty had witnessed.

Once she was done, Ruth interlaced her fingers and studied the faces of the people in the carriage. *One of them has to be the murderer, but who?* She found it all thoroughly exhilarating.

She waved Hugo over.

He approached with a look of exasperation. "Yes, Ruth?"

"Have you looked at the CCTV recordings yet?"

His face dropped. "How do you know there's cameras on board?"

"Spotted them in the corridors," Ruth lied. "Well?"

Hugo pulled a phone from his pocket, navigated to a security app, and showed Ruth the display. It was black, with only the date and timestamp in the corner.

Ruth's brow furrowed. "What does that mean?"

"They cut out." Hugo navigated to the recordings before and then after, which showed him and Ruth in the first-class corridor outside Miles' compartment. "I'll hand a copy over to the police anyway." He slipped the phone back into his pocket. "If you'll excuse me."

As he left, Ruth stared at him with incredulity. "Someone deleted those recordings."

That surely meant a staff member was the culprit.

Does Waylon have access to the CCTV?

Ruth gasped. "That reminds me." She pulled her phone from her pocket, navigated to the Kat's Kitty Hotel website, and typed the log-in details.

A live feed of Merlin's room popped up, with a worker placing bowls on a stand. Merlin slinked over, sniffed the food, and then tucked in.

Ruth beamed. "He's fine." She checked the time on her phone. "I only have twenty-five minutes to uncover the killer."

"So, it must be a member of staff, right?" Greg asked.

Ruth pocketed her phone, and her gaze rested on Mr Price, the biggest unknown in all this. He slouched in a high-backed armchair. "With me." Ruth leapt to her feet.

"What now?" Greg followed her.

Ruth headed over to Mr Price. "Morning," she chirped. "How are you feeling?"

He groaned and squeezed his eyes shut. Sweat glistened on his bald pate.

"That good, huh?" Ruth gestured Greg to one chair opposite, and she sat in the other.

Mr Price took deep breaths and opened one eye. "What do you want?" He looked far more sober than earlier, and a billion times more hungover.

"I won't take much of your time. Pun intended." Ruth lowered her voice against prying ears. "Speaking of which, how did Miles come to have your watch?"

"Stole it," he said through gritted teeth.

"Yes. Right. But how?"

He rubbed the back of his neck. "Not sure. Must have happened when we were playing cards. Miles was seated next to me."

"And this was after dinner?" Ruth asked.

People had gathered in the salon the night before, but she hadn't stayed. Ruth had her usual date with Mrs Beeton.

Mr Price rubbed his temples. "Only played a few hands. Damn near lost everything." He looked away and grumbled, "No wonder Zoey kept insisting we drink so much. Bet she was in on it with Victoria."

"Victoria?" Greg frowned. "How can she play cards?"

"That's the point, isn't it?" Mr Price said. "Victoria is the perfect dealer. Allegedly."

"So," Ruth said. "Zoey forced you to drink?"

"That's an old gambler's trick," Greg said. "Ply your opponents with alcohol so they make mistakes, and you take them to the cleaners."

Ruth cocked an eyebrow at him. "And how would you know that?"

Greg cleared his throat. "Saw it on TV."

"Hmm." Ruth studied him for a few seconds, not sure

she believed his excuse, and then refocussed on Mr Price. "So, you were playing poker."

"Miles won. Every single hand." He shook his head. "Never seen luck like it."

"Miles?" Ruth said. "Not Zoey? Who else was playing?"

Mr Price's gaze drifted to the ceiling. "Me, Miles on my right, Victoria on the left, Zoey next to her, and that Lord Hamilton fella too. He sat next to Miles." He sighed. "Something fishy was going on. Miles cheated, if you ask me. Maybe he was in on it with Zoey and Victoria."

"You can prove that?" Greg asked.

"Of course not." He shuffled in the chair, winced, and rubbed his temples again.

Ruth now had a good idea how Miles had wound up in possession of Lady Hamilton's earrings and a stack of cash, and she considered this strange assortment of impromptu poker players. "What about your watch? How do you think Miles came to have it?"

"He gambled it away and forgot," Greg said.

"I did no such thing," Mr Price snapped. "It belonged to my great-grandfather. It means the world to me."

"When did you notice it missing?" Ruth asked.

"Not long after Zoey helped me back to my compartment."

Ruth raised her eyebrows.

"Oh, it was nothing like that. She noticed I was a little worse for wear. Probably felt guilty for encouraging me to drink. She was calling it a night, so made sure I got settled okay."

"Why are you here?" Ruth asked. "Sorry, I mean, why did Hugo invite you on this maiden voyage of murder and mayhem? How do you know him?"

Mr Price hesitated and glanced over at Hugo. "We go way back."

Ruth was about to ask him to elaborate when Victoria screamed.

She crouched by her chair, with her hands rested on her assistant sprawled on the floor. "Zoey?"

Several people leapt up, but Ruth reached them in three strides. She knelt and felt the girl's wrist—pulse steady and strong—and then Ruth placed a hand to Zoey's forehead—clammy and hot. "She's fainted. Get some water."

Zoey groaned, and her eyes fluttered open.

"You're okay." Ruth helped her into a sitting position and took a glass from Waylon. She placed the water to the girl's lips. "Sip."

Zoey trembled. "What happened?"

"Is she all right?" Victoria asked in a shaky voice.

"She'll be fine," Ruth said in a soothing tone. "Poor girl fainted."

It really wasn't surprising, given all the goings-on. Most people were not used to dealing with murders, especially in such confined proximity.

Hugo paced, looking about ready to pass out too.

Once some colour had returned to Zoey's cheeks, Ruth helped her back into her chair, where she slumped.

"How are you feeling?" Victoria asked her.

Zoey closed her eyes. "Got really hot and dizzy."

"Take it easy," Hugo said. "When we get there, we'll have someone look at you."

Satisfied the girl would be okay, Ruth returned to her seat next to Greg.

Jane Minchent asked to use the bathroom, and Waylon escorted her from the salon.

Seizing her chance, Ruth murmured, "Back in a

moment," to Greg and hurried over to Robert. She dropped into a seat opposite and smiled at him. "Good morning."

He frowned. "Good?"

Ruth nodded. "Fair point. It's a terrible morning."

Robert looked away.

Ruth cleared her throat. "I hear there was bad blood between you and Miles."

Robert's gaze shifted back to her, and his eyes darkened. "Let me guess, Hamilton told you that."

Ruth pressed her lips together.

Robert snarled. "He's a fine one to talk."

"What do you mean?"

"It's true, I hated Miles—we both did after what he did to us, the way he stitched us up and almost ruined our business—but not enough to kill him. If that's what you're getting at?" Robert's nostrils flared. "Lord Hamilton, on the other hand..."

Ruth inclined her head.

"Yeah, not so forthcoming about his own history with Miles, is he?" Robert said in a scathing tone. "What a surprise."

Ruth kept her voice level. "Did Lord Hamilton have bad blood with Miles?"

"Worse than all of us." Robert bared his teeth. "And he has the nerve to gossip about Jane and me? Typical Hamilton." He leaned forward. "If you want to know who murdered that man, look no further than Lord and Lady Snootypants." Robert took a breath. "Years back, Miles did some work at their guesthouse. Interior design. And that's when he met Annabelle Chamberlain. Have you heard of her?"

Ruth shook her head.

"She's Lady Hamilton's sister." Robert sneered.

"Annabelle fell for Miles. Goodness knows why. The man didn't have a redeeming bone in his body."

Ruth hated it when people spoke ill of the recently deceased.

"They got engaged," Robert continued, "Annabelle and Miles, and their relationship went well for a couple of years. Right up until the altar."

Ruth raised a hand to her mouth.

"Yep. Miles jilted Annabelle. Left her standing there at the church, with hundreds of witnesses, and he never gave her a reason why. Broke her heart. Lord Hamilton threatened to kill Miles." Robert's gaze bored into Ruth. "Said he'd make it his life mission to destroy the man." He sat back. "Guess Hamilton finally got the opportunity to fulfil his promise."

"Robert?" Jane appeared next to them and stared down at Ruth. "What's going on?"

Ruth stood and gestured to the chair. "Sorry to disturb you." Walked away, she pursed her lips. Had everyone on board the Finsbury Flyer been enemies with Miles.

It certainly seemed that way.

10

In the salon, Ruth rushed back to Greg and sat next to him.

He eyed the Minchents. "Why do they look so angry?"

"Not sure," Ruth muttered. "Everyone loves my winning personality."

Greg snorted.

Princess Mary swept into the carriage, escorted front and rear by protection officers. "I was so bored cooped up in my gilded cage," she said to Hugo as she passed him. "It was ridiculous."

The black-haired officer glared at the back of her head.

Much to Ruth's amazement, Princess Mary stopped in front of Greg and motioned to the chair opposite.

"Is this seat taken?"

He gawped at her, then stood, and bowed.

Ruth contained a chuckle. "All yours."

Princess Mary lowered herself into it and looked about. "Tragic."

"W-What is?" Greg sank into his chair.

"The murder, of course."

"Oh, right." Greg flushed. "Yeah. Tragic. Really tragic. Terrible."

"You're tragic," Ruth murmured to him through the corner of her mouth.

"Would you care for a drink, Your Highness?" Waylon asked in an over-the-top posh accent.

"I could murder an orange juice," she responded with a glint in her eye.

"Make that two," Ruth said.

Princess Mary focussed on her. "Who are you?"

"Ruth Morgan," the black-haired protection officer said before she could respond. "Ex–Met police."

"Oh, you're retired?" Princess Mary asked.

"Sacked," the officer said, again before Ruth could reply.

Ruth gave him a sweet smile. "Thanks."

He lifted his chin.

"Ooh, how exciting." Princess Mary's eyes sparkled. "Do tell me what you did to elicit your firing. Was it ghastly?"

"Investigated her husband's death," the black-haired officer said.

Ruth now frowned at him. "I can answer for myself."

"Yes, she can." Princess Mary waved him off.

The officer took a step back with obvious reluctance.

"What do you do now?" Princess Mary enquired.

Ruth gazed up at the officer, waiting for his response, but he looked away, so she took a breath. "I'm a food consultant."

"I see." Princess Mary nodded. "Police officer to culinary expert. Quite the change. And what about you?" she asked Greg. "Do you cook?"

Ruth snorted. "Greg's idea of cooking is waiting for the smoke alarm to go off, which lets him know his toast is ready. He can't boil an egg without burning down the house."

"That was one time, Grandma," he muttered. "One time."

"He doesn't have a job," the officer said.

"Greg is about to attend Oxford University," Ruth said to Princess Mary. "To study archaeology and history. He's very talented." She winked at him. "Like his late grandfather."

"How enthralling," Princess Mary said with an expression of keen interest. "Who knows, you may dig up one of my ancestors."

Waylon returned with their fruit juices.

Ruth peered up at the black-haired officer again. "Seeing as you've done background checks on everyone here, I assume no one has a criminal record?"

He glanced at Hugo and Waylon, and then gave a small shake of his head.

Waylon hesitated, bowed, and left the carriage.

Ruth sighed. *That would've been too easy.* "And you're positive you didn't hear a commotion last night?"

Another small shake of the officer's head.

Ruth's gaze moved around the salon, and she met eyes with Mr Price, but he looked away. She was about to make her excuses and head over to him, to ask a few more questions, when Hugo returned.

"Breakfast is served."

Everyone filed into the dining carriage, heads bowed, mournful, and took their seats. A minute later, the servers handed out their orders.

As Ruth picked at her cereal, she eyed Lady Hamilton across the table. "Lord Hamilton said you didn't hear anything strange last night. Is that right?"

Lord Hamilton spread jam on toast and shook his head.

"As a matter of fact, we did." Lady Hamilton looked at him askance.

He glanced uneasily at her.

"Go on," Ruth said.

"Well, my husband didn't want us to say anything." Lady Hamilton gave him another sidelong look of disapproval.

"It's none of our business," he mumbled.

"We heard raised voices," she said.

Ruth nodded. "Hugo and Miles."

"No," Lady Hamilton said. "Hugo, but not Miles."

Ruth dropped her spoon into the bowl. "Excuse me?"

Even Greg's attention moved from devouring his full English.

Lady Hamilton whispered, "It was between Hugo and the night porter." She sat back with a scandalised expression.

"Marty?" Ruth blinked and then scanned the dining carriage, but he wasn't there. She refocussed on Lady Hamilton. "Are you sure?"

"Positive. I spotted them arguing in the next carriage."

"The first-class single sleeper?" Ruth asked, now abandoning her cereal altogether.

"Precisely," Lady Hamilton said. "Through the connecting door. Could not make out exactly what they were saying above the noise of the train, but Hugo waved a finger in the poor man's face. Clearly berating him."

Ruth frowned.

Why would Marty not tell me this? What does he have to lose? Was he embarrassed or hiding something?

The train slowed, and flashing blue lights filled the carriage.

Outside, five police cars, a van, an ambulance, and

several black saloon cars, including a hearse, were parked next to a row of train sheds.

A sign glided into view.

WELCOME TO
FINSBURY VILLAGE STATION

"It appears we've reached our destination." Ruth only hoped the police would listen to what she'd uncovered.

Greg's eye widened. "I thought we were going to Penzance?"

"This is in Penzance," Lord Hamilton said. "Hugo's exclusive stop. An isolated indulgence, as it were."

A few minutes later, a stocky man with a bushy grey beard, wearing an ill-fitting suit that almost burst at the seams, stepped into the salon carriage. "Good mornin'." Uniformed officers, two male and one female, flanked him. "My name is Detective Inspector Kirby, and I would appreciate yer full cooperation at this time." He had a deep, commanding voice, and a strong hint of a west country accent shone through.

Greg finished his breakfast in record time and pushed the plate aside. "This should be fun." He wiped his mouth on a napkin and looked at Ruth askance. "Please don't get us into more trouble."

She gasped. "Whatever do you mean?"

"You can be reckless," he said, hushed. "Mum warned me. She said you've got worse after the Ocean Odyssey fiasco."

Ruth gaped at him. "Sara warned you?" She didn't know how offended she should be at such a revelation. Her daughter had a mistrust of Ruth and her mystery-solving predilections.

All unfounded, of course.

"Mum said you do things in the heat of the moment sometimes, without thinking through the consequences. I'm supposed to tell her when you go off the rails again."

"Your grandfather was the reckless one." Ruth straightened the tablecloth and mumbled, "I've always been cautious."

Greg snorted.

Inspector Kirby shot him a look, and then scanned the rest of the faces peering back at him. "As yer'll know, there's been a death on board this train."

"A murder," Ruth said.

The inspector eyed her. "Cause to be established."

Ruth nodded and murmured, "Definitely a murder."

"Grandma," Greg breathed through the corner of his mouth.

Princess Mary chuckled from her table at the end of the carriage and winked at him.

"Whatever the case may be, I can assure everyone 'ere we'll get to the bottom of it." The inspector studied Ruth for a few seconds and then addressed the rest of the carriage again. "We ask that none of yer'll speculate. Let the professionals take care of it. Everyone's in safe 'ands." He smiled weakly. "Yer to remain 'ere until called upon. No one is to leave this carriage, understood?"

He received several nods in reply.

Inspector Kirby jerked a thumb, and the officers stood guard at either end of the carriage, blocking the exits.

"What if I should need to powder my nose?" Princess Mary asked.

"Yer can 'old it in fer a bit, Yer 'ighness." Inspector Kirby bowed and then nodded at the female officer. He gestured for Hugo to follow him out.

The officer glanced around the salon at the numerous pale faces. Her gaze rested on Ruth. "Madam?" She pointed to the door. Ruth got to her feet, and Greg went to stand too, but the officer waved him back down. "One at a time. Thank you."

Ruth squeezed her grandson's shoulder, and the officer led the way from the salon, outside onto a platform with a Victorian-style ticket office, and a waiting area packed full of police officers and equipment.

Several crime scene investigators, wearing white overalls with hoods and latex gloves, talked to Inspector Kirby and Hugo. Hugo pointed toward the first-class double-sleeper carriage.

The train's driver sat on a bench farther down the platform, talking to another man in an identical uniform—likely his relief.

They had a lot of catching up to do.

The female officer motioned Ruth through an archway.

Baskets of flowers hung from the eaves of a covered walkway, and they headed down a slope, and through a door on the right, into the station manager's office.

Two chairs sat behind a desk facing a third.

The officer indicated for Ruth to sit in the latter.

She lowered herself into it.

Is being chosen first for an interview a bad sign?

They sat in awkward silence for a full ten minutes before Detective Inspector Kirby finally entered the office and closed the door behind him. Then he sat on the other side of the desk next to the officer. The inspector set a portable recorder between them, while the officer removed a notepad and pen from her pocket.

Ruth gave her full name, address, and status, all without being asked.

This, however, didn't seem to impress Inspector Kirby.

He sat back, folded his arms, and glowered at her. "Yer a retired police officer, I take it."

"Sacked," Ruth corrected.

The officer looked up at her with interest.

Ruth returned her gawp with a smile.

Inspector Kirby huffed a breath through his nose. "Why were ye on board the Finsbury Flyer?" He sounded uninterested.

"Hugo invited me," Ruth said. "I'm a food consultant. He hired me to look over the menus and work with Chef."

"What's yer verdict?"

Sheepish, Ruth fiddled with her fingers. "I haven't had a chance to do anything yet."

"And 'ow does a disgraced police officer wind up as a food consultant?" Inspector Kirby asked, matter-of-fact.

Ruth ignored the sleight. "Followed my passion, and a lot of luck."

The officer scribbled notes.

Inspector Kirby stared down at the red light on the recorder for several seconds before his eyes rose to meet Ruth's again. "How did ye know the deceased?"

"I don't," Ruth said. "I mean, I didn't. We only met yesterday. Although, we didn't actually meet. He was a fellow passenger."

Inspector Kirby stared at her. "What was your impression of 'im?"

Ruth shuffled in her seat, and chose her next words carefully. "He seemed . . . passionate."

"About what?"

"Working with Hugo and the Finsbury Flyer," Ruth said. "I think he was the head designer or something along those lines."

The inspector cocked an eyebrow. "'ow do you know that?"

"Overheard him speaking to Hugo. Well, arguing." Ruth would leave out some of the less relevant information for the time being, but since this answer would elicit some questions, she elaborated a little. "You'll have to get the details from Hugo, but Miles seemed to have some safety concerns with the train. Hugo dismissed them." She took a breath. "And the train seems fine to me."

Much to her surprise, this didn't cause a reaction or a request to elaborate.

"Likeable?"

"Who? Miles?" Ruth shrugged. "Didn't know him long enough. Like I say, we didn't talk. He seems to have a history with everyone else on the train, though, in one way or another."

Inspector Kirby stared back at her, unblinking. "Who found the body? You?"

"No." Miles' lifeless corpse lying on the floor of his compartment flashed into Ruth's mind. "Well, not exactly." She composed herself, and then explained the sequence of events, with the drunk guy, Mr Price, banging on the door in the small hours of the morning, waking everyone up, followed by Ruth and Hugo's gruesome discovery.

Inspector Kirby listened to all this with an expression of passive interest. Once Ruth was done, he said, "Ye were the last one to see the victim alive."

Ruth baulked at the accusation. "Sorry?"

"What did ye say to one another? Did 'e seem agitated? Did you argue?"

Ruth widened her eyes.

Has Hugo lied? Did he say something to the inspector just now? Why would he say that? Or is Inspector Kirby baiting me?

Am I the prime suspect? Is that why they're interviewing me first?

Inspector Kirby leaned forward, rested his elbows on the table, and interlaced his fingers. "There's no use denying it."

The female officer looked up at Ruth, pen poised.

"I have no idea what you're talking about," Ruth said. "Are you suggesting I'm a suspect?"

"Everyone's a suspect," the officer said. "You of all people should know that." Inspector Kirby shot her a look, and she bowed her head. "Sorry, sir."

He refocussed on Ruth. "Yer denying ye spoke to the victim?"

She lifted her chin. "I most certainly am. We never exchanged a single word." If Ruth didn't know better, she'd swear Hugo was trying to pin Miles' murder on her. "There were plenty of people who spoke to him last night. Ask Hugo. Ask any of them."

Inspector Kirby continued his cold study for several more uncomfortable seconds, and then he switched off the recorder. "Ye may go fer now."

Ruth stared back at him, dumfounded. "That's it?"

He waved her to the door. "There's no way out of Finsbury Village, so don't bother trying. Ye can't leave the area until we give the say-so."

"Right." Ruth stood.

She assumed officers covered the exits anyway. No one could run, least of all her. Besides, Ruth's motorhome was back in Edinburgh.

The officer saw her out.

Greg waited with a second officer.

Ruth winked at him. "Good luck."

"I'm not being interviewed."

Sure enough, both police officers left.

Flabbergasted, Ruth watched them go. "Something very odd is going on. That has to be the briefest witness interview in history." She then got a grip of herself and motioned down the path, away from the station. "Come on, before they level more unfounded accusations my way."

"What happened?" he asked as they followed a footpath from the train station.

"I'm not sure." Ruth huffed out a breath.

"Something was going on with Mr Price," Greg said.

Ruth frowned. "What do you mean?"

"When you left, Inspector Kirby came back on board and practically dragged him from the train." Greg gestured at the station. "Outside, Inspector Kirby looked really angry. Couldn't hear what he was saying, but he waved a finger in Mr Price's face and sent him off to another room."

"That must have happened right before the inspector interviewed me. It's why it took him so long to show up." Ruth pursed her lips. "He didn't seem flustered."

Did Hugo say something about Mr Price to send Inspector Kirby into a rage?

"I wouldn't want to be in that room right about now," Greg said. They rounded the corner, and the path opened onto a road. "Mr Price looks to be in a lot of trouble."

11

Finsbury Village was less of a village and more of an idealised slice of Victorian life, seen through a rose-tinted lens.

Three-storey-tall brick buildings flanked a wide high street with tram lines down the middle. Sure enough, a little farther down sat a horse-drawn tram, sans the horses.

Shops lined the road on either side, each under the cover of awnings and with old-fashioned advertising signs, tempting hopeful patrons with a variety of home ointments and potions.

White and Sons dispensing chemist advertised a mercury-infused cream to remove warts, lead-infused powder to brighten a complexion, and an opium-infused cure for stubborn headaches.

Ruth peered into a shop window boasting an array of labour-saving kitchen appliances, such as a toaster with heated plates like some kind of medieval torture device, and an electric fan that begged to slice hapless fingers.

However, something beyond the displays caught her eye.

Ruth opened the door and went in to the tinkle of a bell,

finding shelves packed full to bursting with knickknacks: souvenirs of the "Finsbury Experience"—everything from postcards and plastic ornaments of the train itself, to coasters and key rings with pictures of the train.

Greg entered and closed the door. Clearly the window display was a facade masking the modern shop beyond.

"Clever." Ruth turned back, and her eyes widened. "Yes." She snatched a fridge magnet from a stand. "Here we go." It outlined the shape of the steam engine, complete with a jaunty puff of smoke from the stack. Tiny gold letters along the side spelled out *Finsbury Flyer*. "That's Margaret's birthday sorted." She grinned at Greg. "Pick anything you like."

He rolled his eyes. "I'm okay, Grandma. Thanks."

"I'm serious." Ruth motioned around at the myriad tat. "Absolutely anything. My treat."

Greg pointed at a model kit. "Can I have this?"

Ruth squinted at the price label: £89.99.

Glue not included.

She staggered back a step, and then headed to the rear of the shop with Margaret's present in hand, before Greg found something more expensive among the junky souvenirs. "Ninety quid for something you have to put together yourself?" she grumbled under her breath. "They're insane."

Greg chortled as he followed her.

At the farthermost reaches of the shop they found a grey-haired woman behind a wooden counter. She wore a floral-patterned dress and a shopkeeper's apron, her hair up in a tight bun.

On the counter sat a brass cash register.

Greg leaned in, examined it for a second, and then straightened. "Replica."

Ruth smiled at the lady. "Good morning."

"M-Mornin'," she replied, and shot a glance toward the door.

Ruth placed the fridge magnet on the counter and fished in her pocket for her wallet. "I take it you've heard what's happened?"

The woman swallowed and nodded.

"Terrible business, of course." Ruth opened her purse ready.

The shopkeeper stared at her.

Ruth smiled back.

The shopkeeper didn't flinch.

This went on for several more seconds before the smile slipped from Ruth's face. "How much?"

"Sorry?"

She nodded at the fridge magnet on the counter.

"Oh. Yes." The shopkeeper's fingers trembled as she picked it up and rang in the price. "It's 7.99."

"See, Gregory?" Ruth grumbled as she handed over a ten-pound note. "A reasonable price for a gift."

He snorted. "Aunty Margaret will be thrilled."

"I know, right?" Ruth beamed.

Before they'd left Ivywick Island, she had snuck into her sister's attic, filled bags full of the unwanted gifts Margaret had stashed up there, then had strategically placed the items around the house. Some were proudly on display, others in more hidden and unexpected locations.

Margaret would stumble across them for months to come.

Ruth expected an angry text at any moment.

The shopkeeper handed over her change, then placed the item in a brown paper sack with the shop's logo stamped on the side.

"Thank you." Ruth went to leave but turned back. She leaned across the counter and whispered, "We didn't kill him, if you were wondering." She winked and ushered Greg outside.

By the time they continued their saunter along the high street, peering into shop windows, several other Finsbury Flyer passengers had been released from purgatory.

A very pale Robert and Jane Minchent offered Ruth a curt nod from the other side of the road, before heading into a shop fronted as a haberdashery.

Ruth stopped outside a dressmaker's.

In the window were several lovely Victorian gowns, but beyond sat displays of T-shirts and caps with the Finsbury Flyer emblazoned on them. However, although clearly modern clothes, some blouses, skirts, and trousers had callbacks to Victorian times. For instance, Ruth eyed a pair of jeans with black lace at the pockets. She reached for the door handle, when Greg spoke up.

"Can we get breakfast first?" He motioned to the end of the high street and a sign with a carved wooden hand and finger pointing the way. "I'm starving."

"You have got to be kidding me." Ruth tottered after him. "You've literally just eaten." However, a minute later she found herself staring up at a sign above a café. "Inspired name for an eatery. I wonder how on earth Hugo dreamt it up."

Gold lettering on a dark green background read:

FINSBURY CAFÉ

Ruth's gaze dropped to her grandson. "I expect the Finsbury Bus Service will show up at any moment to take us on a grand tour of thrilling sights such as the Finsbury Watermill, Finsbury Castle, not to mention the Finsbury Carpet Warehouse with its half-price sale, using a one-time discount code of..."

Greg smirked. "Finsbury?"

"How ever did you guess?" Ruth threw her hands up. "My grandson is a genius." She waggled a finger at him. "You know, if the whole archaeology and history career path doesn't work out, you should go into marketing. Hugo would snap you up in a heartbeat."

The two of them stood in a courtyard surrounded by red brick buildings. In the middle loomed a circular fountain, complete with an angel, her outstretched hand holding a chalice, which trickled water into a shimmering pool at her feet.

"Guess what her name is?" Ruth said.

"Hmm." Greg pursed his lips. "Miss Finsbury?"

"Don't be ridiculous, Gregory." Ruth opened the café door and waved him in. "Everyone knows that's Archangel Hugo."

Greg stepped through the door, hesitated, and turned back, now frowning at her. "Where do you get this stuff from? Like, what makes you think the way you do?"

"Just kinda springs up." Ruth shrugged one shoulder. "A gift, I suppose. Genetics. Although, no one in our family has ever been as side-splittingly funny as me." And that was the truth. In fact, her sister Margaret was the absolute antithesis.

Greg walked into the café. "I thought someone might have dropped you on your head as a baby."

Ruth couldn't dismiss that theory.

She followed him into a compact and cozy space with wooden tables covered in chequered cloths. No two chairs matched, and LED candles flickered in coloured jars.

Pictures of varying shapes and sizes plastered one wall, images of steam trains, the countryside, and tracks leading into tunnels and across viaducts. Among them hung a picture of a seahorse, for some crazy reason.

Chalkboards filled the other wall, crammed with a billion suggested sandwich varieties, pies, and snacks, plus another trillion dessert choices.

Ruth eyed the drinks menu and opted for a humble mug of milky tea. She'd add the sugar in liberal amounts herself.

A glass-covered counter showed off an impressive array of cakes, buns, and breads.

Greg drooled.

A young man stepped through a back door and smiled in welcome as he approached the counter. He wore a white shirt and a green apron. He'd slicked his dark hair to his head with oodles of oil, in keeping with the Victorian ethos. "What can I get for you?"

"I'll have a pot of tea, and one of those." Ruth pointed to a Danish pastry. "My teenage companion will take one of everything else."

"My treat," a soft voice said.

Princess Mary stood behind them. She wore a long red coat and a matching hat. Her protection officers waited outside, flanking the door, arms crossed, scowling at passersby.

Ruth went to remove her purse, but the princess touched the back of her hand.

"I insist." She looked back at the door and lowered her voice. "Besides, I'll admit to an ulterior motive. Do you have time for a chat?"

Ruth cocked an eyebrow.

Just when she'd thought the day couldn't get any more interesting.

She and Greg sat at a table in the corner of Finsbury Café, opposite Princess Mary.

A surreal experience, and one Ruth was unlikely to forget in a hurry. It wasn't every day you got to chin-wag with someone in line to the throne. Ruth considered asking for a personal tour of Buckingham Palace.

Greg polished off his BLT in record time, along with a large sausage roll, and an extra-large Cornish pastie, and then he worked his way through a chocolate brownie.

Ruth sipped a giant mug of tea—once she'd attacked it with five spoonfuls of sugar—and picked at her Danish.

Princess Mary watched Greg in astonishment. She had only ordered a fruit juice and hadn't yet touched it. "You should charge for the show."

"We tried that," Ruth said. "But people kept asking for refunds once they'd realised how disgusting it was to see Greg eat like a starved animal. They'd seen pigs with more grace."

The princess snickered.

"Don't know what you mean," Greg mumbled through a mouth full of cake.

"You used to be a detective," Princess Mary said to Ruth as she unclipped her hat and set it to one side. Strands of brown hair cascaded down her face, and she brushed them aside.

"I was a police officer," Ruth corrected, taken aback by the sudden change in conversation. "I never made it as far as detective." Ruth inclined her head. "Why do you ask?" It was clearly a loaded question, and she braced herself.

Princess Mary's narrowed blue eyes moved to her protection officers waiting outside. "Neither of them has interest in what I have to say on the matter." She refocussed on Ruth. "I propose an exchange of information."

"Sounds intriguing. What subject do you have in mind?" As if Ruth couldn't guess.

"Murder, of course." Princess Mary glanced at the front door again. "It's both thrilling and horrifying in equal measure."

"What do you know?" Ruth asked in what she hoped came across as a casual tone, when really her insides squirmed with anticipation.

A wry smile played on Princess Mary's lips. "You first."

Ruth shook her head. She'd fallen for that trick one too many times during her time on the Met, and in her family life too.

In fact, one memorable occasion had involved Chloe—Greg's twin sister—when she was young.

The four-year-old had sidled up to Ruth in the kitchen. "Grandma?"

"Yes, sweetie?" Ruth turned from the mixing bowl to gaze down at her oh-so-cute, butter-wouldn't-melt-in-her-mouth, demure, innocent granddaughter.

Chloe tugged at the hem of her dress. "I want a fairy cake with rainbow sprinkles."

Ruth had made a batch the previous evening. "It's not lunchtime yet, my darling. You can have one after. If you eat all your fruit."

There were no worries on that score. Both Chloe and her brother hoovered up anything remotely edible, including broccoli and sprouts. They'd probably eat the plates and cutlery given half a chance.

"I can tell you what Mummy and Daddy got you for your birthday," Chloe said in a shy tone.

This got Ruth's full attention. "What have they bought?"

Chloe smiled, showing her dimples.

Ruth huffed out a breath. "Fine. You can have one fairy cake now, but don't tell your mum and dad. Got it?"

Chloe gave her an innocent nod.

Ruth opened a tub, extracted a fairy cake with rainbow sprinkles, and set it on a plate. She sat Chloe at her mini table next to the adult's breakfast table, and then watched the girl eat with unrestrained enthusiasm.

A few minutes later, Chloe finished her fairy cake and wiped her mouth on a paper towel.

"Okay," Ruth said. "Spill it. What did they buy me?"

Chloe eyed the cake tub. "A present."

"Yes, but what present?"

"I don't know. I heard Mummy tell Daddy it was a present." Chloe hopped from the chair and skipped from the kitchen.

Ruth's face fell as she watched her go. "Duped by a four-year-old."

Back in the current moment, she recognised that streak of devious charm running through the princess too.

"Please?" Princess Mary asked in a sickly sweet voice like Chloe's. She poked out her bottom lip. "I've been so isolated and out of the loop on that train. It's been driving me crazy. No gossip whatsoever. Torture. I promise what little information I have in exchange could be significant to your investigation." She sat forward. "Tell me what you've discovered thus far."

Ruth sighed, unable to resist the girl's charms. "Someone hit Miles on the back of the head. That's how he died."

"How horrible. How positively ghastly." Despite the gruesome subject matter, Princess Mary's eyes lit up. "Which means he knew the murderer." She lifted her chin. "I thought as much. What else?"

Ruth studied her reaction with some bemusement. "I'm not sure. Miles seemed to have rubbed a few people the wrong way last night. Now it's your turn. What do you know?"

The princess tucked a strand of hair behind her ear. "Well, I think the whole sordid affair has something to do with jewellery."

"Yours?" Ruth nodded to her diamond necklace.

Hugo wanted the princess on board for marketing clout, that much was obvious, and it was also clear he'd pulled out all the stops to accommodate her. No doubt rich clientele would pay a premium on future journeys to stay in the royal suite first occupied by the princess. A safe on board was a logical addition.

"Nothing to do with my jewels, no." Princess Mary touched her matching earrings. "As I said to Hugo yesterday when he offered to lock them away for the night: why would I need to place these inside a safe when I have two armed officers at my side?"

"I—I don't understand." Ruth sipped her tea and slid her half-eaten Danish to Greg. "What was in your box, then?" For some random reason, she pictured a set of antique duelling pistols.

"Box?" Princess Mary's brow furrowed. "Oh, you mean the one Luke took last night? That wasn't mine."

"Whose was it, then?" Greg asked.

"Victoria's."

Ruth blinked. "Excuse me? And which one is Luke?"

Princess Mary gestured to the dark-haired protection officer. "Victoria's assistant asked him whether he wouldn't mind placing her valuables in the safe. Luke agreed. Said he'd be happy to once his shift was over."

"Zoey?" Confusion washed over Ruth. "When did she

ask him to do that? I mean, when exactly?" Now she came to think of it, Victoria hadn't been wearing her impressive necklace this morning.

"Last night," Princess Mary said. "When we played poker."

Ruth sat forward as a rush of interest coursed through her. "No one told me you played too."

Princess Mary gave her a coy look. "I'm partial to a few hands now and again. Luke carries cash for such purposes. My pocket money." She sighed. "I lost it all last night, though." The princess's pretty blue eyes glazed over. "That Miles fellow was certainly lucky. What a winning streak."

12

In Finsbury Café, Princess Mary smiled at Greg as he wiped his mouth on a napkin and sat back, rubbing his belly. "All done?" she asked in a sweet voice.

He shrugged.

"He's never done. Gregory is perpetually hungry." Ruth had spent the last couple of minutes picturing the princess at the poker table with the other passengers.

Mr Price had neglected to say she'd been there.

Greg sipped a cola, and his cheeks flushed under Princess Mary's gaze. He avoided eye contact and stared at the picture of the seahorse.

"Going back to Victoria's jewellery box." Ruth composed her thoughts. "You're saying Luke placed it in the train's safe?"

"Precisely." Princess Mary's expression turned serious again. "But there's more." She lowered her voice. "Earlier in the evening, I noticed Miles couldn't keep his eyes off Victoria's necklace. He kept staring at it while we played poker. Even joked at one point that she should add it to the pot." Princess Mary glanced at her protection officers. "I think that's why she asked Luke to lock it away. She didn't trust Miles not to try something funny."

"Makes sense," Greg said. "He probably took that drunk guy's Rolex."

"I assume by drunk guy, you mean Daniel?" Princess Mary sat back. "Daniel Price?"

"What do you know about him?" Ruth asked. "He played poker too, right?"

"He did. Victoria invited him. And other than his name, nothing. Never met him before. Odd fellow. Very quiet." Princess Mary looked wistful. "I bet Miles had Lady Hamilton's earrings in his compartment. Am I correct?"

Ruth's eyebrows shot up. "How did you know?"

"I have no idea what happened with Daniel's watch," Princess Mary said. "But I know for certain Miles didn't steal Lady Hamilton's earrings." She rolled her eyes. "Her wayward husband gambled them and lost. He seemed determined to beat Miles at all costs. Grabbed the earrings from their compartment and brought them to the table. I wonder if Lady Hamilton knows yet?" She snickered, "Too funny," and then straightened her face again. "Well, that's my information. Interesting, yes?"

"Extremely," Ruth said.

Could Lord Hamilton have regretted the loss of his wife's earrings, gone to Miles' compartment and demanded them back? Did one thing lead to another and Lord Hamilton hit him over the head in a fit of rage?

Ruth's brow furrowed.

Lord Hamilton would have grabbed the earrings after killing Miles, and not have left them in the drawer for investigators to find.

The sequence of events still made little sense.

"Was Luke nearby during the poker game?" Ruth asked,

glancing at the protection officer. "Might he have seen or heard something suspicious?"

"Even if he did, he wouldn't tell you or me." Princess Mary huffed. "He's already written a statement and handed it over to his colleagues." She took a breath. "They both wanted to whisk me away as soon as the murder occurred. I had to beg them not to tell my father."

"I can understand that," Ruth said. After all, it was their job to protect her. "How come you're still here, though?"

The devious smile returned to Princess Mary's lips. "I have all the security I need. No one is getting through those two."

She had a valid point.

The princess gazed at Ruth. "May I explain my theory?"

Ruth waved her on. "Please."

The princess sipped her orange juice and set it down again, as though composing her thoughts. "I believe Miles won a lot of money. I left the poker game before its conclusion, but he was on a hot streak." She took a breath. "After the game, I would bet Daniel followed Miles to his compartment—wanting his money and watch back—where they argued, and then Daniel murdered him. After all, he was very drunk. Could hardly focus on the game."

Ruth considered this possible version of events, but couldn't figure out where Zoey would then fit in. After all, she'd apparently escorted Daniel to his compartment.

"If that's true, then how does it make sense?" Greg said. "Why would Daniel knock on Miles' door hours later, and wake everyone up?"

"Subterfuge," Princess Mary said with a knowing look. "I don't think Miles won or stole Daniel's watch at all. Daniel coming back later this morning made it seem he demanded his watch back, when in reality—"

"He'd murdered him." Greg looked at Ruth with raised eyebrows.

However, she'd already thought of this scenario a couple of times and still wasn't convinced. There were a few holes in the theory. "If Daniel really had killed Miles, why not just keep his mouth shut? Why draw attention to the murder?"

A crease formed on Princess Mary's brow. "Maybe someone heard them arguing at the poker table. Perhaps it was—"

Hugo entered the café, with the relief train driver hard on his heels.

"I'm telling you, Mr Finsbury," the driver said in a heavy Scottish accent, "it'll take twenty minutes and we're done. I promise." He scratched his bulbous nose. "We can be back under way in no time."

Hugo smiled at the princess, but ignored Ruth as he passed the table. He then ordered two coffees and donuts from the lad behind the counter.

"What do you say?" the driver pressed. "We can get on it immediately. Minimal disruption."

Hugo faced him. "I'm not sure, Alan. I'll think about it."

"We have the spare first-class carriage. It's ready. We can swap it out and be on our way." Alan looked at his watch. "We have plenty of time."

Hugo turned his back on Ruth and lowered his voice. "I mean, I'm not sure the police will go for it."

"Of course they will," Alan the driver said. "We can roll the entire crime scene into the shed. Then they can examine it as much as they like. Take as long as they want. It won't affect us. We can move everyone's belongings across. No fuss." He took a breath. "Once the police figure out who did it, we'll be back on target. No harm done."

"I guess it's not the worst idea." Hugo rubbed his chin.

"Get everything prepared, but don't act until you've heard from me. I'll put the proposition to the inspector. It'll be his decision."

Alan bowed his head and rushed from the café.

"Your coffee and donut," Hugo called after him, but the driver had gone.

Greg raised a hand. "I'll take them, if they're going spare."

∼

Ruth and Greg made their way up the other side of Finsbury High Street, passed another souvenir shop, and a store selling crystals, with incense wafting from the open door strong enough to strip paint.

Ruth pulled out her phone and navigated to the Kat's Kitty Hotel website. She entered her log-in details, and a second later a video of Merlin's hotel room sprang up.

"There he is." Ruth beamed and zoomed in.

Merlin lay curled up on the sofa, fast asleep, while a TV on a wheeled stand played a nature documentary about penguins.

Greg peered through the window of a bakery.

"You cannot be serious," Ruth said, incredulous. She pocketed her phone. "You have literally just eaten. Twice." If Greg and his sister hadn't been like this their entire lives, any normal grandmother would've sought out immediate medical attention.

"I'm planning ahead."

"What's wrong with the food on the train?"

"We're not going back on the train."

"Of course we are."

Greg's expression turned dubious. "You sure about that?"

Ruth adjusted her coat. "Positive."

"Then, like I say, I'm planning ahead." Greg gazed through the baker's window at all the buns and loaves. "Anyway, you promised to buy me a giant bag of snacks when we reached Penzance. I need snacks. Don't know what might happen."

Ruth sighed. It was a fair point. Besides, a hungry, whiney Greg in a confined space would drive her nuts.

"I'll pay you back," Greg said.

"When you're a rich historian or a famous archaeologist?" Ruth extracted her wallet.

"Mum owes me from working last summer."

Lord and Lady Hamilton approached.

"Well, that was an experience," he said.

"Police questioned you?" Ruth only hoped they'd been treated fairly compared to her.

"Indeed, they did." Lady Hamilton sniffed. "We couldn't shed any light on the matter. How could we? Murder?" She shuddered.

Ruth handed Greg her wallet and focussed on Lord Hamilton. "You played poker last night, I hear."

Lady Hilary's face darkened. "Yes, he did," she said through clenched teeth.

Lord Hamilton tugged at his collar.

"Sorry to bring it up." Ruth looked about and gestured them to a bench between the shops, in a tiny park, of sorts, with an apple tree dominating a small green surrounded by a foot-high picket fence.

While the three of them sat down, Greg signalled he'd return once he'd emptied the bakers of their wares.

"I don't mind admitting I lost a fair amount on that

game," Lord Hamilton said with a grimace, avoiding eye contact with his wife.

"To Miles?" Ruth asked.

"Never seen a run of luck like it." Lord Hamilton's eyes widened in remembered awe. "If Victoria hadn't been dealing, I would've cried cheat several times. She must have brought the worst luck to the table."

"Yes, that's exactly why you lost so much." Lady Hamilton rolled her eyes. "Don't blame your terrible hands on Victoria. You only have yourself to blame."

"And you started playing soon after dinner?" Ruth asked, eager to keep the temperature down, and the answers rational.

Lord Hamilton bobbed his head. "Quite so. After I'd seen Hilary to bed."

And after finding Robert Minchent pacing the corridor, Ruth thought.

"Who invited you to the table?" Ruth doubted it would have been Miles.

"Victoria." Lord Hamilton's expression glazed over. "Perhaps she marked the cards. Worked in cahoots with someone."

"She did no such thing," Lady Hamilton said through the corner of her mouth, and watched Mr and Mrs Minchent through narrowed eyes as they strolled past arm in arm.

They headed into the crystal and incense shop.

Brave, brave people.

Ruth refocussed on Lord Hamilton. "Who else was at the table?"

He blew out a puff of air, and his eyes wandered to the sky. "Victoria, her assistant—"

"Zoey," Lady Hilary said. "Lovely girl. So sweet and

polite."

"Yes. Right. Zoey." His gaze lifted again. "That Daniel fellow, he'd had a few too many. Miles, of course. The ever-charming Princess Mary . . . and the other chap." He clicked his fingers. "What was his name? Wayne, I think."

"Waylon?" Ruth said, aghast. "Hugo's assistant? I thought he was ill and in bed?"

"Don't know about that," Lord Hamilton said. "But he was the last to join the table." His forehead wrinkled. "Now you come to mention it, he did seem rather peaky. Only stayed for a few hands before making his excuses."

Another player Daniel Price had neglected to tell Ruth about.

Lord Hamilton pointed across the road.

Sure enough, Waylon marched through the archway, heading to the café.

"A fine player," Lord Hamilton said. "Not enough to end Miles' run, unfortunately, but a gallant effort. Good bluffer."

"Handsome man too," Lady Hamilton said with a deadpan expression.

Lord Hamilton cleared his throat.

Ruth rubbed her chin as she pondered this new piece of information. *Does Hugo know his assistant played several hands of poker? Is that allowed? Perhaps he was off duty, so to speak, but only due to illness. Was he faking?*

Greg dropped to the bench next to Ruth, breaking her thoughts. He clutched a paper bag as large as his torso. "They had pies too."

Ruth caught scents of sweet pastry, bread, and steak. She took her wallet back, opened it, and peered into the empty slot where she'd once had a twenty-pound note. Ruth then turned to Lord Hamilton again. "What time did you leave the table?" She opted to omit the fact she knew he'd gambled away Lady Hamilton's earrings.

"I suppose around one. Maybe a little before."

"You woke me," Lady Hamilton said.

"Don't I know it," he muttered.

"Were you the first to go?" Ruth asked, placing their whereabouts in the sequence of events that unfolded shortly after.

Lord Hamilton tugged at his shirt collar. "As I say, Wayne left before me."

"Waylon," Lady Hamilton corrected.

Ruth pictured the people seated at the poker table. "And did you happen to see Daniel Price take off his watch at any point?"

Lord Hamilton shook his head. "I must confess I never noticed he wore a watch. First I heard of it was when he accused Miles of stealing. The same time you did. But if he had a watch, my bet is he gambled it away. That can happen in the excitement of the moment. High stakes. Perhaps I missed him adding it to the pot." He gave his wife a sidelong glance, but she paid him no mind. "Well . . ." Lord Hamilton stood. "We'd better be going. Souvenirs to buy for the grandkids. You understand." He and Lady Hamilton headed across the road to an art gallery.

Greg watched them go. "Souvenirs?"

Ruth again pictured the poker table in her mind's eye with the players gathered, and Victoria dealing cards. "Odd group of people." She stood. "Come on."

They sauntered up the high street.

Greg clutched his bag of goodies. "How will we get back to Scotland if they don't sort out the train?"

"I don't know," Ruth murmured. "A taxi, I suppose." Although, she dreaded to think how much a five-hundred-mile journey would cost. Perhaps they were better off catching a ride to the nearest train station and heading back that way.

Ahead, Daniel Price dove into a sweet shop, and Ruth sped after him.

Inside, jars crammed with colourful sweets filled the shelves, everything from gobstoppers, strawberry swirls, and lemon drops to liquorice sticks and shoelaces.

Ruth giggled with excitement. "All sweet shops used to be like this back in my day."

"Yeah, in your dreams." Greg examined a chocolate bar the size of a hardback novel. "Can I borrow some more money, please?"

"Whatever you want," Ruth murmured, and kept her attention on Daniel as she handed over her bank card. "Back in a minute." She made a beeline for him as he examined the label on a bag of peppermint humbugs.

Daniel saw her coming, glanced at the exit, and, clearly realising there was no easy escape, his shoulders slumped.

"Hello." Ruth beamed at him.

He mumbled something unintelligible.

"I wanted to ask you something else about your epic poker game," Ruth said in a casual tone. "An incident interrupted us earlier."

"I can't talk about it." Daniel squeezed past Ruth and hurried from the shop.

She stood frozen to the spot, not quite comprehending. "What's wrong with him?"

Greg returned and thrust the oversized chocolate bar into his diabetes-inducing snack bag, along with some other colourful packets.

"You figured out who murdered Miles yet?" he asked as they left the sweet shop.

"No." Ruth took her bank card from Greg before he did any more damage. "But I can tell you who didn't kill him." She turned to face her grandson. "First of all, it wasn't either you or me."

Greg rolled his eyes. "Obviously."

"Zoey's door squeaked, which would've woken me up. She couldn't have left her room without it making a noise. The metal piece is on the outside. Which leaves us with Robert and—"

Waylon rushed up to them. "The police have arrested someone. Mr Finsbury wants us all to meet back at the train station. In the waiting room. Immediately."

As he raced off, Ruth called after him. "Who did they arrest?"

"Zoey," he said over his shoulder. "She confessed to the murder."

13

Ruth and Greg raced after Waylon, back toward Finsbury Station. However, at the last moment, Ruth steered her grandson away from the covered walkway, and continued down the high street.

"Where are we going?" he asked as he stumbled along, clutching his snack bag.

"I want to check something out," Ruth said with determination.

"Now? We're supposed to be going back to the waiting room." Greg looked over his shoulder as Lord and Lady Hamilton frowned at them and strode along the walkway.

A little farther down, Ruth stopped.

Ahead, visible through the gap between two buildings, three sets of train tracks ran side by side, each ending in a giant metal shed.

Eight disconnected carriages remained on the main track: the first-class single-sleeper, salon, and dining carriages, and then the three economy carriages, what Ruth assumed was a crew carriage, and the luggage carriage at the end.

The Finsbury Flyer backed the remaining two carriages—the royal carriage and the first-class double sleeper—into the nearest train shed.

"Like Alan the train driver talked about back at the café," Ruth said. "They're swapping the carriages over."

Both drivers then hopped out, disconnected the first-class carriage, and pulled the train forward, leaving the double sleeper carriage in the hangar with several police officers.

"Quite a clever idea," Ruth said.

That would give the crime scene officers all the time in the world and allow the Finsbury Flyer to be on its way.

"They're carrying on?" Greg said. "After what happened?"

Sure enough, the drivers switched the tracks and backed the Finsbury Flyer into another shed to collect a replacement first-class carriage.

"Come on," Ruth said. "I've seen enough."

"Do you think Zoey really killed Miles?" Greg asked as they headed back to the station.

Ruth shook her head. "Someone jammed something in her door hinge. I don't know why, and perhaps it's not related, but Zoey could not have removed it without making it squeak again first. I'm sure I would've heard her leave her compartment or remove it earlier, when she went to bed around one."

Greg frowned. "She's confessed, though. Why would Zoey do that if she's not the murderer?"

Ruth let out a slow breath.

There were some things she could sleep through, like Greg's snoring from the other room, but squeaking doors was not among them.

"You didn't hear him get murdered, though, did you?" Greg continued. "Not even his body when it hit the floor."

Although he made a good point, Ruth wasn't so sure. The low rumble of the train as it trundled along could have masked the deep thud of Miles collapsing to the floor of his compartment, that was true, but no way would she miss the high-pitched, ear-splitting squeak of Zoey's door opening.

Ruth and Greg strode onto Finsbury Platform and into the waiting area, where everyone gathered.

"Now that we're all here . . ." Hugo didn't look best pleased, and it was apparent which direction he aimed the jibe. He still did not make eye contact with Ruth. "As you probably know by now," he said to the group, "the police have arrested a suspect."

All eyes moved to Victoria, who stood by the far wall, hugging herself, a glum look etched onto her face.

Ruth couldn't blame her for being upset. If Zoey had murdered Miles, then Victoria had placed her trust and well-being in a killer's hands, without realising, only to have this tragedy occur. *Surely, she must be wondering if the same could've happened to her?*

A few people in the crowd muttered to one another.

Hugo raised his hands. "They're confident they have the right person in custody."

Robert Minchent leaned in to his wife. "Yeah. Because she admitted it."

Jane screwed up her face. "She was so nice and polite. Just goes to show you."

"We have fully cooperated with the authorities," Hugo said. "And with their permission, we have swapped over the first-class double-sleeper carriage for a replacement. All your belongings are being moved across from one to the other as we speak. We should be done in the next ten minutes."

"If you think I'm getting on that blinkin' train again," Robert Minchent said, "then you've got another think coming."

This resulted in a few more mutterings, some in agreement.

Waylon leaned against the wall, far from everyone else, arms crossed, expression unreadable.

"I understand how upsetting this must be," Hugo continued. "Therefore, I have arranged for a coach to take those of you who wish an alternative route back to Edinburgh. However . . ." He held up his hands again. "I implore you to continue the journey on board the Finsbury Flyer. Everything is under control."

Ruth could understand Hugo's desperation, but given the circumstances, he'd handled the disaster well. Inside he must be freaking out. The maiden voyage would be the stuff of legends.

In fact, from the inevitable social media hype, along with some positive spin, Ruth expected ticket sales would be bolstered, rather than harmed. But that still meant the rest of this trip had to go smoothly. Couldn't have any more people dying unexpectedly.

"Where are the rest of my cases?" Daniel Price asked.

"We'll have them packed and brought to you." Hugo nodded at a porter.

The Hamiltons conducted a murmured exchange.

"We'll continue the journey," Lord Hamilton then said. "You have the murderer in custody. That's good enough for us. We'll support you through this tragic time, Hugo."

Hugo placed his palms together and gave a slight bow of his head.

"I'm staying too," Princess Mary declared in a loud voice from the corner of the room.

Her protection officers both scowled.

Hugo mouthed, "Thank you."

As the Finsbury Flyer pulled into the station, Jane and Robert Minchent were in a heated discussion. Robert's face had turned red and blotchy, while Jane wore an expression of dogged determination.

"I'm not travelling all the way back to Scotland on a coach," she hissed. "It's a gruesome idea." Her husband went to answer, but Jane waved a finger in his face. "Man up, Robert. The murderer is in police custody. We've got nothing to fear now." She turned from him, and lifted her chin. "We're coming too, Hugo."

"Excellent." He smiled and rested a hand on Victoria's shoulder.

"I don't know, Hugo," Victoria murmured. "Do you think I should stay for Zoey? She might need me."

Hugo seemed to ponder this. "I'm not sure what you could do for her. The police will be interviewing Zoey for the next few days. If you like, I could bring you back down to Penzance then, should the need arise. But it's totally up to you."

Victoria didn't say anything for several long seconds, and then she let out a breath. "You're right. There's not much I can do for her. I'll return to Edinburgh on the Flyer."

"Are you sure?" Lady Hamilton said. "This must be a terrible—"

"I'm fine. I'll be okay. Thank you."

Hugo waved over his assistant. "Waylon will take care of your needs from here on, Victoria."

"I'll be happy to. May I take your arm?"

Victoria recoiled at Waylon's touch, and then, seeming to get a grip of herself, she allowed him to link arms with her.

"Let me escort you onto the train," he said.

As far as Ruth was concerned, Hugo had got off lightly, with only Daniel Price refusing to get on board and face the return journey by rail. *Why was that?* Ruth hoped she got a chance to speak to him before they left.

"Are we going back on the train too?" Greg asked.

"Of course." It was a given. Ruth had a job to do and hadn't met with the chef yet. Besides, she felt compelled to show her support for Hugo and his endeavours. It was the least she could do.

Hugo checked his watch. "We leave in twenty-eight minutes."

Everyone filed from the waiting room onto the platform.

Princess Mary and her protection officers climbed on board the train first, followed by Lord and Lady Hamilton, and the other guests.

A porter wheeled Daniel's suitcase to him. He mumbled a thanks, and disappeared around the corner, no doubt off to wait for the coach.

Ruth went to hurry after him, but halted as another porter wheeled their suitcases over to them. "Oh, that's okay," she said. "We're coming back on the train. Greg and I prefer the Finsbury Flyer over a coach."

The porter looked confused, and then he backed away as his boss approached.

Hugo extended a hand to Ruth. "Thank you for your help," he said in a stiff voice, and looked a foot above her head.

Puzzled, she shook his hand. "I haven't done anything."

"You've done enough." Hugo released her, nodded to Greg, and walked away.

"Hugo?" Ruth called after him, but he didn't turn back. "Hugo? Come on. Can we talk about this, please?"

"I guess he's angry with you," Greg said in a sage tone. "He did ask you like twenty times not to investigate, but you kept slipping off when his back was turned."

"Yeah, yeah." Ruth rubbed her chin. "I didn't do anything harmful, though. Disturbed nothing at the crime scene, did I?"

"Maybe not." Greg fished into his paper bag and pulled out a sausage roll. "But you wouldn't listen to him. Guess he's mad about that. He did employ you to do a job, after all." He took a bite and returned the roll. "Technically, Hugo was your boss for a couple of days. You should've done what he asked."

Ruth glared at him. "Whose side are you on?"

The station manager sauntered over to them. "The coach is delayed. Will be here in another couple of hours." He waved the porter back over, who promptly wheeled their cases into the waiting room. "We'll watch your luggage for you. May I suggest a visit to our charming village?" He motioned to the covered walkway.

"We've already seen it," Ruth said, but did as he indicated. As they headed away from the platform, she glanced back at the train, contemplating another round with Hugo. Surely, he'd see sense once she explained she'd only been trying to help. He had to understand.

"Leave it," Greg warned.

"But— He—" Ruth harrumphed. "It's not fair." She stopped short of stamping a foot.

"Are you irritated because Hugo thinks badly of you, or because you were wrong?" Greg asked, deadpan.

Ruth spun to face him. "How dare you."

He smirked.

Ruth straightened her collar. "I'm never wrong."

Greg cocked an eyebrow. "You sound like Aunty Margaret."

Ruth's face fell. "Take that back, you nasty boy. Anyway, I'm not wrong about mysteries or murders."

Greg lifted his other eyebrow.

"Well, hardly ever." Ruth plodded down the covered walkway. At the end, she came to an abrupt halt, and Greg almost bumped into her.

"What now?"

"Something's still not right." Ruth's stomach twisted. "I don't believe Zoey killed Miles. Not for one second." No matter how hard she tried, she couldn't picture the sweet girl clubbing him over the head.

"Why would she admit to it?" Greg asked with a look of incredulity. "I mean, if she didn't murder him? Seems like a pretty absurd thing to do otherwise."

"Precisely. Someone put her up to it."

"Victoria?" Greg asked.

"I don't know." Victoria seemed pretty upset about what had happened, but Ruth couldn't rule her out until she'd questioned her. *Could Zoey have been cheating at poker, and someone else found out? Blackmailed her into confessing to Miles' murder?* Ruth peered up the high street, in the direction of the train sheds.

"Leave it all to the police," Greg said. "They'll get to the bottom of what happened."

"No doubt," Ruth said. "But now Zoey's claimed responsibility, that could take days."

"So?" Greg said. "What's the hurry? Miles can't die twice."

Ruth glanced about to make sure they were alone, and then pulled him aside. "If Zoey isn't the killer, that means the perpetrator could still be on board the Finsbury Flyer." She took a breath. "And if they're on board that train, they could..."

"Kill again?" Greg whispered.

Ruth nodded.

"Oh no." Greg clutched his bag of food. "I know that look. We're about to get into a lot more trouble, aren't we?"

Ruth frowned. "Why do you say that?"

"Because now is about the time you usually want to do something reckless or dangerous. Probably both."

Ruth grinned.

Greg shook his head and stepped back. "Whatever it is, Grandma, I won't do it." He held up his bag. "All I want is some quiet time."

Ruth sighed. "It's an enigma."

"What is?"

"How you remain so rake-thin with the amount you consume. Where on earth do you put the calories?"

"Probably burn them off chasing after you."

Ruth marched up the high street. "Come on, Gregory. We haven't much time."

He swore under his breath and trotted after her, snack bag rustling.

At the end of Finsbury High Street, Ruth hurried down the alleyway to the fence and peered at the train sheds. "When I looked into the spare compartment earlier, Miles had covered the walls and desk with drawings and photographs. Blueprints of train carriages. Designs. Lots of notes."

Greg joined her. "So? Didn't he have something to do with building it?"

"Designer." Ruth gripped the top of the fence. "I should've taken pictures with my phone because I want more time to decipher his notes and get to the bottom of what's going on. There was a lot to take in."

Greg leaned against the fence. "You think they have some sort of significance? They hold clues as to why someone did him in?"

Ruth paced with her hands clasped behind her back. "Don't you think it's strange that the very person who had concerns about the Finsbury Flyer is now dead? That he brought those concerns to Hugo, and yet the train is still in operation and about to return to Edinburgh? Even after a murder, they found a way to keep going? Swapped carriages."

"The Death Train," Greg murmured. "All the more reason we shouldn't be on it."

Ruth stopped pacing and lifted her chin. "I want another look at that compartment."

Greg stared at her, then his gaze drifted to the train sheds, and his eyes went wide as he cottoned on. "You can't be serious, Grandma."

"Deadly serious." Ruth faced the sheds with renewed determination. "I believe the answers are in that first-class compartment."

Greg swallowed. "It's a crime scene."

"Not true. The only crime scene is compartment 1A, where Miles stayed. The others are fine. Porters were allowed to remove our belongings, remember? I want another peek inside 7A. That's nowhere near 1A. They're far apart."

Greg closed his eyes. "Please. No. Don't do it. Why do you always have to take these risks?"

It was true Ruth was a thrill-seeker at times. Something her late husband, John, had passed onto her. *But what is life without a little adventure?* "You can stay here." Ruth softened her voice. "I'll be fine." She slumped her shoulders and did her best vulnerable grandmother impression. "If I get into an accident, I'm sure I will . . ."

Greg's eyes snapped open and glared at her. "I'll save you the bother of what would've been a very endearing speech, I'm sure." He waved a finger in her face. "I'm not going to prison for you, though. I am serious. And the moment I see a police officer, I'm out of there. Got it?"

Ruth pointed to the front of the nearest train shed. "Like her?"

A police officer stood guard, with her back to them.

Greg turned to leave, but Ruth grabbed his arm.

"I need another peek inside that compartment," she insisted. "See if there's anything I've missed. You know it's unlikely Zoey killed Miles."

Greg didn't look convinced. "What laws are we about to break?"

"Small laws," Ruth said. "Minor. Absolutely nothing to worry about. The worst that will happen is they'll tell us to go away." Although, that would depend on several factors—primary among them being how far they were from the crime scene. "A slap on the wrist," Ruth murmured. "Maybe a bit of community service. Hundred hours or so."

Greg's jaw dropped. "No way I'm getting a criminal record."

"You won't," Ruth said with a dismissive wave. Although, every ounce of her police training told Ruth not to go into that shed under any circumstances, and that the entire carriage would likely be deemed an active crime scene, but that was all pushed aside by her sense of justice and overwhelming curiosity.

Greg grumbled under his breath, clearly realising there was no way she was about to back down, and she would be better off with him at her side. He set his bag of food by the nearest wall. Greg then took a deep breath and, with a huge amount of effort, hauled himself over the fence, almost tearing his shirt in the process.

Once he'd finally dropped to the other side, he outstretched his hands to Ruth and panted, "Careful not to hurt yourself. There's splinters and rusty nails."

"Sure. Duly noted." Ruth strolled down to a gate, opened it, and popped out on the other side. "How about I lead the way from here on?"

Greg squeezed his eyes shut.

14

With only twenty minutes left to uncover a definitive clue and catch up to Hugo, Ruth waved Greg on, and they hurried down an embankment, away from the fence, and toward the train sheds. All the while, Ruth kept a close eye on the police officer standing sentry out front. So far, she hadn't had cause to turn in their direction.

When the two of them reached the side of the first shed, out of sight of the officer, Ruth allowed herself a few calming breaths.

She beamed at Greg and whispered, "All this feels so delightfully bad, doesn't it? It's like we're a couple of spies." Her insides squirmed with excitement.

Greg shook his head. "No government would want us working for them."

"Oh, I don't know." Ruth pointed farther down the shed and motioned for Greg to follow. "Once they get a load of my boiled sweets laced with cyanide, the dart-firing lipstick, and my handbag with the concealed grenade launcher, they'll jump at the chance." She reached the corner, held up a hand, then peered around it.

The back yard stood empty, save for a couple of skips. There were only fire exit doors and no windows at the rear of the buildings.

Ruth swore under her breath and pulled back.

"Language," Greg muttered.

"No way in. Fire exits don't have handles on the outside."

"We can go, then?" Greg asked with a hopeful expression.

Ruth pursed her lips. "We need a distraction."

He groaned. "You do realise there could be like fifty more police officers inside."

"I don't think so. It's too quiet. The three officers we saw in there earlier have gone. It's only that one standing guard for now." Ruth took a steadying breath. "I bet the crime scene team won't be back here until later today." She glanced at Greg. "We need to get into the shed without anyone spotting us."

"Won't someone have locked it? The train carriage, I mean. Sealed?"

"Only one way to find out." Ruth pressed her back against the wall and thought it through.

The female officer looked young—early twenties—which meant she likely hadn't had much experience on the force. However, the newest recruits tended to be the most eager and attentive to their surroundings.

Ruth shimmied her way along the wall and peered round the corner again, to the front of the sheds. She eyed the crates to the left of the officer, and the police tape strung across the open roller door behind her.

The side door to that was closed, so no way to tell if someone had locked it too, but no tape secured it shut either. A good sign. The connecting door at the nearest end was also closed.

"I have an incredible idea." With a rush of enthusiasm, Ruth beckoned Greg close, and then whispered her plan in his ear, making sure to spell out exactly how the events should go, step by step.

When she was done, Greg shook his head. "No way I'm doing that. You're crazy. Lost your mind. That's the worst plan I've ever heard." He glared at her. "And you've come up with plenty of other loopy ideas in the past."

Ruth let out a long breath, ignoring the dig against her impeccable character. "Do you remember that time in the New Forest?" She watched his reaction.

Greg's cheeks flushed, and he looked away. "No."

"Oh, sure you do." Ruth smirked. "It was the first week after we left Morgan Manor and started our grand tour of the countryside. We'd parked up at that campsite, if you recall, and while I connected the electricity, you trundled off to fetch water." Ruth acted out his trundling by waddling side to side and swinging her arms about.

"Why are you bringing this up now?" Greg said through gritted teeth.

"You'd been gone ages," Ruth continued in a whisper. "I was getting very worried. When ten minutes turned into twenty, I decided to come find you." She inclined her head. "And where did I find you, Gregory?"

He looked away again.

"On a bench, next to the water tap, with your arm around a beefy biker guy. One of those Hell's Angels types."

Greg's attention snapped back to her. "He wasn't a Hell's Angel."

"But he *was* sobbing his eyes out, if my memory serves." Ruth kept a straight face. "Why was the biker crying, Greg? Be a dear and remind your sweet grandmother what happened, would you?"

"Fine," Greg snapped. "I'll do it. I will go do something stupid and get arrested, just because you want to stick your nose somewhere it doesn't belong. Happy?"

"Extremely. Thank you."

He edged round her and muttered, "Why do I always feel like a guinea pig in a coal mine?"

Ruth patted his back. "That makes no sense."

"Sure it does," Greg said. "You either experiment on me or send me into dangerous situations first. Sometimes both. Like now. This is both." He thrust a finger at himself. "Guinea pig." And then round the corner. "Coal mine." He took a deep breath, lifted his chin, and strode round it.

Ruth chuckled to herself.

Back at that campsite, Greg had gone to fetch water, as planned, but had wound up helping a rather attractive girl fill her own bottles first.

That was when the aforementioned biker, her boyfriend, her very large and mean-looking boyfriend, had shown up and flipped out at the pair. He'd accused his lady of flirting with Greg, which Ruth could well believe had gone both ways, and the biker was about ready to smash the poor lad to a teenage pulp.

Greg had then proceeded to talk down the burly hooligan, and the two of them had started an impromptu therapy session, right there on that bench by the water tap, delving deep into the man's psyche, and getting to the bottom of his anger issues.

Whether he liked it or not, Greg had a way of connecting with people when he wanted to. When he made the effort. He was a charmer when he put his mind to the task. It was a shame Greg didn't put that gift to good use more often. He would make a good hostage negotiator. Or a nursery school teacher.

Ruth steeled herself and peered around the corner.

The officer turned at Greg's footfalls. "Stop. This is a crime scene. You're trespassing."

Greg raised his hands and continued his approach. "You'll want to hear this." He spoke in a calm but determined voice. Relaxed posture. Slow movements. Casual and nonthreatening.

The officer squared up to him. "Please, sir. Go back the way you came." She reached for her radio.

Greg kept his distance while he circled her. "I thought you should know my grandmother is going to break in."

The officer stared at him. "Excuse me?"

"Right here." He motioned over her shoulder to the carriage. "She's determined." Greg sighed and lowered his hands. "She wants to get in there at all costs. Completely lost her mind, if you ask me."

The officer frowned. "Why does she want to do that?"

Greg circled her some more, and plonked himself on the nearby crates, facing forty-five degrees away from the officer, keeping his threat status to a minimum, palms open and away from his pockets. "She has some crazy notion the real murderer is still at large, and that they'll kill again, and that she's the only one in the entire world smart enough to stop them."

"Hmm." Ruth wasn't sure whether she should take that as a compliment or a thinly veiled insult.

She chose . . . *compliment*.

Greg then proceeded to tell the story, in excruciating detail, right from their arrival in Edinburgh. ". . . we dropped her lunatic cat off at the kitty hotel. Kitty hotel? Can you believe it? Nuts. It had all these different themed rooms." He rolled his eyes. "Goodness knows how much that place costs. Merlin lives better than I do. That's his name, by the way—Merlin. Like the wizard from King Arthur's court..."

With the officer's back to her, Ruth tiptoed to the shed door, ducked under the police tape, and crept over to the train carriage.

She held her breath and tried the handle.

An enormous wave of relief then washed over Ruth as the door opened.

After another furtive glance over at Greg and the officer, who removed a notepad from her pocket and attempted to take Greg's statement, Ruth stepped on board.

She didn't waste a second pulling on her gloves and opening the door to cabin 7A.

As before, drawings, blueprints, photos, and notes lined the walls, desk, and bed. The only light came from the window, but despite the gloom, everything looked in its place and undisturbed from the last time.

Ruth frowned and murmured, "Why hasn't Hugo cleared this away?" After all, if there really were some kind of health and safety concerns, he should have got rid of it all when he had the chance. "Or is he confident the police won't look in here?" If so, that was a mistake. They'd check all the compartments as a matter of routine.

However, the police had released the passengers' luggage, which meant they'd allowed the removal of some items. So that either meant they'd seen this compartment and not linked any significance to the murder—perhaps they'd already spoken to Hugo about it—or they'd deliberately left the space intact for further forensic investigation.

Whatever the case, Ruth would be careful not to disturb anything.

She pulled her phone from her pocket and edged her way around the compartment, taking plenty of pictures with the flash activated, and moving slowly so as not to touch anything.

She stopped at the desk, and a drawing of the luggage carriage. It had the futuristic safe outlined, with details of it bolted to the floor inside a cage. A hand-drawn red circle enclosed a device at the end of the carriage.

Ruth leaned down for a better look.

It seemed to be the coupler—the heavy mechanism that connected train carriages. Miles had highlighted part of it.

A scrawled note attached read:

Why is this nonstandard? It could be forced apart when the train is in motion. Who authorised this change? How did it pass official inspection?

Ruth's eyes drifted to another drawing. This showed the side elevation of another train carriage with its coupler highlighted too. "Same problem with all the carriages?"

Miles had drawn another red circle around a rectangular section beneath. An attached note read,

What's going on here? This pushes the conduit to one side and is too low to the tracks. What's its purpose? It's not part of my original design. Why have the fabricators added this section? Looks to be storage. Of what? Tools? Parts? Why there? This will not pass official inspection.
What are the rails for?

"Wow. He was not a happy chappie." Ruth took pictures of Miles' various complaints, and then finally found what she was looking for. "Ah, here we go." She made her way to the far end of the desk and took a picture of the electrical wiring diagram. Then she activated the torch function on her phone and leaned in for a better look.

It might as well have been random squiggles. She had no idea what all the symbols and numbers meant.

However, Miles had gone to town with his red pen, making a lot of notes, squeezing them into gaps and margins.

Although a lot of it still went over her head, Ruth pieced together what she could.

The gist was the technicians had connected the electrical system in such a way it was prone to intermittent failure or attack.

Ruth focussed on that last word, as Miles had underlined it twice. This was what she'd come back to see. What she'd assumed had been paranoia before, could also contain a premonition of what was to come.

As far as she could tell, Miles felt the electrical and security systems were vulnerable.

"Someone's going to attack the train's systems?" Ruth murmured. "Why? To make sure the train fails and Hugo looks bad?"

Was murder not enough?

Or is the killer planning to do it again?

She had to tell Hugo.

Ruth took a few more pictures, capturing all the items in the room, and then she snuck out of the carriage.

Greg was still blabbering away to a now bewildered-looking officer, who held the pen loosely poised over her notepad and gaped at him.

Ruth tiptoed to the police cordon and ducked under the tape.

"My grandmother is a total lunatic, of course," Greg said. "Lost. Her. Mind. Mad as a bicycle."

Ruth's step faltered, and she looked over at him.

Greg glanced up at her and half smiled.

The officer turned to look, but Greg broke out into a coughing fit. "Are you okay, sir?"

"Fine," Greg wheezed. "One of those days."

Not wasting a second more, and vowing to have strong words with her grandson, Ruth jogged around the corner of the building.

A few moments later, Greg appeared, looking pleased with himself. Some would say extremely smug, in fact.

"Yes, yes. Very amusing, Gregory." Ruth glanced at the time on her phone, and her eyes almost popped from their sockets. "The train leaves in three minutes. We have to warn Hugo." She raced up the embankment. "Quickly."

"What did you find?" Greg hurried after her. "Warn him about what?"

The Finsbury Flyer's whistle sounded.

Ruth mumbled several swear words.

"Hey," the officer shouted. "Stop." She ran up the embankment toward them.

"Run, run, run." Ruth pushed through the gate, and then raced along the alleyway.

"Wait."

She spun back as Greg darted round the corner. "What are you doing?"

He appeared again a few seconds later, clutching his bag of snacks.

Ruth glowered at him. "Are you kidding me?"

The pair of them jogged from the alleyway and along Finsbury High Street.

"Stop," came the officer's shout as she gained on them.

"You seriously want us to get on board a train with a killer?" Greg panted.

Ruth kept up her pace, even though her lungs burned. "Would you ever forgive yourself if we did nothing?"

"Yes."

"Gregory."

"Okay, fine," he grumbled. "No. No, I wouldn't."

They jogged up the covered walkway and onto the train platform.

The Finsbury Flyer pulled away, gaining speed.

Ruth snatched the bag of food from Greg.

"Hey. What are you doing?" He went to grab it back, but she pulled away from him.

"Our suitcases." Ruth waved a hand at the waiting area, and then the train. "Hurry. She's coming." Ruth turned and raced after the Finsbury Flyer, her short legs pounding the platform, arms pumping the air. As Ruth drew level with the last door, she grabbed the handle, threw the door open, and scrambled on board.

Panting, lungs about to explode, she looked back.

Greg ran along the platform, a suitcase in each hand, face red.

Ruth beckoned. "Hurry up." She then waved the bag of snacks back and forth as an extra incentive.

The police officer appeared on the platform, spotted Greg, and hurried after him.

The Finsbury Flyer continued gaining speed, and then the platform ended.

Greg stumbled down the ramp, released the suitcases on the gravel, and sprinted after the train. He caught up to it and launched himself on board.

Ruth peered down at him as he rolled onto his back, breathing hard. "What exactly will we do without our luggage? My toothbrush and pyjamas were in there."

"I could've made it with mine," Greg wheezed. "But your suitcase was way too heavy."

Ruth gasped. "Mrs Beeton." Her favourite book in the entire world, the one she never left behind, under any circumstances, was in that suitcase. Ruth contemplated jumping from the train, but it was now going way too fast.

The officer stopped at the edge of the platform and stared wide eyed at them. However, she did not lift a radio to her mouth. *After all, how would she explain this to her superiors?*

Greg clambered to his feet. "At least we didn't lose this." He snatched the bag of food from Ruth. "Thanks."

Ruth hurried past racks of boxes and crates.

"Wait."

She whirled.

"We could've seriously hurt ourselves back there, Grandma." Greg panted and clutched the snack bag to his chest. "That was completely reckless. We should've just told the police what we found and let them deal with it."

Ruth was about to argue when she stopped herself. She drew in a long breath and let it out slowly. "You're right." Ruth had once again been so focussed and determined to unravel the mystery, she'd risked both of their well-being. She gripped his shoulders and levelled her gaze. "I promise, from now on, I'll think things through more carefully before I act."

Greg snorted. "Yeah, right."

Ruth released him, and her attention shifted to the corner of the luggage carriage. Taking up a six-foot square was a mini jail. At least, that was how Ruth first interpreted it, with its thick steel bars from floor to ceiling, and a lock with both fingerprint and code protection.

High on the opposite wall, near the corner of the ceiling,

was a security camera, sealed inside its own cage, pointing directly at the cell.

Lastly, inside the cell sat an impressive safe with a heavy door and more high-tech protection in the form of a keypad and biometrics.

Ruth pressed her face against the bars and whispered to the safe, "Have you been naughty? Is that why you're locked up? What did you do that was so bad?" She stepped back. "Well, I would say it's safe to assume the safe is more than safe in there." She looked over at Greg and winked. "Safety first."

He rolled his eyes.

Ruth smiled. "Better safe than sorry."

"Have you taken your medication today?" Greg asked. "Because I think you may have missed a few of the vital pills."

Ruth waved a finger at the cell. "It's in safe hands."

"Please stop." Greg strode to the door.

Ruth followed him and mumbled, "Safe as houses." She couldn't help herself.

15

Greg followed Ruth as she made her way through the crew carriage—a narrow corridor with doors a few feet apart. "Are you going to tell me what you uncovered in the compartment back at the train sheds? After all, I just risked my life to distract that police officer. She could've shot me."

Ruth raised one eyebrow. "Not without a gun."

"Arrested me, then." Greg swallowed. "I would not do well locked up."

"Because you're meant to be free?" Ruth asked as he opened the door at the end and continued through an economy-class carriage. "Or is it because you're a scrawny teenager who wouldn't last two seconds in prison?"

"Neither," Greg said. "Well, both. But worse than that is the grub always looks terrible." He shook his bag of junk food. "Don't think they'd let me take this with me."

"That's a good point."

He would not survive five minutes without a sausage roll.

"If they had caught us," Greg continued, "I would've

blamed it all on you anyway. It was your stupid idea, and you're the one who snuck into a crime scene, not me." He tugged at his shirt collar. "I mean, I only did what you told me to, didn't I? It was all your idea. Your fault."

"Thanks."

"You bullied me into it," Greg said with conviction.

Ruth gasped. "I did no such thing. Take that back."

Although, he had a point there too.

The door at the other end of the carriage opened, and a man in a white double-breasted jacket, trousers, and a toque blanche stepped through. "Good morning," he said as he slipped past Ruth and Greg. He also wore a pair of thick-rimmed glasses. Judging by his attire, he must be the chef or one of the kitchen assistants.

"M-Morning," Ruth replied in a tremulous voice. As soon as the man left the carriage, heading toward the back of the train, she pulled her phone from her pocket, navigated to the photograph of the electrical wiring diagram, and held it out to her grandson. "This is what you risked your liberty for."

He took it from her and frowned. "What is it?"

"I thought you might know. Someone deliberately cut the CCTV right before, during, and after the time of the murder. Hugo showed me the blank recording on his security app. It was back to normal by the time Mr Price woke us up. Does this explain how they might have done it? Got to Miles, and away unseen?"

Greg's lips moved as he read the various notes and parts of the diagram, zooming in to each section and turning his head from side to side like a curious dog.

"There's not a dedicated CCTV room on board," Ruth added.

Greg nodded. "Controlled via a computer, by the look of

it. Wouldn't need to be very big." He outlined an imaginary box a few inches on each side with his fingers. "A Raspberry Pi would be enough. Doesn't have to be sophisticated."

"I'll take your word for it," Ruth said, urging him on. "Well?"

Greg tapped the screen. "This is the motherboard, connected to the network, but it doesn't say where on the train they installed it. Could be anywhere. Maybe hidden in a wall."

Ruth considered if that was what the box beneath the first-class carriage Miles had mentioned could be for: storing the added electronics. Additions he hadn't approved. She recalled his notes about how the box was easy to access from outside.

"The wiring seems to have been modified beyond the original designs," Greg said, confirming Ruth's suspicions. "And the CCTV cameras added later. These red sections are all extra parts. There's a lot of them. It's very complicated."

"Additions requested by Hugo?" Ruth asked. Although, that was one of the things she planned to bring up with him.

"Hard to tell," Greg murmured. Then his eyes widened. "Are you saying the killer was a member of staff? They had access to the CCTV and switched it off during the murder?"

"It does seem a possibility. Or an almighty coincidence."

"And you don't believe in coincidences."

"Not when it comes to murder."

Greg whispered, "It has to be Hugo, right?"

Ruth took the phone from him. "I don't believe that." She then spun on her heel, opened the door, and marched through the next economy-class carriage.

All seemed quiet, and Ruth couldn't help but shudder as a foreboding washed through her.

"We can't confront him," Greg said. "He might try and do us in."

Ruth shook her head. She refused to entertain the idea her old friend would commit murder, especially on such an important occasion.

Greg still looked dubious. "I hope you know what you're doing."

"Not even a little bit," Ruth murmured.

After hurrying through the next two economy-class carriages, she stepped into the dining carriage, marched past a compact reading nook, a closed door to the kitchen, and into the main dining area.

Hugo stood at the far end, going through a list with Waylon. When Hugo spotted Ruth, his eyes almost popped from their sockets. He thrust the list into his assistant's hands and shooed him away.

Waylon glared at Ruth and Greg as he passed them.

Hugo bounded to Ruth in three strides. "What the hell are you doing here? I thought I'd made it perfectly clear your services are no longer required."

"I get your anger," Ruth said in a placating tone, even though her insides demanded a snappier retort. "I really do, Hugo. You think I've been meddling, risking your business."

"You damn well have."

Ruth took a zen-like breath. "You're absolutely right. And I am sorry." She offered him a weak smile, which wasn't reciprocated. "But I wouldn't be back here and annoying you if it wasn't vitally important."

Hugo folded his arms. "You don't give up."

She held out her phone. "I found something."

Hugo squinted at the screen. "What's that? Another wild theory?"

"Don't you recognise it?" Ruth asked, confused by his reaction.

Hugo shook his head. "Never seen it before in my life."

Ruth checked the phone's screen to make sure she had the right photo. She did. "It's the train's wiring diagram, including the camera system you've installed."

"Where did you get that from?" Hugo's brow furrowed, and he seemed genuinely puzzled.

Ruth looked back at Greg.

He shrugged and helped himself to a mini chocolate bar out of his snack bag.

Ruth cleared her throat and refocussed on Hugo. "Last night, you had an argument with Miles."

"This again?"

"Please, hear me out," Ruth said.

Hugo stared at her for several seconds and then lowered himself into a dining chair. He motioned to another opposite. "You have one minute."

Ruth did as he indicated while Greg sat at a different table, munching away and watching them as though they were a mildly interesting TV program.

"You deny you had an argument with Miles?" Ruth asked Hugo in a soft tone.

"We had an argument, all right," he said. "That's all we've done for the past couple of months—argue and bicker." He rubbed his temples. "It's been a trying time for everyone involved, and you're making it harder."

"You argued about the design of the train?" Ruth pressed.

Hugo glared at her. "What does this have to do with anything?"

"Please, Hugo."

"If you must know, Miles wanted to control everything

from fabrication to testing. Each step of the process. I only hired him as a designer. Nothing more. He's stuck his nose in at every level." Hugo adjusted the place setting in front of him, lining up the cutlery with the edge of the mat. "At first, I made the mistake of allowing Miles to do what he wanted. I thought by giving him free rein, it would help make the Finsbury Flyer the best it could be. I trusted his judgement." Hugo ground his teeth. "But Miles put a lot of noses out of joint. Chief of all, mine. I should never have signed that contract."

"What's with all the pictures and notes in the compartment?" Ruth asked. "It looks like a serial killer decorated."

Hugo let out a puff of air and shook his head. "Miles tried to show me last night, but I refused to listen. Didn't look at what he'd put together. I regret that now, of course, but he had been drinking. Slurred his words and staggered about the place. I told him to calm down and sober up. That we'd discuss it in greater detail once we'd arrived at Finsbury Village."

"He wanted to show you all the changes to the train's design," Ruth said. "He clearly had deep anxieties about them."

"Look, as far as I was concerned, and still am," Hugo said, "his worry was overblown and unjustified." He motioned around them. "You can see as well as I can the train is in excellent condition. Exceeds all health and safety requirements. Passed all the tests."

Ruth sat back. "Why do you think someone killed him?"

Hugo stared at the table. "That's been bothering me a great deal. I can't get over it. I know Miles could be hard to deal with, but his heart was in the right place. He was passionate." Hugo's gaze rose to meet Ruth's. "I have no clue. Murder? It doesn't make sense. He didn't deserve to die. I'm sure Zoey will explain her actions. I'm as eager as you are to know what provoked her attack."

Greg gave him a dubious look, but Hugo didn't notice.

However, Ruth believed her old friend. "Who else has access to the CCTV app?"

Hugo's gaze wandered to the ceiling for a couple of seconds. "The drivers and other staff members."

"Which ones?" Ruth pressed. "It's important. Be specific."

Hugo pondered the question some more. "The porters and Waylon."

"How come so many people?" Greg said through a mouthful of chocolate. "Why not just you?"

"We're on a train," Hugo said. "It was another safety requirement, given the fact we're pushing technology and dealing in the public arena. We had to jump through many hoops and pass a tonne of regulations to arrive at this day."

"I need to speak to the people with access," Ruth said.

Hugo stared at her. "I thought by answering some of your questions you'd back down from this nonsense. I can see I was mistaken." He went to stand, but Ruth waved him back down.

"Please hear me out." Ruth cleared her throat. "I think someone deliberately switched off the cameras, or wiped the recordings."

"Not possible."

"Why not?" Greg asked.

Hugo pulled his phone out, navigated to the CCTV app, and handed it over to him.

Greg examined it for a few seconds. "This is playback only. No way to change settings, stop the recordings, or switch off the cameras." He returned the phone to Hugo.

Hugo set it on the table in front of Ruth. "See for yourself. I don't know if it was a coincidence or not, the CCTV blacking out, but DI White knows all about it now. I told him everything. He's handling the case."

"Detective Inspector White?" Ruth said with confusion. "Who's that?" The assigned detective back at Finsbury Village, and the one conducting the interviews, was named Kirby.

"I've said too much." Hugo straightened his tie. "Suffice to say, DI White has taken care of everything. I've worked with the police for the last couple of weeks."

Ruth blinked up at him, struggling to belive her own ears. "You have? To what end?"

Is that why Hugo has been so angry with me getting involved?

He folded his arms. "It's all under control, Ruth. That's as much as you need to know."

She begged to differ. "There was a murder on board this train," Ruth persisted, getting to her feet. "How on earth is that *under control*?" She fought to keep her voice from turning shrill.

Hugo looked about. When he spoke, the harshness had left his voice, but he still sounded wary of her antics. "DI White wasn't on board because of an imminent murder, Ruth. He was here because—"

"The detective was among us? Who?" Ruth glanced at Greg.

"Look," Hugo said. "I'm terribly sorry for how I spoke to you earlier. That was bad of me, but you were snooping about. I couldn't have you interfering with an investigation. DI White was working on a credible tip-off about something else, when Miles was . . ." His voice trailed off.

"Done in," Greg murmured.

Ruth's mind reeled.

Hugo's expression hardened again. "It's over, thank goodness. Now, if you'll excuse me . . ." He turned to leave.

Ruth shook herself. "Wait, Hugo."

He growled under his breath and faced her.

"I came back here to tell you that Miles had deep concerns about the electrical system too," Ruth said. "You must admit that it could be linked to what happened to the cameras. He felt the system was open to attack."

Hugo let out a slow breath. "Another unfounded worry." He held up a hand before Ruth could answer back. "I addressed all of Miles' questions, in full, but he wouldn't see sense." A vein throbbed at Hugo's temple. "I can't explain the timing of the cameras blacking out, but I will have the system checked over again in Edinburgh." He motioned around them. "As you can see, everything is working perfectly."

Ruth wanted to press on with her questions, but the best thing she could do right now was calm the situation and pretend everything was back to normal, so she composed herself. "If you can forgive my snooping, how about we reset and reinstate our original deal?" Ruth glanced at a clock on the wall. "We're coming up for dinner in a couple of hours. I could work with Chef, as we'd originally planned."

Although, given their evening's prior meal, she didn't think she had much to offer. It had been delicious and cooked to perfection. Clearly, Hugo had found top-class talent to go with his no-expense-spared train.

What Ruth wanted to do was demand to know what the detective had been investigating prior to the murder because she was sure it would help solve the mystery of Miles' untimely demise.

Instead, she ground her teeth, fighting back the urge to fire a thousand questions at Hugo. She needed to play it cool for the time being. Bide her time. Do everything she could to stay on the train. She forced a smile.

Hugo stared at her for several more seconds with a wary look, which soon gave way to a relenting one. "Let me speak to Chef. He was rather flustered earlier." Hugo left for the kitchen.

"Flustered?" Ruth murmured.

"Maybe an asparagus emergency," Greg said. "Not enough thyme on the pasta? Burnt sauce? A pea soup catastrophe?"

Ruth clucked her tongue. "Where do you get your odd sense of humour from?"

"Wonky genetics."

"Not from my side of the family." Ruth stared out the window and thought about the strange sequence of events that had transpired over the last twenty-four hours. There were huge gaps in her understanding that she itched to fill.

A few minutes later, Hugo returned. "Follow me."

Ruth glanced over at Greg, who looked bemused.

"Did you bring your luggage back on board?" Hugo asked him.

Greg's cheeks flushed. "Almost."

"Ruth can take back her compartment in 3A," Hugo said. "You can have pride of place in 1A."

Greg screwed his face up. "The murder room?"

"Different carriage," Ruth reminded him.

Greg's expression relaxed. "Oh yeah. Even so . . ."

"Take 7A, if you'd prefer," Hugo said.

"Go freshen up," Ruth said to Greg. "I'll come find you when I'm done." She followed Hugo to the end of the dining carriage, and into the kitchen.

The kitchen area had stainless steel worktops and rows

of compact ovens with hobs, along with a bewildering assortment of pots and pans.

Ruth gaped at it all and made a few mental notes. After all, she'd itched to upgrade the kitchen in her motorhome, and this gave her plenty of grand ideas.

"This is Chef Carlos Perez," Hugo motioned to the nearest of two men dressed in white. "And his assistant, Boyd."

Boyd, with his thick-rimmed glasses, who'd passed them earlier, gave Ruth a jaunty wave as he unloaded a giant dishwasher at the far end of the kitchen, setting plates in a rack above.

Hugo really hadn't spared any expense.

"Chef Carlos, this is Ruth Morgan," Hugo said. "The food consultant we discussed last week."

"Ah, yeah. All richt?" Despite his Spanish-sounding name, Carlos had a Scottish accent. He outstretched a hand. "Pleased to meet ye."

Ruth shook it and smiled. "Likewise."

Carlos had a reassuring set of calluses that showed he was not only accustomed to grabbing hot pans, but also not afraid of hard work.

Ruth's husband, John, had also had calloused hands. Although, his came from a life of adventure and hunting for artifacts.

"I'll leave you to it." Hugo bowed and left.

Carlos unclipped a tablet computer from the wall and set it on the worktop. "It's all in here. Everything we planned. Sorry not to have come found ye earlier, but we had a faulty oven to deal with."

"Is that why you were flustered?" Ruth asked.

"Understatement," Boyd said with a cheeky smile.

"Yeah." Carlos cleared his throat. "I may have launched a few cuss words at it. Sorted now, though."

Ruth scrolled through the recipes on the tablet. "Impressive."

"My twist on a few classics." Carlos navigated to a page. "Tonight's meal. How about we start here?"

It was a recipe for lobster in vinaigrette with mixed vegetables.

"Looks delicious." Ruth then scrolled through each recipe, talking over the ingredients and preparation with Carlos, making a few suggestions and adjustments where she could, which he accepted with good grace. He seemed to genuinely take pride in his work, so Ruth found the whole experience enjoyable.

After she'd covered the main meals and side dishes, Ruth moved on to the dessert section, where she had more input, and a proposal for expanding the range using ingredients they had on board. And then she addressed the health and safety aspects of the kitchen.

Although, during her whole time with Carlos and Boyd, the back of Ruth's mind was still on the subject of murder. On top of that, she wanted to know who the mysterious Detective White was, and why he'd really boarded the Finsbury Flyer.

16

An hour later, after Ruth had finished with her kitchen checks and found everything in perfect order, Chef Carlos returned the tablet to its holder.

"Mr Finsbury was richt," he said. "Ye were a big help."

Ruth smiled. "If there's anything else you need, let me know." Truth was, all she wanted to do was find a link between the train's modifications and Zoey's murder confession.

She bid Chef Carlos and Boyd goodbye and headed toward the salon carriage. However, before Ruth reached the connecting door, Angus the night porter stepped through.

"Hello." He yawned. "What do you make of that Zoey girl? Strange, huh?"

"What do you mean?"

Angus' eyebrows lifted. "You don't know?"

Ruth's heart sank. "Know what?"

"I can't believe Mr Finsbury hasn't told you." Angus looked away and muttered, "Guess he's still afraid to get a bucketload of bad press. Can't blame him, really."

Ruth took a calming breath and inclined her head.

Angus noticed her expression. "Mr Finsbury really should've said something, to you at least." He scratched his head. "That Zoey girl recanted."

Ruth stiffened. "She what?"

His brow furrowed. "That is the right word, isn't it? Recanted?" Angus yawned again. "Zoey took back her confession before the cops could get an official statement."

Ruth stared, incredulous, thoughts sluggish.

I was right. She's not the killer.

"Mr Finsbury really didn't say a word?" Angus asked.

Ruth slowly shook her head. "When did it happen?"

"Right after we pulled out of the station. I overheard his conversation with Inspector Kirby on the phone." Angus's expression turned sheepish. "I couldn't help it. Mr Finsbury was standing in the first-class carriage, right by the alcove."

Ruth wished Hugo had mentioned it earlier. If Zoey had taken back her confession shortly after they'd got underway, that meant Hugo had only just received the phone call when she'd caught up to him.

"Police will meet the train back in Edinburgh," Angus said. "Guess we'll all be interviewed for a second time. Won't that be fun?" He cleared his throat. "If you ask me, Zoey still did it and she is messing about."

Ruth stared through Angus. Now it was doubly imperative she speak to Victoria and try to figure out what was really going on.

She snapped out of her daze. "Do any of the other passengers know?"

"Not as far as I'm aware," Angus said. "I've been in the alcove since we left Penzance. Mr Finsbury asked me to make sure everyone was settled before I headed off to bed. No hint as to what's really happened." He half shrugged.

"Guess he's afraid to cause a panic." Angus's expression darkened. "I'll bolt my compartment door to be safe."

Ruth nodded. "Wise idea." Although none of the compartments had locks, they did have the bolts on the inside. "You definitely look like you could do with some sleep."

Angus yawned again. "Should have been in bed ages ago. Anyway, see ya."

He trudged through the dining carriage, and wave after wave of anxiety washed through Ruth.

She had left her grandson, on his own, with a killer on the loose. Now it was confirmed, the reality of her mistake sank in. What had only been a vague theory before, now turned to an almost certainty. She had to get back to Greg immediately, before something terrible happened.

Ruth sent an urgent text to him, demanding he lock himself inside his compartment, and not open the door to anyone other than her.

Anxious seconds went by, and she was about to call him, when a typical Greg-style text came in response:

I AM IN THE SALON!

He'd attached an emoji with its tongue poking out.

"Charming." Even so, Ruth sighed with relief, pocketed her phone, and continued through the connecting door.

In the salon sat Princess Mary—her ever-present protection officers hovering nearby— next to an uncomfortable-looking Greg. Mary giggled and playfully punched his arm.

Greg squirmed in his seat, spotted Ruth, and raised a hand, indicating for her to rescue him at once, but instead she gave a jaunty wave in return.

After all, he was safest with the princess and her officers.

Greg's face fell.

Ruth scanned the rest of the carriage.

Everyone else seemed to be here too: Jane and Robert Minchent, Hugo and Waylon. Victoria sat in the corner, both hands cupped round a mug of hot chocolate.

Lord and Lady Hamilton smiled at Ruth in welcome.

"Thought we'd left you behind at Finsbury Village," Lady Hamilton said. "Glad to see you're still with us."

"Can't get rid of me that easily," Ruth murmured, her attention fixed on Victoria.

"Would you care for a drink?" Lord Hamilton got to his feet.

"Not right now. Thank you." Ruth was about to make her way over to Victoria when Lord Hamilton took Ruth to one side.

"I take it from your expression that you've heard about Zoey?"

Ruth gawped at him. "You know too?"

"If you ask me . . ." Lord Hamilton glanced over his shoulder, and then breathed, "The Minchents put her up to it."

Ruth furrowed her brow. "Up to what?"

"The murder, of course. Zoey used to work for them. Did you know?" Lord Hamilton tugged at an earlobe. "Was their PA for several years before she went to work for Victoria." He then raised his eyebrows. "It's no secret the Minchents loathed Miles. You saw for yourself. They hated every bone in that man's body. Vowed vengeance, and now they have it. Pay someone enough money and they'll do anything."

Ruth ignored that last comment and pictured the note sent to Miles, telling him Hugo had lied and to come to the station at once.

Did the Minchents send that to him?

"You said Miles designed their shop interiors, right?" Ruth left out the fact she knew he had worked for the Hamiltons too, and jilted Lady Hamilton's sister at the altar. Now was not the time or place to bring it up.

"Miles sued the Minchents, and they counter-sued," Lord Hamilton breathed. "All very messy. They held grudges from then on." He looked over at Hugo. "I'm surprised he invited them all."

"He didn't," Ruth said. "Well, that wasn't Hugo's original intention." Although back in Edinburgh he had made the last-minute offer to Miles, who had accepted. No doubt all to the killer's plan.

"I believe the Minchents paid Zoey to shut him up once and for all," Lord Hamilton pressed. "But she's now welched on the deal. They must be reeling."

Ruth nodded slowly, not sure what to make of his theory. Right now, anything and everything was possible. "Can you excuse me?"

As she headed toward Victoria, Waylon's narrowed eyes followed her. "Yeah, you're next, sunshine," she murmured.

However, Hugo stepped into her path. "What's wrong? Did all not go well with Chef?"

"What? Oh, no. It's good." Ruth brightened her face, which took some effort. "Better than good. The menu is great. So are Chef Carlos and Boyd. Nice guys. Know what they're doing. The kitchen is in safe hands." She let out a slow breath and opted not to confront him about Zoey.

At the moment, Hugo had no idea Ruth knew about Zoey's confession retraction, and that gave Ruth a little wiggle room to investigate unimpeded.

So, despite the fact a murderer was still likely on board, Ruth wouldn't let on, for fear of causing a panic, and of

Hugo forcibly ejecting her and Greg from the train . . . while it was in motion.

"Delighted to hear it." Hugo gave a small bow and joined Lord and Lady Hamilton. "Everything to your satisfaction?"

"Splendid." Lord Hamilton raised a glass of brandy. "Now that grisly business is behind us."

Lady Hamilton screwed up her face. "Ghastly."

Ruth made her way to the corner of the salon before anyone else stopped her. "Hi, Victoria." She sat in a chair opposite.

"Mrs Morgan?"

"Call me Ruth." She smoothed the creases in her blouse. "Am I disturbing you?"

"Not at all." Victoria felt for the side table, and then placed her mug down. "You're here to ask me about Zoey?"

Ruth sighed. She'd ease Victoria into the questions. "I guess this whole murder business has me a little on edge." And that was an understatement.

"Tell me about it," Victoria said. "I feel like I'm in a nightmare." She grimaced. "I can't believe Zoey would confess to something she wouldn't do. Not in a million years."

"She's taken back her confession," Ruth said, before she could help herself.

Victoria gasped and raised a hand to her mouth.

"That's why I came to see you. Thought you should know." Ruth glanced in Hugo's direction and back again. Keeping her voice low, she added, "I want to understand why Zoey would confess in the first place."

Victoria swallowed and lowered her trembling hand. "I have no idea why she did that. It's completely out of character, and has been driving me crazy. Now she's taken it back?" Victoria fiddled with her white cane. "What is she playing at? Zoey has never shown the slightest hint of any criminal wrongdoing. An odd moment of madness I can't get my head wrapped around." She let out a tremulous breath. "Thank goodness she's seen sense. I suppose she'll still be in a lot of trouble for lying. Whatever was she thinking?"

"How did you meet?" Ruth asked.

Victoria blinked back tears. "Recommendation through a friend."

"Did you know she used to work for the Minchents?" Ruth plucked a tissue from a box on the side table and pressed it into Victoria's hand.

"What?" A crease formed between Victoria's eyebrows as she mopped away tears. "Jane and Robert? Really?"

"You had no idea?" Ruth studied her reaction, but Victoria seemed genuinely surprised.

"Well, that explains it," she murmured.

Ruth leaned forward. "Explains what?"

Victoria tucked a loose strand of hair behind her ear and spoke in barely a whisper. "Last night, before dinner, I waited for Zoey in my compartment, but when she didn't turn up, I opened my door to call for her. That's when I heard them in a whispered argument."

"Who?"

"Zoey and Waylon."

Ruth gaped at her. "They knew each other?"

"Apparently so." Victoria gripped the tissue. "I didn't hear what they argued about, but when I later confronted Zoey, she told me they'd worked together before she joined me as my assistant. I had no idea."

Ruth's mind reeled as she tried to piece together the connections.

Waylon worked for the Minchents too?

"Zoey didn't do it, Mrs Morgan," Victoria said with

conviction. "I've known that all along, and I'm glad she's seen sense. She's a good girl."

"If you knew she was innocent," Ruth said, "why did you agree to get back on this train?"

Victoria hesitated. "I'm not sure. I believe the murder wasn't premeditated. I think it was a crime of passion. Miles wasn't a nice man, and a small part of me can understand why someone may want to hurt him in a moment of anger and frenzy." She pocketed the tissue and gripped her cane with both hands. "At first, I wasn't coming back. I don't want to be within a million miles of Waylon, but I thought I could get him to confess, or at least slip up. Admit to what he's done, and Zoey would be let off." Her expression turned sheepish. "I know that's foolish now."

"You think Waylon did it?" Ruth blinked at the theory. It certainly had come out of left field. "What motive could he have to kill Miles?"

"I don't know, but he put Zoey up to confessing, of that I'm sure." Victoria sighed. "As I say, the idea to confront him was incredibly dangerous and silly of me, but I had to try."

Although Victoria should have stayed back in Penzance, Ruth could understand her wanting to defend Zoey. "I heard you played poker with Miles."

"Several of us played, yes."

Ruth sat back. "Did he say anything to anyone that may have upset them? To Waylon in particular?"

Victoria seemed to consider the question for a moment and then took a breath. "Miles was an obnoxious man. Gloated every time he won a hand, which was most of them. But if you're asking me if he said something heinous enough to warrant being attacked, then I have to say no." She found her mug of chocolate, took a sip, and set it back on the table. "Waylon only joined us for a few hands and then left. I guess they must have argued later." Victoria's expression turned to worry. "If he realises I suspect him, will he come after me?"

Something still felt off, but Ruth couldn't quite put her finger on what. Only an annoying hunch that she was overlooking something obvious.

Miles angered Waylon enough to warrant murder, and no one overheard their argument?

Ruth shook herself and softened her tone. "Everything will be fine. Would you like Greg and me to sit with you at lunch?"

Victoria's face brightened. "That would be marvellous."

"Victoria?"

Both women jumped.

Waylon stood nearby. He glared at Ruth, and then turned his attention to Victoria. "I'll escort you to your compartment now, so you can change for lunch."

Anguish and fear swept over Victoria's face. "I-I'm not f-finished." She picked up her mug of hot chocolate in her shaking hands.

"I'll wait." Waylon folded his arms.

"I can take her when she's ready." Ruth stood. "I'm going that way." She looked to Victoria. "Would you like me to?"

Victoria's shoulders relaxed. "Thank you."

"No problem." Ruth glared back at Waylon until he left. "Back in a moment, Victoria." She hurried over to her grandson and the princess.

The latter squeezed the former's knee, giggled, and whispered something in his ear.

"May I borrow you for a moment?" Ruth asked him.

Greg leapt to his feet.

Princess Mary slouched and pushed out her bottom lip. "Must you?"

"I'm afraid so." Ruth forced a smile. "Won't be long." She strode back to Victoria and assisted her up.

"Hurry back," Princess Mary said to Greg. "I want to hear all about your studies and where you'll be staying on campus."

He mumbled something unintelligible and followed Ruth and Victoria across the salon.

"Everything okay?" Hugo asked as they strode past.

"Fine," Ruth said over her shoulder. "Off to get changed." Even though her suitcase currently resided back in Finsbury Village.

Jane and Robert Minchent watched them go in silence.

In the first-class double-sleeper carriage, Ruth opened the door to compartment 4A. "Here you are." As Victoria stepped inside, Ruth said, "Bolt your door. Don't open it to anyone other than me."

"Thank you." Victoria closed and bolted it.

Ruth marched to 7A and ushered Greg inside.

Lord and Lady Hamilton returned to their compartment. They waved to Ruth as she followed Greg and closed the door.

Greg dropped onto his bed. "How did you get on?" he asked as she sat at the desk.

"Zoey took back her confession."

"What?" Greg's face fell. "You were right after all?"

"Don't sound so surprised." As Ruth brought him up to speed with what else she'd uncovered, frustration gnawed at her. She was missing a giant piece of the puzzle. "Apparently, the police will interview everyone when we get back to Edinburgh."

"Talking of police." Greg leaned forward. "The undercover detective; I bet I know who it is."

Even though Ruth had an idea too, she was eager to hear his thoughts. "Go on."

"It's Daniel. Daniel Price. That drunk guy."

Ruth nodded. "Great minds think alike."

"The way he sat at that table alone and watched everyone at dinner," Greg said. "And then he invited himself to the poker table. You think he faked being drunk?"

"No, he was definitely inebriated." Ruth rubbed her chin. "I smelled it on his breath." If she had to guess, Daniel was a whiskey kind of fella.

Greg's brow furrowed. "Is that legal? Drinking on the job? He's a police officer."

Ruth shrugged. "I guess he took the undercover part seriously. It's not the best idea, but whatever works, I suppose." Having never worked undercover during her time on the force, only uniformed, she wasn't aware of the rules. In fact, Ruth suspected some undercover jobs required the officer to bend the boundaries of legality, just to get inside a criminal enterprise.

"Why did Daniel make a big fuss of Miles stealing his watch?" Greg asked, breaking Ruth's thoughts.

"I'm not sure," she said. "But I now wonder if he knew something was afoot, and it was his way of getting Hugo to open the door to Miles' compartment. He wanted witnesses."

She stared at the wall as she remembered what Greg had told her about Daniel back at the train station—*was that why Detective Inspector Kirby berated him? For drinking? For allowing a murder to take place, right under his nose? Did he know someone had it in for Miles?*

"I guess we'll never know what he was up to." Ruth let out a puff of air. "He's back at Finsbury Village with Zoey."

"He isn't."

Ruth's gaze moved to her grandson. "What?"

"He's not back at Finsbury," Greg said. "He's here. On this train. I've seen him."

Ruth sat upright in the chair. "Are you sure?"

"Positive."

"When did he come back on board?"

Greg shrugged one shoulder. "Must have been when we were at the train sheds almost getting shot by the police."

"Daniel changed his mind about returning on the coach?" Ruth said. "But he wasn't in the salon."

"He was earlier," Greg said. "When you were in the kitchen. He looked angry about something and left."

"Where did he go?"

"Well, last night he was staying in a compartment in the single sleeper. Few doors down from mine. Guess he's there."

Confusion swept through Ruth. "But the police had a suspect in custody when they allowed the train to leave the station." She frowned. "Why would he be back on board?" Ruth's breath caught. "Unless the police suspected the same thing I did." She stood. "That the killer is still among us. It's why Daniel has returned. He wants to flush them out."

"Or maybe he only wants a lift back to Edinburgh," Greg said in a flat tone. "Anyway, I guess you can ask him yourself. He'll be in compartment 14A."

17

Ruth hurried into the first-class single-sleeper carriage and raised a fist to bang on the door to 14A when the train slowed. "What now?" She peered out the window, only to be greeted by a brick wall.

They were in a tunnel.

The lights in the carriage snapped off, plunging them into inky blackness.

Ruth stood rooted to the spot. The only sound came from the wheels on the track, up until the moment the train stopped inside the tunnel, and then all that remained was the blood pounding in her ears.

"Greg?" she said in a hoarse whisper.

A light appeared, like a glimmer in a cave. "I'm right here." He held up his phone, illuminating their faces. "What's going on?"

Ruth pressed her cheek against the glass, looked to the left, and then the right, but couldn't make anything out other than the faint brickwork of the tunnel wall lit by Greg's phone. "We appear to have broken down."

"And I bet you think this is no coincidence either."

"I do not."

Greg let out a low groan and checked his phone's display. "No signal. We're doomed."

Ruth held up a hand. "We must remain open-minded and calm." Footfalls and deep voices made her spin toward the door at the far end of the carriage. "Get back." She ushered Greg into his compartment and stepped inside with him.

The door to the connecting gangway opened, and Luke, the dark-haired royal protection officer, marched through with a torch. He shone it in Ruth's face as she peered out at him.

She shielded her eyes. "What's going on?"

"Stay in your compartment, ma'am."

"No one knows what on earth is happening," a posh female voice from behind him said.

Officer Luke lowered his torch, and Ruth's eyes adjusted.

Princess Mary followed him along the corridor, with the second protection officer bringing up the rear. She stopped when they reached Ruth. "If you ask me, my armed goons here are overreacting." She rolled her eyes and then smiled at Greg. "Hello. I was waiting for you to come back so we could carry on from where we left off."

Greg swallowed and fiddled with the light switch.

"Please keep moving," Luke said to the princess.

Princess Mary huffed. "Yes, yes." She addressed Ruth. "They're taking me to the panic room. Can you believe it? A total overreaction."

"You've got a panic room?" Greg asked with incredulity.

"In the royal carriage. The security office doubles as one. Metal carbon walls or some such. Bombproof. I don't think it is at all necessary, but what do I know? It's not as if I ever get a say in the matter." Princess Mary winked at Greg. "Like to keep me company? It's rather cozy in there. Would be just the two of us. No interruptions."

Despite the meagre light coming from the officer's torch, it was clear Greg's cheeks flushed scarlet.

"Absolutely not," Officer Luke said before Greg had a chance to respond. He gestured down the passageway. "Please, Your Highness."

"Oh, very well," Princess Mary said. "Always spoiling my fun." She waved at Ruth and Greg and continued along the corridor. "We'll have lunch together once this nonsense is over with. You can bring me up to speed with all the gossip."

"We'll be delighted. Victoria will join us too, if that's okay?"

"Of course."

As soon as the princess was out of earshot, Ruth grinned at her grandson and murmured, "Prince Gregory. It certainly has a ring to it."

"I have a girlfriend," he said through a tight jaw.

"Queen Ruth sounds even better. Anyway, it's always good to keep your options open."

Greg stared at her. "Did you keep your options open when you were my age?"

"Of course," Ruth said. "Well, up until I met your grandfather. Then I only had eyes for him."

"I've only got eyes for Mia."

Once the princess and her protection officers had disappeared through the door to the double sleeper, Greg switched his phone back on and held it up. "What should we do? We don't have a panic room."

"Why would we need one with you about?" Ruth said. "In situations like this, you can panic well enough without the need for a room."

"That's not funny." Even so, Greg's eyes darted about.

Ruth pursed her lips and was about to suggest they locate Hugo, when light glinted over Greg's shoulder. Ruth slipped past him, farther into his compartment. "Turn off your phone."

Greg did as she asked.

Careful to watch her footing, Ruth inched over to the window and peered out. "Someone's there." A light bounced off the walls of the tunnel.

"Who?" Greg joined her.

The light in the tunnel brightened.

"Someone's outside with a torch," Ruth breathed. "It's exciting, no?"

"You and I have very different ideas as to what's exciting," Greg mumbled.

They watched in silence as the person picked their way along the other track.

Ruth squinted. "I can't make out who they are. Can you?"

"No. Looks like a man, though."

The person moved under their window and continued along the track, heading toward the back of the train.

Ruth activated the torch function on her phone. "Let's go." She hurried from the cabin, along the passageway, and through the door at the end. In the gangway, Ruth tried the door on the track side, but it was locked. However, the door on the wall side was not. She opened it as quietly as she could and peered down.

Without a train platform to step onto, the ground—a carpet of gravel—was a few feet below.

"We shouldn't leave the train," Greg whispered.

"I want to know what's going on."

"Because you're nosey?"

"Not nosey, curious," Ruth said. "And I don't want someone to get away with murder." She pointed. "Let's go."

Greg grumbled. "Why do we always have to do things your way?" He squeezed past her, sat on the floor, with his legs out of the train, and jumped down. Then he turned back and raised his arms to Ruth. "Come on, then."

Ruth edged to the door, squatted, and allowed him to assist her. Once both feet were on terra firma, she whispered, "Stay behind me and switch off the light." Ruth raised her phone, with only the screen activated, which gave them just about enough illumination to see the ground ahead.

Ruth hurried alongside the train, holding the phone low. Ahead, light spilled from the salon carriage.

Hugo and his staff had switched on LED candles, which bathed the carriage and passengers in warm, flickering lights.

Ruth peered through the nearest window.

"Careful," Greg whispered. "They'll see us."

However, none of the guests looked in their direction, and they all seemed agitated, drinks in hand, animated conversations in full flow.

Hugo obviously had tried to convince them the situation was in hand, and failed miserably.

All the passengers were there, save for Daniel Price, Victoria, who was in her compartment with the door bolted, and Princess Mary. The Hamiltons had dressed and were huddled in the corner, shooting nasty glances at the Minchents.

Waylon wasn't anywhere to be seen, but Carlos and Boyd stood in the doorway at the other end, both wearing scowls, their arms crossed. The power cut had interrupted their lunch preparations.

Ruth motioned for Greg to follow her, and they

continued down the tunnel. When they reached the luggage carriage and the end of the train, Ruth turned back to her grandson and placed a finger to her lips.

Then she took a deep breath and peered around the back of the train.

A bright light shone in Ruth's eyes. She let out a small shriek and staggered back, bumping into Greg.

"What the hell are you doing out here?" a deep voice boomed.

The beam of the torch lowered, and Ruth blinked away annoying crimson patches that danced and flashed across her vision.

The faint outline of the relief train driver—Alan—swam into view.

"I'll ask you again," Alan growled. "What are you doing out here? What are you playin' at?"

"We might ask you the same thing." Ruth rubbed her eyes, and the red patches turned to bright sparkles. "Why have you stopped the train?"

"I haven't stopped anything," Alan said. "It did that by itself."

"Really?" Ruth scratched her head. "Why?" She wasn't aware trains had minds of their own, but technology advanced by giant leaps every day, so anything was possible.

Greg waved a hand about. "And we stopped in a tunnel, where we can't call for help."

"I'm here trying to figure out what happened for myself," Alan said, sounding annoyed they'd interrupted his fault-finding mission. "Best guess is it has something to do with the live rail pickup. I was about to check it all over when I heard you two thumping about."

"How dare you," Ruth said. "We do not thump. We glide, light-footed and fancy free."

Greg stifled a laugh.

Alan looked between them. "If you can't sit tight for five minutes, and you're so desperate to make a phone call—" He thrust a finger down the tunnel. "Walk back half a mile that way. Can't guarantee we'll still be here when you return."

Greg mumbled something about not wanting to trudge half a mile in the dark.

"Well," Alan scolded, "I suggest you both return to your carriage and let me do my job. I'm trained for this kind of thing, and you're slowing me down." He motioned along the track. "We can't hang about here all day. Isn't safe."

Now it was Ruth who mumbled, this time an apology, and then she nudged Greg. "Come on." As they walked off, she called over her shoulder to the driver, "Sorry to hold you up."

"Just make sure you're back on the train by the time we get going. Wouldn't want to leave you stranded, would we?"

Alan sounded as though he wouldn't mind that at all.

Ruth waved in acknowledgement, and when she and her grandson reached the open door to the first-class double-sleeper carriage, she stopped. "Hold on." Ruth flipped through the pictures on her phone until she found the one with the modified first-class carriage. "This extra box thing." She tapped the display. "While we're here, let's see what's inside."

"Not a great idea," Greg said. "It's on the other side. If that driver sees us..."

However, Ruth hurried alongside the carriage, and at the far end, before it reached the royal carriage, she peered underneath. "Is that it?"

Greg looked too.

On the other side, fixed to the undercarriage, was a metal box around six feet in length, a few wide.

"Go look at it," Ruth whispered.

"Are you serious?"

"Quickly," she said. "Before the driver comes back this way. Watch out for the live rail, though."

Greg muttered several inventive swear words, climbed under the train, and with some effort, he reached the box.

"Well?" Ruth asked.

Greg peered around it. "No idea. It's sealed." He gripped either side, but it wouldn't budge. "No way to tell what's in there."

Ruth huffed out a breath. "Okay. Come back."

It had been worth a shot.

Greg climbed back across the tracks and popped up again. "Can we stop doing dangerous stuff, please?"

At the other end of the carriage, he hauled himself on board. Then, with a huge amount of effort, and grunts of overexaggerated exertion, plus a few more swear words, he finally managed to help Ruth back into the train.

She closed the door. "That was an experience."

Greg rubbed his arms and winced.

Ruth glared at him. "I am not heavy. Stop being so dramatic. Young lad like you should be able to carry two of me with ease."

"Two of you?" Greg's eyes widened.

"Hello?" a female voice called.

Ruth stuck her head around the corner of the connecting gangway and raised the light of her phone.

Victoria stood at the door to her compartment, wearing a pastel blue dress with a pearl necklace and matching earrings. "Anyone there? What's going on? Why have we stopped?"

"It's okay," Ruth said in what she hoped came across as a relaxed tone. "We've broken down. A power cut. The driver is on the case. Nothing to worry about."

"Oh, thank goodness." Victoria sighed. "I heard a noise when the train stopped and wondered what on earth was happening."

Ruth hurried over to her. "Ready for lunch? Would you like us to escort you to the salon?"

"That would be wonderful. Thank you, Ruth." Victoria held on to her cane with one hand and stuck out her other arm.

Ruth took it and guided Victoria along the corridor.

Greg opened the doors for them, and they headed into the salon carriage. The LED candles flickered, sending shadows dancing across people's pale faces and the walls.

On any other day, it would've been a fun and cozy atmosphere.

Ruth escorted Victoria to a chair, and then indicated for Greg to sit with her. Ruth smiled at the passengers' anxious expressions as she passed them and walked over to Carlos and Boyd. "Is lunch ruined?"

Carlos, with his arms folded, gave a brief shake of his head. "We have it all mostly prepared, just waiting on people's orders. It can keep for an hour. Then we'll have to throw it out and start again."

Ruth exhaled. "Let's hope it doesn't come to that. If it does, though, I'd be happy to help where I can."

"Thank you." Carlos eyed Hugo as he moved between passengers with murmured reassurances.

Waylon appeared at the door, and the lights snapped back on.

The assembled passengers let out a cheer and clapped.

Hugo smiled and held up his hands. "It appears the

driver has solved the issue. Nothing to worry about. I'm sure we'll be back underway in a few moments' time."

Sure enough, five minutes later, the train accelerated down the tunnel and punched back into daylight.

"We'd better get to it." Carlos bowed his head at Ruth and left with Boyd.

"Can I have a word?" Ruth asked as Waylon strode past her.

"I'm busy." He headed into the dining carriage without a backward glance.

Ruth considered hurrying after him but thought better of it and plonked herself in a chair next to Greg and Victoria. She stared out the window as the train gathered speed, racing past houses. "I wonder if Alan is trying to make up for lost time?"

Because it felt a lot faster than before.

∼

Twenty minutes later, Ruth sat at a table in the dining carriage next to Victoria, opposite Greg and Princess Mary, who'd insisted he sit next to her.

The princess's protection officers stood sentry by the doors at either end of the carriage, not taking their eyes off her. Given the recent craziness, Ruth understood their diligence and didn't envy the impending responsibility of reporting to their superiors.

Ruth's gaze returned to Princess Mary. "Nice to see they let you out of your panic room."

"Only after I threatened them with expulsion from the British realm if they didn't let me eat soon," Princess Mary said with a twinkle in her eye.

A server took her order, then Victoria's, before facing Ruth.

"My grandson will have the steak sandwich and fries."

"And my grandma will have a Caesar chicken wrap with a side salad," Greg said.

Ruth smacked her lips. "I will." She handed the menus to the waiter.

Princess Mary smiled. "You know each other so well."

"Relatively." Ruth sipped water.

Greg pinched the bridge of his nose.

Victoria chuckled.

"Did I miss something?" Princess Mary looked between them.

"I'd say we know each other relatively well." Ruth smirked. "Relatively? You know, because we're relatives. He's my grandson . . ." She trailed off at the princess's blank expression. "Never mind. I'm not funny."

"You've got that right," Greg murmured.

Under the table, Ruth kicked him in the shin.

"Ow."

She then thought about Daniel Price, who simply had to be the elusive detective, and she turned in her seat, but couldn't see him among the other passengers.

He must be in his compartment.

"Tell me, Victoria." Princess Mary opened a napkin and placed it across her lap. "Why did your assistant confess to killing a man, and then take it back?"

"How did you find out?" Ruth asked.

Princess Mary gestured to her protection officers, but kept her attention on Victoria. "What could possibly have gone through her head?"

Victoria shifted in her seat. "I—I don't know."

The princess's eyebrows lifted. "I'm sure you know her best."

"Two years."

"And in all that time," Princess Mary pressed, "Zoey showed not even the slightest hint of violence?" She glanced at Ruth with a disbelieving expression.

Greg sat ramrod straight in his seat.

"She did not," Victoria said in a small voice.

"How odd." Princess Mary's gaze moved to Ruth. "What do you make of it? If she didn't kill him, why confess? A very strange thing to do, wouldn't you say?"

Ruth nodded. "I'm still trying to figure that out."

"During your time as a police officer, how many false confessions were you later aware of?" Princess Mary asked. "Was it a common occurrence?"

"I'm not sure," Ruth said. "Some people would claim the officers had coerced a false confession, but it wasn't common, no." At least not with modern interrogation techniques and practises.

Princess Mary nodded slowly and then gazed at Victoria again. "Doesn't smell right, does it, Victoria? Something's off, wouldn't you say?"

Victoria didn't respond.

Ruth cleared her throat. "Did Zoey know Miles prior to this journey?"

Victoria hesitated. "I think so. She didn't mention him by name but told me how she'd worked with a very obnoxious man during her time with the Minchents."

Princess Mary smiled. "There are plenty of obnoxious people in the world. Could've been anyone."

Ruth nodded, but if one person may have the answers, other than Zoey, that would be Detective Inspector White, and she vowed to seek him out the moment lunch was over.

***

Ruth stopped outside 14A with Greg, and she knocked on the door.

No answer.

She knocked again.

When there still came no reply, Ruth tried the handle.

Surprised to find the door unbolted, she called, "Yoo-hoo. Detective?" Ruth peered into the gloomy interior.

Someone had drawn the curtains, so it took a few moments for her eyes to adjust. Then she gasped as her gaze rested on a form sprawled across the bed at an odd angle.

Blood soaked the sheets, and Daniel Price lay motionless.

Greg looked over Ruth's shoulder and groaned. "Not again."

18

Ruth continued to stare at the detective's lifeless form. Although Ruth knew in her heart he was dead, her gaze shifted to the man's chest, hoping for a slow rise and fall, but it didn't move. His skin was pale and waxlike, eyes closed.

"I'll find Hugo and tell him to call the police." Greg went to leave, but Ruth grabbed his arm.

"Wait," she said. "I want a few minutes."

Greg gave her an exasperated look. "Have you lost your mind?"

"No doubt," Ruth said. "But not recently." Her brow furrowed. "I think it happened sometime in the nineties. Your grandfather—"

"Grandma. Seriously."

"Come on." Ruth hurried along the corridor and then stopped outside the salon door. "Stay right here. Don't move." She indicated the connecting window. "Any trouble, bang on this and alert the other passengers."

"Where are you going?"

"Back in one minute." Ruth tried to look casual as she

sauntered through the salon, smiling at people as she went, but as soon as she reached the other side, Ruth jogged through the dining carriage, and into the kitchen.

Boyd loaded plates and cutlery into the dishwasher, while Carlos cleaned surfaces.

"What did ye think of lunch?" Carlos asked Ruth.

"Huh? Oh, splendid. Well done." She nodded at a box of disposable gloves. "May I have a pair of those?"

"Of course." A small frown creased Carlos's brow. "Is something the matter?"

"No. Well, yes." Ruth took a pair. "Thank you." And she hurried off again.

At the door to the dining area, she slipped the gloves into her pocket, took a few deep breaths, and then stepped through.

She almost bumped into Hugo and staggered back a couple of steps.

He frowned at her. "Are you okay?"

Ruth swallowed. Of course, she could tell him here and now what was going on, but she wanted some time alone with the crime scene first. "I'm fine. Why do you ask?"

"You seem flustered."

"Me? No. No, not flustered. Not flustered at all." Ruth forced a tremulous smile. "All good. Superb." Her insides squirmed.

Hugo folded his arms. "Anyone ever tell you you're a terrible liar?"

Ruth's cheeks burned. "Not recently."

"Has someone else been murdered?"

Her blood ran cold.

Hugo noticed Ruth's expression. "I'm joking."

"Oh." She let out a breath. "Yes. Good. Fine." Ruth

glanced around at the passengers, but none of them paid any attention to their conversation.

She eyed the door at the far end of the carriage.

Seated next to it, Princess Mary waved.

Ruth returned the gesture.

"What did you think?"

She refocussed on Hugo. "Sorry?"

"Of lunch," he said. "It's why you're here."

Ruth's stomach now did a full backflip. "It was excellent. Chef Carlos is very talented."

"He is, isn't he?" Hugo's expression glazed over. "Should be. Heaven knows I pay him enough." He snapped out of it and gestured to the bar. "May I get you a drink?" Hugo looked about. "Where's your grandson got to?"

"In his compartment," Ruth lied. "A little under the weather." She really needed to practise her poker face in the mirror.

"They've probably worn off." Hugo fished in his jacket pocket and pulled out the bottle of travel sickness tablets. "Give him another couple of these, and he'll feel right as rain."

Ruth took the bottle from Hugo, smiled, and then stepped round him.

"Ruth?"

Shoulders hitched, she braced herself, and turned back.

"Come straight back for that drink," Hugo said. "I want to hear your every thought about the lunch menu."

Ruth tipped an imaginary cap, and then hurried along the carriage, with the exit door in her sights, but Princess Mary held up a hand, stopping her. "So close," Ruth murmured, and faced her.

"Do you think I offended Victoria?" Princess Mary asked. "At lunch. With all my questions?"

"I don't think so," Ruth said as Waylon strode past them. "Why?"

"She seemed off." Princess Mary adjusted her dress and crossed her legs. "A distant expression came over her face when I mentioned Zoey."

Nearby, the Minchents sat in silence. Clearly listening to their conversation.

"It's been a tough day," Ruth said. "If you'll excuse me." She curtsied and returned to Greg in the first-class carriage. "Stand guard. Don't move, don't let anyone in, and certainly don't tell them what I'm doing." Ruth pulled on the disposable gloves.

Greg opened his mouth, but Ruth closed the door on him, switched on the light, and faced the compartment.

The door to the en suite bathroom stood open, wet towels on the floor inside, condensation on the mirror, beard trimmings in the sink. Various bottles of shower gel, shampoo, and aftershave sat on a nearby shelf.

Ruth's gaze moved from the bathroom to the bed.

The man was bare-chested, his shirt on a hanger nearby, along with a jacket. He wore dark trousers, a black belt with a silver buckle, and black socks. He'd placed a pair of polished shoes by the nearest leg of the desk.

On the desk sat a tie, laid across a cuff link box.

Ruth examined the label inside the jacket—rented from Foxworth Tailors on Princes Street in Edinburgh.

She then scanned the man's body from toe to chin. Apart from an appendectomy scar, he appeared healthy, trim, as though he'd taken care of himself.

His face also seemed healthy, pockmark free, clean-shaven, no reddening or swelling around the nose or mouth. Not a regular drinker. His hair greyed at the temples, and Ruth gauged him to be in his early fifties.

She took a breath, edged over to him, and leaned down for a closer look.

As with the other body, a fresh red mark crossed the man's face, the right-hand side this time, and then an impact to his head, above the left temple. Dried blood matted his hair and stained the sheets.

Blood spatter covered part of the wall and ceiling. He'd been standing when struck and had fallen backward. Judging by his posture, his death had been instant—a single blow and then oblivion.

"I'm so sorry this happened to you." Ruth straightened and faced the desk.

She lifted a notebook and opened it. Inside was a shorthand scrawl she couldn't read. Perhaps Greg could look on the internet later and try to decipher the pages. Ruth set the notebook back down, and took pictures with her phone, each leaf in turn, until she reached pages with photographs taped.

She leaned in.

Someone had taken snapshots of train carriage interiors mocked up out of wood. She frowned at them. "What are these for?" They were in a warehouse, each carriage represented, with tables and chairs in the dining room, a sectioned-off area for the kitchen, and even the salon, with cardboard boxes representing the bar and seats.

Ruth snapped pictures of all these too, and then closed the notebook.

Once she'd scanned the room several more times—including the floor, inside the wardrobe and drawers, and even peeking behind the curtains—Ruth stepped back into the passageway with Greg. "Let's go give Hugo the bad news."

"You don't think he did this?" Greg asked.

Ruth shook her head.

Truth was, although Waylon was at the top of her suspect list, she still wasn't sure who was responsible. All Ruth knew for certain was she had to trust Hugo and tell him the latest bad news.

Greg looked at his phone. "Great. Now I don't have a signal." He held it high and turned on the spot. "Not a single bar. Are you kidding me?"

Ruth checked her own phone. "Neither do I."

Greg's voice turned shrill. "We can't call the police."

"Let's take that as a sign."

"What do you mean?"

"Most people are in the salon," Ruth said in a level tone. "They're together. The killer is probably among them and unlikely to strike someone else."

"Why?" Greg said. "They've now murdered two people. They could wait until someone else goes to the toilet or something." He glanced about and shuddered.

Ruth paced back and forth a few steps as she thought it through. "The killer is still up to something. Something Miles and then the detective threatened to uncover."

"Like what?" Greg asked.

Ruth huffed out a breath. "I need to speak to Hugo. Come on."

The two of them headed through the carriage and into the salon.

"Ah, there he is." Princess Mary beamed at Greg.

"Feeling better?" Hugo asked Greg as he handed the princess a drink.

"I—"

Ruth nudged him. "He is much improved." She held up the travel sickness tablets. "Thank you, Hugo. These worked perfectly."

"Oh, yeah," Greg said, cottoning on. "Thanks."

"Don't mention it." Hugo waved Ruth's hand away. "Keep them."

She pocketed the pills. "Can I have a quick word about the dinner menu?"

Hugo's eyebrows lifted. "Is there a problem?"

"No," Ruth said. "But I have a wonderful idea for a surprise." She tapped the side of her nose.

"Sounds positively exciting." Princess Mary pointed to a seat opposite. "Stay with me, Greg. I need entertaining."

Greg hesitated, glanced at his grandmother, then sat in the chair.

Ruth led Hugo across the salon and into the dining carriage. Once there, she faced him, and kept her voice low. "You need to tell me everything you know about the detective. Mr Price, right?"

Hugo's face dropped. "How did you find out?"

"Never mind that now. What is he investigating?"

"We've already talked about this, Ruth. I—"

She held up a hand. "He's dead."

Hugo stared at Ruth for almost a full ten uncomfortable seconds without blinking. "What—" He cleared his throat. "Detective White is dead? How- How do you know?"

"The general lack of breathing." Ruth winced at her own callous remark. "He's gone, Hugo. I'm sorry. I wish it weren't true."

"Wh-What happened?"

"Same fate as Miles. Someone hit him across the head. From the front this time." She tapped her left temple. "Must have been someone he knew." Which was no surprise, given the fact they were on a train with so few suspects. "He didn't have time to defend himself. A single blow."

Hugo staggered sideways and grabbed the back of a

chair. Ruth went to take his arm, but he waved her off. "I'm fine." He breathed deeply. "She really didn't do it."

"If you're referring to Zoey, then no, she didn't."

Hugo shook his head. "Why did she admit to it?" His eyes glazed over. "Because of her foolishness, we still have a killer on board. If only Zoey hadn't interfered . . ." Hugo collapsed into the chair and buried his face in his hands. "This is a nightmare. What have I done to deserve this?"

Ruth sat opposite and felt a twinge of pity for him. Hugo had worked so hard, and the very worst had happened. "Why was the detective here? What was he looking into?" Clearly, he'd got too close to something, and the killer had put a stop to his investigation.

Is that what happened to Miles?

Hugo lowered his hands, composed himself, and then levelled his gaze at Ruth. "There was a rumour." His jaw tightened. "I say, a *rumour* about some gang or another." He looked out the nearest window as trees and houses glided past. "I didn't believe it, but what choice did I have? The police insisted they let him investigate, or they'd shut me down entirely."

Ruth leaned forward. "Go on."

"I told them the idea was preposterous."

"What idea?" Ruth gripped her knees.

Hugo sighed and looked back at her. "They claimed to have knowledge of a gang planning to target the Finsbury Flyer. Some wild idea the gang had in motion since I first announced plans five years ago."

"Target it in what way?"

Hugo folded his arms. "The police came to me a year ago. They thought a gang would use the Flyer to transport illicit items across the country, north to south, and vice versa."

Confused, Ruth said, "Why would criminals want to use a train that travels so slowly?"

"It's not about the speed," Hugo said. "The police have the motorways under surveillance. The Flyer is the last place they'd think to look for such things." He ground his teeth. "However, I explained to them, several times, that wouldn't be possible anyway. Not with all our security precautions. They wouldn't listen. So, to be safe, I insisted extra measures be put in place."

"The box under the train carriage," Ruth murmured.

Hugo's forehead wrinkled. "What box?"

Ruth showed him the design on her phone.

Hugo stared at it. "I don't know what this is."

"It's definitely there," Ruth said. "Under the first-class double-sleeper carriage." She left out the fact Greg had tried to look inside.

Hugo shrugged. "I've not seen it. But even if such a box exists, it makes no difference." His determined expression intensified. "I'm telling you, Ruth, smuggling is impossible." He adjusted his tie. "We only stop in Finsbury Village for a short while. It's a secure compound. Guards vet everyone and everything that comes in and out of those gates. There's no way anything sneaks past them." Hugo let out a breath. "Even if someone smuggled something on board in Scotland, they'd have no chance of offloading it in Cornwall. Our operation is watertight. The police know that. They inspected everything before we left."

Ruth scratched her head. "So why the need for the onboard detective?"

"They insisted. Intimated if I didn't agree to their demands, those smuggling rumours may leak to the press."

Ruth screwed up her face. "That's terrible." Although,

she wasn't sure she could believe the threat was real. It seemed like a risky gamble for the police to take.

Intimidation? Unlikely.

"I wonder if one of the gang members could be on board?" Ruth asked, half to herself.

Hugo shook his head. "I don't want to believe it. Everyone is here at my personal invitation."

"Miles wasn't very well liked," Ruth pressed. "And everyone here seems to have had run-ins with him to varying degrees. What about all those blueprints and photographs?"

"I don't see the connection," Hugo said. "Miles loved to worry about health and safety. I have no idea why someone would want him dead. Makes no sense."

Ruth stared down at her phone and the drawing with the box under the double-sleeper carriage. *If the gang really planned to use that for smuggling, was that why Miles focussed on it in particular?*

"Where is the detective?" Hugo stood. "I want to see him."

"Is it necessary?" Ruth had unfortunately witnessed more than her fair share of dead bodies, and wouldn't wish it on anyone else.

Hugo lifted his chin. "We need to secure his compartment and call the police." He balled his fists.

Ruth sighed. "Very well." She stood. "Hold on. The cameras."

Hugo checked the application on his phone, but as with the last time, the recordings were blank. "Must have happened during the blackout in the tunnel." He pocketed the phone. "That can't be a coincidence."

"No," Ruth said. "It cannot." And she led the way from the dining carriage, with ever-increasing unease.

19

In the salon, people chatted as soft music played in the background.

Princess Mary laughed at something Greg was saying and twiddled with her hair, eyes sparkling.

"I'm sorry to interrupt," Ruth said. "May I borrow my grandson for a few minutes?" When the princess's expression turned to disappointment, Ruth added, "I will bring him straight back again." Although, she could not promise that this time.

Ruth wanted Greg at her side from now on, so they could help each other stay safe. And as soon as people found out about this latest murder, chaos could well ensue.

Greg mumbled a half-hearted apology to the princess, and then followed Ruth and Hugo from the salon.

In the single-sleeper carriage, Ruth stopped outside compartment 14A.

Hugo pulled a deep breath and opened the door.

He then stood there for several long seconds, taking in the scene before him: everything as it was before, with the detective's body across the bed, blood soaked into the pillow and sheets.

"I don't believe it." Hugo's jaw dropped.

"I know it's hard to take in," Ruth said in a sombre voice. "But we—"

Hugo rushed into the compartment, pressed two fingers to the man's neck, and looked back. "He's alive."

A wave of shock ran from the top of Ruth's head to the tips of her toes. In a daze, she squeezed past Hugo and knelt next to Daniel. "We need to call a doctor." Hugo turned to the window with his phone. "Still no signal."

The door at the end of the passageway opened, and in walked Jane Minchent, her arm linked with Victoria's.

Waylon appeared behind them. "I said I could take Victoria to her compartment. I can wait outside for her to freshen up, and escort her back."

"I told you it's fine," Jane said. "I'm happy to help."

As the three of them approached, Ruth tried to step around Hugo and shut the door, but it was too late.

Jane gasped.

Victoria stiffened. "What's wrong?"

"An a-accident," Hugo said in what he clearly thought was a relaxed tone, but actually came across as a little shaky. "N-Nothing to alarm you. We're dealing with it. All under control." He swallowed and studied her reaction.

Victoria's expression turned panicked. "Who is it now?"

"Daniel," Greg said.

Ruth shot her grandson a look. "But we'll get him some help. Right, Hugo?" Once they'd figured out how to contact the outside world.

"Right." Hugo looked to Waylon. "Fetch Boyd."

Waylon hesitated, and then hurried off.

Hugo noticed Ruth's puzzled expression. "Boyd is our

designated first-aider. He'll take care of him until we can get him some proper medical attention."

Victoria raised a hand to her mouth. "Daniel will be okay?"

"He's alive," Greg said. "Barely."

"Where are you going?" Ruth asked Jane.

"I'm escorting Victoria to her compartment, so she can freshen up."

"Perhaps you can take me to an economy-class bathroom instead." The colour drained from Victoria's face. "I— I do not want to be in the way, and it means we don't have to come back this way." Her fingers trembled on the white cane.

Hugo addressed Jane. "That's not a bad idea. We need to keep the corridors as clear as possible."

"You can leave me in the bathroom," Victoria said. "I may be a while."

"I can't do that," Jane said.

"I'll be fine." Victoria raised her cane. "Take me to the first economy-class bathroom. I know the way back to the salon from there." She turned her face to the ceiling. "Past the kitchen, through the dining carriage, and then I'm there. Right? There's plenty of staff. Someone can help me."

Jane looked to Hugo.

Hugo pursed his lips.

Ruth wasn't comfortable with that idea either, especially with a killer on board. "We should leave no one on their own."

"I've done nothing to deserve being hit over the head," Victoria said. "I lead a pretty boring life."

Hugo refocused on Jane. "Please wait at the dining carriage door for Victoria's return."

Jane nodded and led her back along the corridor.

Ruth took the detective's wrist and felt a pulse, slow and weak, but unmistakable. "I'm so sorry," she whispered to him. "I should have checked." With guilty tears in her eyes, Ruth glanced at Greg. "Why didn't I check?" She'd never forgive herself if the detective now died because she'd not been observant enough. She'd been so focussed on the crime scene.

"Don't blame yourself," Greg said. "It's not your fault."

"For once, your snooping may have done some good." Hugo held his phone up. "I still don't have a signal."

Greg checked his phone too. "Neither do I."

Ruth rested Daniel's arm back on the bed, stood, and checked her phone. She frowned. "How can none of us have any bars?" She stepped from the compartment and peered through the windows. They travelled past a town, where there should be plenty of phone masts nearby and a powerful signal. "This is absurd." She swore under her breath.

With head injuries, every second was vital, and they'd wasted a lot of time.

Hugo pressed a palm to the detective's forehead. "Clammy. I don't know how long he can stay like this. He should be in a hospital."

They could elevate Daniel's head and legs onto the bed, to make him more comfortable, but Ruth was afraid any movement may cause further brain damage.

If he made it through the day, he would have a serious concussion at the very least, severe cerebral swelling at the worst.

The wound had stopped bleeding, so there was no need to interfere or try and stem the flow.

Waylon returned with Boyd, who clutched a first aid kit.

Boyd's eyes almost popped from their sockets when he

took in Daniel's motionless form and the blood-soaked sheets. "What happened to him?"

"Unknown," Hugo said before Ruth could answer. "Head injury."

"The bleeding has stopped," Ruth added.

"Then we shouldn't touch him," Boyd said. "Let the paramedics deal with this."

"Speaking of whom." Hugo pocketed his phone. "It's an emergency. We must ask the driver to stop at the next station." He peered out the window. "I'm not sure how far that is, but we have no alternative."

Ruth nodded her agreement. Without phone signals, it was the only remaining logical step.

Hugo gestured Ruth and Greg down the passageway. "Please return to the salon and wait with the others. I ask you not to tell them what's happened. We don't want to cause a panic."

"We're coming with you," Ruth said.

Greg groaned.

Hugo looked as though he was about to argue, but Ruth cut across him. "No one should roam about the train on their own. Greg and I will accompany you. All three of us will speak with the driver."

Hugo glanced at Daniel, rubbed the back of his neck, and then gave a reluctant bob of his head. He addressed Waylon and Boyd. "You two wait here. Monitor him. Don't let anyone into this carriage, no matter who they are. It's off-limits." He then motioned to Ruth and Greg. "This way."

As they followed Hugo along the passageway, through the connecting gangway, and into the first-class double-sleeper carriage, Ruth said, "Hugo. We shouldn't leave Boyd alone with Waylon."

"Why ever not?" Hugo's eyebrows then rose. "You can't

be suggesting . . ." He stopped at the door to the royal carriage. "Ruth, I'd trust Waylon with my life. He's not the killer." Before Ruth could protest some more, he knocked.

"They're all in the salon," Greg said.

"Ah, yes. Of course." Hugo unlocked the door, and he stepped through.

Greg whistled.

"See what you're missing?" Ruth said to him. "If you responded to the princess's flirtatious advances, all this could be yours."

Greg rolled his eyes. "She's not flirting. She's only being nice."

Ruth grinned.

Hugo marched on through. "You have no idea how much this cost."

"Worth every penny, no doubt." Ruth peered into the royal bedroom suite as they passed by. It had a four-poster bed, plush carpet, velvet wallpaper, gold fittings on the windows and light switches, and a crystal chandelier.

Hugo stopped at another door at the far end of the carriage. He selected a key and unlocked it. Then he typed a code into a panel to the side, and once it had let out a long beep, he opened it.

Wind whipped through the carriage.

Ruth staggered back, shielding her eyes.

The train seemed to be travelling even faster than before, and by Hugo's eyebrows bunching, he'd noticed too.

"Watch your step." He made his way across a short open platform until he reached the faux coal tender. He pressed a button, and a hidden door swung open. Then he ducked through.

Lights inside lit the way to the far end, where Hugo stopped at another door, this time to the driver's cab.

He tried the handle. "Locked." Hugo chose another key from the bunch and placed it in the lock. He frowned, knocked, and shouted, "Alan?" above the roar of the wind.

When there came no answer, Hugo banged a fist on the steel.

Ruth's stomach sank. She cupped her hands over her mouth and called, "Hugo."

He turned back.

"Could he have fallen asleep?" Though that was unlikely.

Hugo shook his head, and then, by his eyebrows rising, clearly realised what she was really implying. "There's a foot pedal."

"A dead man's switch," Greg said.

Ruth winced. "Poor choice of words."

"It's a driver's safety device," Hugo shouted. "It also has a vigilance measure built into it. Meaning, the driver not only has to press the pedal with his foot, but release and press again at certain intervals." His brow furrowed. "Every ten minutes, as I recall. There's a buzzer to alert him." He turned his ear to the door.

"And if it's not pressed, the train comes to a stop?" Ruth asked.

"He must still be in there," Greg said. "Bolted the door from the inside."

Hugo faced the driver's door again and banged with his clenched fists, harder this time. "Alan. Open up. It's an emergency."

Greg leaned in to Ruth and said in her ear, "Or he died under ten minutes ago, and we haven't stopped yet."

Ruth remained stoic. "Perhaps someone else has got in there with Alan the relief driver." She eyed the door and the lock, but it didn't seem likely that had occurred.

Greg's eyes widened. "The killer's in there with him?"

Hugo spun around and gestured for them to go back the way they'd come.

The three of them ducked back inside the faux coal tender, made their way along, hunched over, and stepped back into the royal carriage.

Hugo closed the door, and Ruth stretched as silence fell over them.

"Now what?" Greg asked.

"Nothing else for it." Desperation etched Hugo's face. "I need to bust into the driver's cab. I'll fetch my tools." He marched from the carriage.

"Wait, Hugo," Ruth called after him, but he ignored her.

Greg went to follow but turned back as Ruth sat in a plush armchair. "What are you doing?"

"He won't break in." Ruth picked lint from her blouse. "That driver's door is reinforced steel." She recalled one of Miles' blueprints indicating as much.

"Then what do we do?" Greg wrung his fingers. "We're on a runaway train with no way to call for help."

Ruth motioned him to an armchair opposite.

Greg paced. "Could we short out the motors? Blow a fuse or something? The train lost power earlier—perhaps we can make that happen again. I bet it was something to do with the kitchen. An oven drawing too much power?"

"Sit, Gregory."

He stopped pacing and gawked at her. "Why aren't you worried?"

"I am. But now is the time for clear heads." She thrust a finger at the chair. "You're the one who doesn't want me rushing into things, remember? For once, I'm following your sage advice, Gregory."

Greg huffed and dropped into the chair.

"We have a lot of train track left between here and Edinburgh." Ruth interlaced her fingers. "It's high time we pieced together what is going on." She took several deep breaths. "Let's start at this moment and work our way back." She waved a hand toward the front of the train. "There's no answer from the driver. Which means he's either ignoring us banging on the door, or someone has rigged the safety pedal."

Greg gaped at her. "Someone's really killed him?"

Ruth shrugged. "We don't know that." There were no handy windows that could easily be reached to confirm anything, and Ruth certainly would not risk their lives trying to find out.

Hugo marched past with his tool bag, heading to the front of the train again with a determined look.

"It won't work," Ruth called after him. "You'll only hurt yourself."

Hugo ignored her, opened the door, and stepped through.

As the door closed, Ruth refocussed on her grandson. "The detective was working on a case. That's why he's on board the train. Something to do with a gang smuggling undisclosed items across the country."

Greg's brow furrowed. "Is that likely?"

"I don't know," Ruth said. "However, someone saw fit to crack him across the skull and leave him for dead, which means he was close to figuring out who was responsible for Miles' murder." She only wished Daniel were conscious so they could ask him questions.

"How did the killer know he was close?" Greg asked.

"A good question." Ruth pursed her lips.

Greg leaned forward. "You think he confronted them?"

"He's in his own compartment," Ruth said. "Blood spatter on the walls. Which means..."

"The killer went to Daniel, not the other way around." Greg sat back, shaking his head. "Who did it?"

"More importantly," Ruth said in sudden realisation, "why didn't the murderer leave the train at Finsbury Village? At that point, Zoey had confessed to killing Miles. If there were any smuggled items on board, they'd already have made it from Edinburgh to Cornwall. The guilty party could have left at that point, under the pretence of not wanting to return on the train of death."

Greg nodded slowly. "Now when we stop in Edinburgh, the police will surround the train. The killer will have no way to escape."

"Right you are," Ruth said. "Which means they're not finished with their plan."

The carriage door opened, and wind whipped through.

Hugo reappeared, hair dishevelled, clutching his hand.

Ruth stood. "What's happened?"

He closed the door, and muttered, "Sliced my palm. Damn it."

Greg got to his feet too. "Shall I fetch Boyd?"

Ruth gasped. "That's it." She pulled her phone from her pocket and scrolled through images of Miles' blueprints until she reached the ones with notes about carriage couplers, and his concern regarding them being easy to disconnect.

Ruth's heart leapt into her throat. "Oh no." She looked up at the men, wide-eyed. "I get it now. The killer isn't smuggling anything."

Greg's brow furrowed. "What are they doing, then?"

Ruth took a deep breath. "This is a train robbery."

20

With her heart hammering in her chest, Ruth raced through the royal carriage. "We must hurry. I know what the killer is doing." She couldn't believe it had taken her this long to figure it out.

"Are you going to explain?" Hugo asked as he and Greg jogged after her. "What do you mean, a train robbery? Who are they robbing?"

Ruth reached the door, but it opened before she could grab the handle. She staggered back as the protection officers and Princess Mary entered.

"What are you doing in here?" Luke, the lead officer, said in a deep bark. "This carriage is off-limits." Then his attention moved to Hugo, and his eyes narrowed. "We heard there's been another murder. Is it true?"

"Attempted murder," Ruth said.

Luke glared at her, and then shot another look at Hugo. "This train is a death trap. The whole thing has been a complete fiasco." He waved a finger in his face. "We demand you pull into the next station and let us off immediately."

"We're working on that very idea," Hugo said through tight lips.

"Working on it? What do you mean?" Luke frowned. "What else has happened?"

"I think this trip has been rather exciting, Hugo," Princess Mary said. "Congratulations. You'll get a rave review from me. Five stars. Minus a few points for the murder, of course."

Greg snickered.

"We don't have time to explain." Ruth went to step around Luke, but he blocked her exit. She let out a juddering breath. "I believe the killer has plans to steal from the train. To be precise, from the luggage compartment. If we hurry, we might stop them. If you keep getting in my way, they'll escape." She gave him a hard look.

He didn't back down.

"What are they attempting to steal?" Princess Mary asked, as though simply enquiring about the weather.

"Something of Victoria's," Ruth said. "Her jewellery." She looked at Luke. "It was in that box you placed inside the safe."

He stared at her for a few seconds. "I'll come with you." His hand moved to the gun under his jacket, to indicate he was armed. "I feel responsible."

"Probably because you are." Princess Mary smiled. "He who touched it last . . ."

"It's a good idea you tag along," Ruth said to Luke. Besides, this could get dangerous, and she would prefer some police protection of her own.

Luke turned to his companion. "Secure the princess in the panic room."

"Not again." She rolled her eyes. "This is getting ridiculous."

"We can't take any chances. It's for your own safety."

"It is definitely for the best," Ruth said in a soothing tone. "Just until we have the killer secured." Inside, she screamed for everyone to hurry up.

"Will you tell me everything that happens?" Princess Mary asked. "The blow-by-blow account? I want to know every minute detail."

Ruth crossed her heart. "You have my word."

"Very well." Princess Mary extended a hand to Greg and offered him a sweet smile to accompany it. "Coming with me this time? I could do with some companionship. I think I spotted a deck of cards in there. If not, I'm sure we can entertain ourselves in other ways." She winked.

Greg blushed.

Luke did not seem amused. "Your Highness. That won't happen. We must follow a strict protocol that dictates—"

Princess Mary huffed. "It's extremely boring in there. Do you have any idea? It doesn't even have internet."

"That reminds me." Luke looked at Hugo. "Our phones don't have signals."

"None do," Greg said.

His eyes widened. "None?" He peered out the window.

"Can we please get moving?" Ruth bounced on the balls of her feet. "We're wasting time."

Once they'd secured the princess inside the panic room and sealed the heavy door, Luke said to his companion, "Stand guard. No one in or out."

He gave a sharp nod. "Understood, sir."

Officer Luke then gestured to the door. "After you, madam."

Ruth led the way back from the royal carriage, and marched into the first-class carriage where Boyd and

Waylon waited. Her concerns about leaving them alone together were unfounded.

She pointed to Hugo. "He needs a bandage."

"I'm fine," Hugo said as blood dripped from his hand.

"Get it fixed, and we'll be back shortly," Ruth said. "We have the right person for the job." She motioned to Luke. "He's trained for this type of thing. We don't want to be in his way when he springs into action."

Hugo hesitated and then nodded.

Waylon looked between them. "What's going on?"

"No time." Ruth raised a hand as Greg went to follow her. "Wait here too."

"No way," he said. "We stick together."

Ruth growled under her breath. "Fine. But you stay behind me."

He shrugged. "How about you stay behind me?"

"Yeah, right," Ruth laughed, and followed Luke out.

When they reached the salon, the passengers were still there, oblivious, chatting in groups while soft classical music played in the background.

Smiles and jolly expressions turned dour as the three of them trooped through the carriage.

"I say," Lord Hamilton called after them. "What on earth is happening now?"

"Police business," Luke said as they headed past the bar.

Victoria sat on a stool next to Jane Minchent. "Police?" she said in a shrill voice. "Did he die?"

This resulted in several gasps.

Jane clapped a hand over her mouth.

"Rest assured, no one has died," Ruth said. "Daniel will be okay."

"Then what are you doing?" Lady Hamilton asked.

"We'll bring everyone up to speed in due course." Ruth followed Luke from the salon with Greg in tow.

They continued their march through the dining carriage. At the far end, Chef Carlos stood in the door to the kitchen, wiping his hands on a kitchen towel.

"Everything all right?" he asked with a look of concern as they approached. "Waylon said there was an accident and fetched Boyd." He indicated an empty hook on the wall where the first aid kit once hung.

"Has anyone been past here recently?" Ruth asked.

"Not that I know of," Carlos said. "Maybe. I've been busy." He nodded to stacks of clean dishes in the racks. "What with Boyd AWOL."

"How about when Victoria came this way earlier?" Greg asked. "She was with Mrs Minchent."

Carlos shook his head. "Didn't see."

"How many any other staff members back there?" Luke asked. "I counted two servers in the salon."

Carlos hung the kitchen towel next to the door. "I suppose there must be another five, including Angus. The servers work shifts." He glanced at a clock on the wall. "I was about to take a nap myself."

Ruth half smiled. "Thank you." As she continued to follow Officer Luke through the economy carriages, she glanced back at Greg. "Whatever happens, promise you'll be careful. Nothing reckless or heroic."

"I'm hardly the heroic type, Grandma." He peered over his shoulder. "Anyway, I was about to say the same thing to you. You're the reckless one."

Ruth swallowed. "I'm trying not to be."

Greg snorted.

They raced through all three economy carriages and into the crew carriage. It seemed quiet—doors closed, the only sound the cla-clat, cla-clat, cla-clat of the wheels on the track.

Ruth considered waking the shift crew members and telling them to go to the salon for their own safety, but she feared drawing the killer's attention.

The three of them needed to keep the element of surprise if they hoped to catch them without bloodshed.

At the far end of the crew carriage, Officer Luke stopped at the door and drew his gun. "Stay back until I give the all-clear."

Ruth stood to one side, although she had no intention of staying back. She simply had to see what was going on with her own eyes.

Luke held his gun high, grabbed the handle and threw open the door.

Wind whipped through the carriage, but instead of it knocking the officer back, he fell forward.

As if in slow motion, Ruth lunged at him and grabbed his jacket, arresting his fall, and Greg appeared at her side a split second later, also grabbing Luke's arm. Together they hauled him back into the crew carriage.

Beyond the door was nothing but open track, with the luggage carriage nowhere to be seen.

Luke leaned against the wall, breathing hard. "Thank you."

"Don't mention it," Ruth said. "Now I'm glad you went first."

Miles concerns of how the carriage couplers could be easily disconnected with the right tools were now confirmed.

"We need to stop the train." Luke peered at the receding track. "The luggage carriage can't be too far behind."

Ruth's stomach tensed as she delivered the bad news to him. "We can't stop." And that couldn't be a coincidence.

Officer Luke looked at the track again and back to her. "Why not?"

"Someone locked the cab and the driver is not responding. We don't know what's happened. We were figuring it out when this happened."

"Is he hurt?"

"Unknown at this time," Ruth said. "There's a safety switch that covers the eventuality, but we don't know if someone has jury-rigged it."

Luke hesitated. "We need to get inside that driver's cab."

"Already tried," Greg said. "That's how Hugo busted his hand."

"But you're right," Ruth said. "Now it really is the only way. We'll have to try harder." She went to close the carriage door, but Greg stopped her.

He stepped around Ruth with his phone held high and leaned through the opening. "Bars. I have bars." He pulled the phone back inside, but the signal vanished. Greg thrust his hand back out, and they appeared again. He looked to his grandmother. "Shall I call someone?"

"I'll do it." Luke straightened. He took his own phone from his pocket and leaned out the door while Ruth and her grandson held on to him. "I have a signal too," he called back to them, then dialled, and pressed the phone to his ear. A few seconds later, he said, "Hello? This is Officer Edwards, assigned to protection duty of . . ." He cleared his throat. "Frisky Kitten."

Ruth beamed at Greg.

"Why am I not surprised she's called that?" He rolled his eyes. "I wonder if she knows?"

"Probably chose the call sign herself," Ruth said. "I guess Flirty Wildcat was already taken."

Greg laughed.

"Sir?" Officer Luke said into his phone. "Can you hear me?" This was followed by an anxious pause of a few seconds.

Ruth grimaced as her arms started to ache.

She really needed to fit a mini gym to her motorhome, but that would likely require freeing up space where the whipped ice cream machine currently resided. A concession she wasn't willing to make.

"Yes, sir. We are on the Finsbury Flyer, as planned, heading back to Edinburgh. There's been a second incident. Yes, sir. Attempted murder . . . That's not all." Luke cleared his throat again, as if steeling himself. "The perpetrator has escaped." His shoulders tensed.

Ruth imagined the inevitable shouting and name-calling on the other end of the phone.

After an agonising, lactic-acid-inducing ten more seconds, Luke added, "It would appear someone unhitched the luggage carriage while we were in motion. We believe the killer is on there and intends to break open the safe. Yes, sir. We can't, sir . . . Because the train is still moving at speed. The driver is not responding. I'm about to go check myself, but the assumption is he's either refusing to answer or is incapacitated."

Ruth could tie a rope around Greg's waist, send him onto the roof of the driver's cab, and see if he could smash a window or something. However, she assumed Greg wouldn't be amenable to such a request, given the day they'd had.

The boy was the absolute antithesis of a thrill-seeker. In fact, Greg still told the story about when he was eight years old and got trapped on the roof of a hotel for a couple of hours. He'd gone up to get some fresh air and admire the view when the door had jammed shut. Of course, Greg had made out as though it had been a life-or-death adventure, akin to John McClane in *Die Hard*, only just stopping short of tying a fire hose around his waist and leaping off the building.

"I'm leaning out the back of the train," Luke continued. "We don't have a signal on board. It's the only way, sir. I'll call back in twenty minutes if nothing has changed."

Greg looked at Ruth, and the colour drained from his cheeks. "Like we crash?"

She shook her head. "We'll be fine." Although, Ruth couldn't completely rule it out.

"Yes, sir. I will . . . Thank you, sir." Luke hung up and moved back into the carriage.

Ruth finally closed the door, cutting off the wind and noise, and faced him. "What's the verdict?" She flexed her stiff fingers and shook her arms.

"They'll locate the luggage carriage." Luke pocketed his phone. "My boss has advised we try to get into the driver's cab by whatever means necessary, but they'll contact the signal engineer. They can divert the train and cut power to the track if necessary."

"At least that's some good news," Ruth said, trying to look on the bright side of their ordeal. "Even if the killer has got away."

"Officers will surround the luggage carriage and arrest them," Luke said. "There's no way someone can open the safe and be gone before they get there."

Greg looked dubious. "The killer went through all this trouble. They must have planned for that eventuality too."

Ruth sighed. "Agreed. They clearly had this whole thing

mapped out and have remained a step ahead of us. There's no way that after all their effort they wouldn't have an escape route in mind."

The killer would have also factored in the time needed to bust open the safe and steal the jewels. They'd have a getaway vehicle ready and vanish before the police arrived on the scene. In fact, they'd probably already escaped.

A pit of despondency gnawed Ruth's stomach.

They'd lost.

She'd lost.

"Come on," Ruth muttered, and headed back along the passageway. "Let's give Victoria the bad news."

Greg hurried after her. "It'll all be insured, though, right? Her necklace?"

"I hope so," Ruth said. "But nothing can make up for the sentimental value." Victoria had explained how the jewellery had belonged to her great-grandmother.

The three of them stepped into the salon to find it empty, save for a couple of servers.

Greg looked about. "Where's everyone gone?"

"To their compartments," a server behind the bar said. "They got spooked. They've all locked themselves away and are refusing to come out until we reach Edinburgh." His gaze shifted to the door at the other end, no doubt about to do the same thing himself.

"That's ridiculous," Luke snapped. "We need to get them all back out here. Now."

"Wait a minute." Ruth faced him and lowered her voice. "It's not such a terrible idea, if they feel safer that way."

"But with the killer off the train," Greg said, "they have no one left to fear."

"Come on." Ruth led the way into the first-class single-sleeper carriage and stopped outside 14A. She knocked, and Waylon answered. "How's the detective?" she asked.

He stepped aside.

The detective was in the exact same position, laid across the bed, and Hugo was seated at the desk with his hand bandaged, while Boyd leaned against the wall, arms folded.

"What happened?" Hugo asked.

"Someone disconnected the luggage carriage," Ruth said. "It's gone."

"What?" Hugo leapt to his feet.

"A train heist." Greg gestured to Daniel's motionless form. "He must have figured it out."

Hugo shook his head. "They told me it was about smuggling."

"Maybe the gang changed their mind once they laid eyes on Victoria's necklace yesterday." Ruth eyed the detective and only hoped he'd one day be in a fit state to answer the numerous questions coming his way. "Clearly he suspected more than he let on."

"We must get to the driver and stop the train," Luke said. "I'm sure we can figure out a way into that cab if we put our heads together."

Ruth agreed. Although, short of explosives, she was out of ideas.

Greg's brow furrowed into a deep line. "The signal operator will stop the train, right?"

"Yes," Luke said. "But I'd prefer we also attempt to do the same. Safer that way."

"Waylon, remain here with Boyd." Hugo slipped from the compartment and closed the door. "Let's go."

Ruth followed Luke along the single-sleeper passageway, with Greg and Hugo behind, on through the double sleeper, and into the royal carriage.

Officer Luke waved a hand to his counterpart, who still stood guard outside the panic room door. "Let her out. It's all clear."

The officer unlocked the door and opened it. "Okay, Your Highness. You can—" His jaw dropped.

The room was empty.

21

Ruth, Greg, Hugo, and both protection officers stared, unblinking, into the compact panic room within the royal carriage.

Greg was the first to unstick his tongue and say what everyone else was clearly thinking. "Where the hell has the princess gone?"

"Language, Gregory." But Ruth had to agree with his sentiment.

The room stood empty, with only its single cot, desk, chair, and a distinct lack of windows.

All eyes moved to the officer who'd stood guard.

"I didn't budge from this spot," he said in a defensive tone. "Was here the whole time." He frowned. "I don't understand how she got out." He scanned the rest of the carriage as though she may be hiding behind a cushion or table lamp, ready to jump out and surprise them.

Ruth inclined her head. "Did you use the bathroom?"

His bewildered gaze returned to her. "No."

"Fall asleep?" Greg asked.

The officer's frown deepened. "Standing up?"

"Did anything distract you at all?" Ruth pressed, imagining a nuclear explosion or aliens landing. "Even for a moment? Turned away for a second? Think carefully. It's important. Can you recall anything odd at all? No matter how insignificant." She peered into the panic room and paid close attention to the floor, ceiling, and walls.

The officer screwed his face up for a second, ran a hand through his short-cropped mousy blond hair, and then shook his head. "Like I say, I was here. Fully awake. I didn't move." He looked at Luke, the lead officer. "Waited for your return, sir. Nothing happened. I swear. Didn't hear anything either. She was in there." He rubbed the back of his neck, and sweat broke out on his forehead.

"You heard no strange noises?" Ruth found that hard to believe. She stepped into the room and scanned every inch of the interior, from floor to ceiling and back again, several times. "Especially from in here? She didn't make a sound?"

"Not a peep." The blond officer scratched his head, looking as baffled as everyone else.

"She definitely went in there," Greg said. "We all saw her. Then you shut the door and stood in front of it. She's a magician."

"Or someone used a shrinking ray on her," Ruth murmured. "Be careful where you step."

"This is no time for jokes," Hugo said. "How could this happen?"

Ruth now thought Greg should have gone in with the princess, kept her company, but he could've wound up vanishing as well, and Ruth would never have forgiven herself if something bad had happened to him.

Sara, her daughter, would not let her hear the end of it either.

"How is this possible?" Hugo muttered.

"I was about to ask you the same thing," Luke said through a tight jaw. "This is your train."

Hugo's brow knitted. "I hope you don't for one second think I had something to do with this?"

Luke faced him, pulled his shoulders back, and straightened to his full height. "Your train, your passengers, your responsibility. I told the princess this was a bad idea from the start. She insisted. Said she wanted to do all she could to support your new venture." He balled his fists. "And this is how you repay her?"

"Why would I want anything bad to happen to Mary?" Hugo's voice rose. "I worked for her family for years. Was their most loyal servant. I would do anything for her. They trusted me"."

"Maybe a little too much." Luke stepped to Hugo, so their noses were only a couple of inches apart. "This is all on you."

"Enough bickering." Ruth examined the doorframe. "You can argue and point fingers later. After we've found Princess Mary." She then spun around and lifted the mattress off the cot, only to find slatted supports and nothing underneath. Ruth faced the desk.

On it was a novel, open to the middle, and the chair pulled out slightly, as if the princess had been reading and set the book down to answer the door.

"This is insane," the officer said. "She was in here. We all saw her go in." He looked panicked.

"Could she be playing some kind of prank?" Greg asked.

"Like what?" Hugo raised an eyebrow. "Hiding under her invisibility cloak?"

"She knows better than to trick us." Luke strode to the bedroom suite and peered inside. "Princess Mary has been through training that covers such scenarios. It's serious business. She may like her little jokes, but she knows better than this." His expression darkened. "Someone else is behind this."

Ruth ran her fingers over the walls of the room, and then crouched on the floor. Nothing seemed out of the ordinary.

She pursed her lips.

All the other passengers were supposedly in their compartments. If the princess had somehow snuck out, she could be with one of them. Ruth's first thought was Waylon, but he had stayed with Hugo and Boyd.

Her next thought was Victoria. *Has Princess Mary gone to sit with her?* They needed to check Victoria's compartment first.

"People don't simply vanish into thin air," Hugo said. "There has to be a logical explanation." And not only did he look desperate to solve it, but quickly too.

Ruth couldn't blame him. She straightened. "We're wasting time." She strode from the room and closed the door. "We'll search the train from front to back before it stops."

"Agreed," Luke said. "We can ask people to leave their compartments along the way and then inspect each one."

"I'll go ahead of you and do that," Hugo said. "I will send them to the salon again and demand they wait there. We'll ply them with complimentary drinks."

"Greg and I can help you persuade them," Ruth said.

"And we'll search each compartment behind you until we find the princess." Luke motioned to his companion. "We'll first see if we can get into the driver's cab and stop the train."

"No." Ruth held up a hand. "While the train is in motion, the princess can't leave. We're better off not stopping for now."

Greg bit his fingernails and muttered, "As long as we don't crash."

"We won't crash," Hugo said. "I can assure you of that."

With renewed purpose, the five of them left the royal carriage and stepped into the first-class double sleeper.

"This one is vacant." Hugo went to open the door, but someone had bolted it from the inside. With a look of confusion, he knocked. "Hello?"

A couple of seconds later, the door opened.

Hugo stiffened. "Victoria?"

She gripped the doorframe. "Hugo? What's wrong?"

Ruth peered over her shoulder. The door to the bathroom stood open, and Victoria was alone.

"What are you doing in here?" Hugo asked her.

"I'm s-so sorry," she said. "I . . . I felt really unsafe in the salon. D-Don't know who to trust." Her hands trembled. "I wanted to come here, and wait until we got back to Edinburgh."

"This isn't your compartment," Hugo said. "Yours is 4A. This is 1A."

"It is? Oh. I'm sorry. I—"

"Have you heard or spoken to Princess Mary since leaving the salon?" Ruth asked.

Victoria shook her head. "Please tell me something hasn't happened to her."

Hugo let out a breath. "Never mind. Jane must have brought you to the wrong compartment. No harm."

"I thought it felt off, but I wasn't sure. Once I was here, I didn't want to leave." Victoria's shoulders relaxed. "What is going on, Hugo?"

"My deepest apologies. It has been a very trying day." Hugo cleared his throat. "We feel it would be best for everyone to return to the salon. It really is the safest place right now." He glanced over his shoulder, through the window behind him. "The train will be stopping soon." Although, it still showed no signs of slowing.

Ruth imagined the signal engineers and police discussing the best place to bring the train to a halt, where they could be sure of no murderers escaping. She expected the train to stop way before they got to Edinburgh, though. Somewhere remote but accessible. That would take time to plan and execute.

Victoria fumbled by the door, found her white cane propped next to it, and gripped it with both hands. "If you think it's best, Hugo, then I suppose I can't argue." She swallowed. "I must say, this whole affair has been stressful and worrisome."

"And for that you have my humble apologies." Hugo went to say something else, but stopped himself.

Ruth guessed he'd been about to inform Victoria about her stolen jewellery but opted to delay the bad news.

"I can escort her back to the salon." Greg looked to Victoria. "If you'd like me to."

A slight smile turned the corners of her mouth upward, and she held out an arm. "Thank you." Clearly Greg was on a very short list of people she felt safe with.

Greg then guided Victoria from the compartment and down the corridor. "I'll stay with her until everyone is back."

The officers went in to search 1A, and Hugo moved to compartment 2A. After a check, he opened the door to Ruth's compartment.

She peered inside. "No princess."

Hugo sighed. "No." He opened the door to 4A, which also stood empty, and moved down the carriage to 5A. Hugo tried the handle and then knocked. "Hello?"

A few seconds later, a male voice answered, "Who is it?"

"Hugo Finsbury."

The door opened, and Robert Minchent stood there. "What's happening?" His eyes darted between Hugo and Ruth. "Let me guess, another gruesome murder?"

"What makes you say that?" Ruth asked in a level tone.

Robert rolled his eyes.

Ruth peered over his shoulder.

Jane sat on the edge of the bed, wringing her fingers, not making eye contact.

"Everything okay?" Ruth asked.

Robert moved into Ruth's field of view. "My wife is scared. Wants to get off this damn horror train, and so do I. We want to get to Edinburgh, where we leave this sordid affair behind us."

Jane sniffed and dabbed her eyes with a handkerchief.

"We would like everyone to wait in the salon," Hugo said.

Robert folded his arms. "We're comfortable here."

"It's for your own safety."

"Oh really?" Robert leaned through the doorframe and peered into the hallway as the police officers left one compartment and went into the next. His eyes narrowed, and he pulled back. "I'm not going anywhere until you tell me what's going on."

"Please." Hugo stepped aside and gestured. "We insist."

Robert glared at him. "I've got nothing to hide." He looked at Ruth. "Fine. Come along, Jane." Robert slipped from their compartment, shortly followed by his wife, who, head bowed, still didn't make eye contact with anyone.

Ruth wanted to take Jane aside and ask her what had her so upset, but with a killer on the loose, it didn't take a genius to figure out.

Once the Minchents had left the carriage, Hugo knocked on the door to room 6A.

Lady Hilary Hamilton answered. "Are we almost there?"

"A little way to go," Hugo said with a forced smile. "Would you mind waiting in the salon, please?" He looked over her shoulder, into the empty compartment. "Where's Lord Hamilton?"

"Already back there, as far as I know. Propping up the bar." Lady Hilary rolled her eyes. "Said he needed a stiff drink. Never mind leaving his poor wife alone in their compartment where goodness knows who could break in."

"Allow me to escort you to the salon." Hugo held out an arm, and he glanced at Ruth.

She nodded.

Lady Hilary and Hugo left the carriage.

Ruth watched the officers as they stepped from compartment 5A. "Anything yet?"

"Nothing out of the ordinary." Luke looked paler by the minute. "We need to speed this up."

Ruth stepped out of the way and allowed them to search Lord and Lady Hamilton's compartment, while she moved to the next.

She opened the door to 7A and stared.

Greg appeared at her side. "What's up?"

Ruth continued to gaze into the empty room. "This was the same compartment number as the other carriage. The one with all Miles' blueprints and photographs."

The protection officers joined them.

"Something wrong?" Luke asked.

"No. It's fine." Ruth stepped aside, allowing them in to check it. She then moved to the last compartment—Hugo's.

The wardrobe door stood open, and someone had

tipped over the tool bag, spilling its contents across the floor.

"What's happened here?" Unable to think of an immediate explanation, Ruth backed out and gestured for Greg to follow her. They hurried through the connecting gangway and into the next carriage—the first-class single sleeper.

Compartment 9A was Waylon's, but he wasn't there, and nothing seemed out of the ordinary.

The protection officers continued checking the compartments behind Ruth, their expressions showing more and more exasperation by the minute.

However, she thought it wise to move slowly and methodically through the train.

She checked the other compartments, finding them all vacant, and then paused outside 14A.

"I'm sure he'll be okay," Greg murmured in her ear.

"I hope so." Ruth took a deep breath, knocked lightly, and opened the door.

Waylon sat on the edge of the bed next to the unconscious detective, while Boyd still leaned against the wall, arms folded.

"Are we stopping soon?" Boyd asked Ruth.

"Working on it." She nodded to the detective. "How is he?"

Boyd sighed. "No change, but he could have brain swelling. I just have no way to know. I'm not a doctor. He needs to go to the hospital."

"Stay here," Ruth said as the protection officers peered into the compartment. "Don't leave under any circumstances. We'll get help as soon as we can." She eyed Waylon for a second. *Has he played a part in all this?* Then she closed the door.

Ruth checked the remaining three empty compartments before finally reaching Greg's—18A.

He opened the door and waved the officers inside. "Be my guest."

Once the men had completed their work, Ruth peered through the connecting door to the salon. "Greg and I will remain here and stop anyone from going beyond this point, while you sweep the rest of the train."

"You won't help us?" Luke asked.

"I think you'd be quicker working alone from here on," Ruth said. "Hugo seems to have all the staff and passengers gathered. He can keep them there until you're finished."

Luke didn't seem convinced, but he let out a breath. "Very well."

The officers left the carriage.

Greg faced his grandmother. "What's going on?"

Ruth rubbed her chin. "I need some time to think this through. It doesn't make sense."

"Of course it doesn't make sense," Greg said. "The protection officers will find Princess Mary though."

Ruth paced. "I'm not so sure."

Greg's brow furrowed. "They won't? Then how did she get past all of us?"

"She couldn't have." Ruth pulled her phone from her pocket and swiped through the images until she reached the various documents and photographs Miles had gathered. Ruth gasped. "Wait. Look at this." She showed Greg the blueprint with the box beneath the train. "I thought it was something to do with electrics, but it only applies to the first-class double-sleeper carriage. None of the others have the modification."

Greg squinted at the display. "Okay. So what?"

"How big would you say this added box is?"

"There's no dimensions listed, but from when I had a look at it earlier . . ." He pointed to the nearest window. "Judging by that, I'd say the box is about six feet wide by—"

"Big enough for a person?"

Greg stared, and then his face fell.

"Maybe even two people at a squeeze?" Ruth's chest tightened as she brought up the image of the royal carriage and pointed to the panic room. "I think that box can slide from under compartment 1A in the first-class carriage, across these rail things, and over to the royal carriage." She zoomed in. "And then it must trigger a secret hatch in the floor, that can only be opened from underneath."

"Which is why you didn't find it," Greg said.

Ruth's stomach then did a backflip as some of the events fell into place. "Someone grabbed the princess, pulled her into the box, and slid back to the first-class carriage."

"Victoria went to that compartment by mistake. Do you think she interrupted their plan?" Greg gawped. "Could the princess still be there? In the box beneath the floor?

With a rush of adrenaline, Ruth pocketed her phone. "Only one way to find out." She waved Greg behind her as she marched along the corridor.

At the end, Ruth hurried through the connecting gangway, threw open the door, and a rush of air knocked her back a step.

Someone must have just unhitched the carriages because the first-class double sleeper, along with the royal carriage and the train engine itself, pulled away from them.

Without a second thought, Ruth jumped.

22

More by luck than any skill or athletic prowess, Ruth somehow traversed the three-foot gap between the parting train carriages. She hit the other side, and almost toppled backward onto the track, but managed to grab the door handle at the last moment and held on for dear life.

Panting, heart about to explode through her chest, she turned back.

"Grandma," Greg shouted. He gripped the doorframe of the other carriage and stared back at her, wide-eyed.

But it was too late—he receded into the distance, and all Ruth could do was offer a remorseful wave as she mouthed, "Sorry."

Greg would never let her hear the end of it.

Powerless to reverse her spur-of-the-moment, and some would say reckless, decision, Ruth peered through the door's window, but the corridor beyond stood empty.

Senses on high alert, Ruth entered the first-class double-sleeper carriage. She stood there for several seconds, the only sound the cla-clat, cla-clat, cla-clat of wheels on the track, and tried to gather her thoughts.

Someone had disconnected all the other carriages save for the royal carriage and this first-class one, and the train sped ever onward with no sign of slowing, all the while increasing the gap between her and backup.

From here on, Ruth was on her own.

She crept along the corridor until she reached the door to 1A. She turned an ear to it. Hearing no sounds coming from inside, Ruth held her breath and opened the door.

She pulled the phone from her pocket and studied the images from Miles' serial-killer-esque setup in the old first-class carriage back at Finsbury Village.

According to the blueprints, the secret box sat under the bathroom, lengthwise, part of it straddling the door's threshold, and now the whole swapping out of the train carriages made sense. The original first-class double sleeper can't have had the box addition, and therefore had passed final inspections, whereas this replacement carriage had flown under the radar. That could only mean a conspiracy.

Is Alan the train driver in on it?

That why he doesn't open the cab door?

Come to think of it, he was the one who suggested swapping over the first-class carriages.

Ruth ground her teeth, took two steps inside the compartment, and knelt. "It must be right here." She pocketed her phone and ran her fingers across the metal threshold strip, and up the sides of the doorframe.

Finding nothing loose or out of place, Ruth crawled on all fours into the bathroom, and over to the vanity unit. She grabbed each side and gave it a tug, but it was secured to the wall.

Ruth examined the floor around the toilet and the shower cubicle. Inside rested an adjustable spanner.

"From Hugo's tool bag?"

Ruth scanned the shower fittings, then rocked back onto her haunches and checked the blueprint again.

"It should be here." Her gaze drifted to the door, and back to the blueprint. "What am I missing?" Ruth zoomed in to study the details. "Hurry up, Morgan."

In the corner of the drawing, at the intersection of the door and bathroom floor, there appeared to be a catch.

Ruth frowned. "Where is it?"

She slipped the phone back into her pocket and crawled across the bathroom floor. Ruth stopped halfway and ran her hand back and forth as a slight breeze caressed her fingers. "Hmm." She leaned down close to the tiles. A thin line ran through the mortar and betrayed a secret hatch. "Knew it."

Ruth made her way to the door and the corner of the room, to a set of three exposed pipes that disappeared into the wall. However, the one on the right not only looked thicker than the others, but someone had loosened a nut at its base. Ruth glanced back at the adjustable spanner, then grabbed the pipe.

First, she twisted it one way, then the other. Ruth pulled, but when she pushed, the pipe moved inward, and there came a heavy clunk, followed by an entire section of the tiled floor lifting by an inch.

Ruth slid her fingers underneath and swung it up, revealing the lid of the metal box below. With her heart now pounding painfully against her rib cage, Ruth hinged the lid up, and let out a strangled gasp—a mixture of shock and relief.

Inside lay the motionless princess, eyes closed, arms by her sides. Ruth reached down into the box, pressed two fingers to the woman's wrist, and sighed at the steady, solid pulse.

Her gaze moved to a tiny spot of blood on the princess's neck. Someone had injected her. Judging by the angle and position, from behind. They'd taken the poor girl by surprise.

Ruth sat back and pictured the assailant climbing into the box on this side, sliding between the carriages and over to the royal suite. From there, they'd popped up from the floor inside the panic room and stabbed the princess in the neck, while she'd been seated at the desk, obliviously reading a novel.

Ruth assumed that meant the cot in the panic room had a hidden trapdoor beneath and could be opened from the inside. She'd not checked it closely enough earlier.

"What's my next plan of action?" Ruth murmured.

As if on cue, the train started to slow.

Ruth leapt to her feet, ran into the main compartment, and pulled back the curtain. The train headed down a siding flanked by tall trees, its brakes squeaking.

In the distance sat a black van, and two masked men waited with a metal gurney.

"They're going to take her." Ruth stepped back into the bathroom and looked down at the princess. "The whole thing, with her inside." She lay on the floor, grabbed Princess Mary under the arms, and, with a huge amount of effort, hoisted the girl from the box.

The princess was only of slight build, but even so it took every ounce of strength Ruth had to then lift her clear of the trap door, across the compartment, and onto the bed.

Ruth then rushed to the door and bolted it.

The train stopped, and she peered back out the window. The men approached the side of the train with the gurney.

Wide-eyed, blood flowing cold in her veins, she looked from them to the princess on the bed, and then the box beneath the bathroom floor, and back again. "They'll know she's not in it."

The weight would be a dead giveaway, and the second the men realised the princess wasn't in there, they'd come on board to grab her instead.

Ruth frantically looked about for something heavy to drop inside the box, but there was nothing. She was running out of time. The men were twenty feet away.

Ruth swore. "I can't believe I'm about to do this." She threw a blanket over the princess, covering her from head to toe, and then with extreme reluctance, Ruth climbed into the box and lay down.

Footfalls drew near.

Before she could change her mind, Ruth gritted her teeth, reached up and shut the lid, plunging her world into darkness.

Her cleithrophobia instantly clawed at every inch of her body and demanded Ruth throw the lid back open and climb out immediately.

Instead, she squeezed her eyes closed, clenched every muscle, and resisted the urge to scream. She felt as though she were suffocating, and her body trembled.

A few seconds went by, each one an eternity in the metal coffin. Blood pounded in Ruth's ears, and sweat blossomed on her forehead, but she still refused to move.

She lay there, trying to concentrate on her ragged breathing, and doing everything possible not to panic.

There came a loud clunk to her left. Something unbolted, and then something else swung clear with a creak.

Ruth's best guess was a hatch on the side of the train that now allowed direct access to the metal box.

Sure enough, the next second the box shook and shifted

sideways, then lifted into the air. It rocked one way, and then another, before it dropped onto what Ruth assumed was the medical gurney with a heavy thud.

She winced at the jolt of pain in her shoulders and back.

Next came a long silence.

Too long.

Ruth braced herself for the capture.

Have they realised the princess isn't in here? That someone else has taken her place? And more importantly, what will they do with me once they find out?

This abduction had clearly been a team effort, as the detective had described to Hugo, with a boss pulling the strings. But instead of smuggling illicit items up and down the country, the plan all along had been to kidnap Princess Mary.

Ruth's ears strained, but she could make out no frantic discussions or hurried whispers, so she kept as still as possible, her body stiff, eyes shut.

More footfalls crunched gravel. This time singular.

A man murmured something Ruth could barely make out. "Where is she?"

Ruth recognised that voice as Alan the relief train driver. She was right—he'd been in on it this whole time.

"Don't know," came a deep reply. "Shall we wait?"

"Not here. Stick to the plan."

And then the gurney, complete with box and Ruth, were in motion, rattling up an incline.

A minute later, her stomach lurched as the men lifted Ruth into the air and slid the box across a hard surface, the scrape of metal on metal sending shivers up her spine.

If they were going to open the box and check its contents, now was the moment, in the relative privacy of the van's interior, away from prying eyes.

Every muscle spasmed as Ruth waited.

To her immense surprise, the back doors slammed shut, and moments later the van's engine roared to life, and they were off, bumping along what felt like a dirt track.

Momentary relief gave way to panic.

Where are they taking me?

Ruth opened her eyes, only to be greeted by total darkness. She pictured herself lying on the floor in a spacious ballroom, in a giant castle, and not with the lid of the box an inch in front of her face.

She tried to focus on all possible scenarios when they would open the box and find their new acquisition.

Will they make me a nice cup of tea, serve biscuits, and then enquire as to how I came to be in the box?

Unlikely.

Will they kill me?

Quite possibly.

Especially seeing as they'd done away with Miles and attempted to murder a police detective. If they'd been happy to do that to an officer of the law, they wouldn't think twice about offing some random busybody food consultant. Even if she did offer up her world-famous Victoria sponge cake recipe in exchange for her life.

One thing was for sure, Ruth would not make it easy for them. She'd go out kicking and screaming, just like Merlin every time she tried to clip his nails or bathe him.

The van bumped and lurched to the right, off the dirt track, and then the wheels touched smooth tarmac—a paved road.

Where are they taking me? How far?

For a horrible moment, Ruth imagined the goons loading her onto a ship and sailing off to a remote island, never to see her loved ones again.

However, that scenario seemed extremely unlikely because the longer they moved her about, the greater the chance they'd get caught.

No, these guys must have a hideout nearby enough to keep their travel time to a minimum, but far enough for the police to not catch them during their initial sweep of the immediate area.

Of course, none of this was useful to Ruth because she had no idea where the train had stopped, how far they'd since travelled, nor what direction they now headed.

Midlands? Over the border to Wales? Northern England?

Ruth stifled a cry as something vibrated against her leg.

And then it dawned on her—*My phone.*

She touched her pocket, feeling the phone's bulk within, and then managed to edge to one side, pull it out, and choosing to ignore the fact the phone now illuminated the interior of her steel confines, Ruth slid the display in front of her face.

Thank goodness she had it on silent.

Ruth blinked and focussed on the words,

Sweetiepie Gregikins
CALLING

Ruth hit the answer button and pressed the phone to her ear.

"Grandma?"

"Gregory," Ruth said in barely a whisper. "I— I need you to listen to me very, very carefully."

"The train carriages stopped, and as soon as I jumped off, I got a phone signal. What were you playing at? You promised not to do anything reckless. You could've died."

"Greg. Please. You must—"

"Hold on," he said. "If you've got a signal too, where are you? Where's the train? Did it crash? Are you hurt?"

"I'm in a box," Ruth breathed.

A couple seconds' pause followed this proclamation.

"Huh?"

"The train pulled into a siding," Ruth said. "About five minutes farther up the track. Part of their plan. Tell the protection officers the princess is fine, but unconscious. She's in compartment 1A, in the bed, under a blanket." At least Ruth hoped she was still there. "They knocked Princess Mary out. Injected her with something. Send paramedics."

"Who knocked her out?" Greg asked in a strained voice. "What's going on?"

"Tell the officers they'll have to break down the door. I bolted it from the inside."

The van bumped over a pothole in the road, and Ruth winced as a sharp pain shot up her spine. "Alan the train driver and someone else are behind this," she whispered. "He's not been working alone. There's a team of goons."

Another few seconds' pause, and sirens wailed on the other end of the phone.

"Police are coming," Greg said.

"Good. They need to catch up to me. These people are taking me somewhere. Have the police come get me"

"Wh-Where?" Now Greg's voice shook. "Where are they taking you? H-How will I find you?"

Ruth ground her teeth. "A great question. Let me think."

"The police can track you," Greg said. "Your phone. Triangulate your signal from phone masts. I'll ask them."

"That will take too long to set up. By which time, the bad guys will have got away."

And probably finished her off.

"I told you to install that family tracking app," Greg said.

"And if I had your laptop, I could use the 'find phone' feature. Wait. I'll tell one of these officers what's happened."

Ruth listened to her grandson recounting the events, and then an idea struck her. "Hold on. Listen very carefully." She squeezed her eyes closed. "They took me from the right-hand side of the train, up a path to the top of a hill, where they then loaded me into the back of a van. We followed a dirt track for a few minutes."

"O-kay," Greg said. "The police will take me. I'm getting in a car." Doors opened and closed. "Farther down the road must be a siding, then top of the hill, and down a track. I can look that up on the map. Let me put you on speakerphone, Grandma."

There came the rumble of car engines and the crackle of gravel under tyres.

Ruth concentrated. "At the end of the dirt track we turned left—no, right. We turned right onto a normal road. Paved. Smooth."

"Yeah, I think I see," Greg said. "It's about a mile from here. We can get onto it sooner by turning down there . . . Yes, this road. Then where, Grandma?"

The van stopped.

It was too late.

"Greg," Ruth whispered. "Tell the police to keep everyone in the salon carriage. Don't let anyone off."

Doors opened.

"Why? The police are seeing to them."

"Because the murderer is still among them. You must radio—" The rear doors of the van opened, and Ruth slipped the phone back into her pocket without disconnecting the call.

A split second later, the box lid swung up, and Alan stared down at her in surprise.

Ruth blinked and forced a smile. "Hello." She sat up, took deep breaths, and looked about an empty warehouse. "Is—Is this Edinburgh Castle? I'm dying for a cuppa."

Alan grabbed her arm and snarled, "Where is she?"

"Princess Mary is nowhere near this dingy warehouse," Ruth said in a loud voice. She peered through the partly open warehouse doors, to a church beyond. "That's a lovely church on the other side of that field. Are we going to mass?" She hoped Greg could still hear, despite the phone being in her pocket. "Wow, what a big oak tree next to the church. Looks old. Where are we?"

The two goons lifted her from the box, set Ruth down, but held on to her with vicelike grips.

"What are we going to do with her?" one asked.

Alan glared at Ruth, then turned away. He removed a phone from his pocket, dialled, and then swore.

"Your boss is stuck on the train with no phone signal?" Ruth asked. "Let me guess, your own signal blockers are working against you?" When Alan turned back around, she added, "That's what you were doing in the tunnel, right? Fitting phone signal blockers to each carriage? Stopping anyone calling in or out after we left the tunnel?"

One of the men redoubled his grip on Ruth's arm, making her wince. "Well?" he said to Alan. "I'm not waiting here all day. Shall we stuff her back in the box and dump it in the nearest canal?"

"Don't worry," Alan shot back. "You'll get paid."

"What's the use of money in prison?"

"Think of all the commissary snacks you can purchase," Ruth said. "You'll be the envy of your cellmates."

"We'll carry on as planned and take her with us." Alan motioned for them to follow him.

"Where are we going now?" Ruth asked as they led her

to a side door. "Are we in a village? I guess if it has that big church with the spire, we must be, but which one?"

"If you don't put a sock in it," the goon snarled, "I'll tape your mouth shut."

The driver opened the side door, and the four of them strode toward a black car.

"Ooh, that's fancy," Ruth said. "What is it? BMW? Mercedes?" A bonnet ornament came into view. "A Jaguar. A black Jaguar. Very good choice. What year? Looks new." She tried to get a peek at the number plate, but the men pulled her back.

Alan stopped dead in his tracks, turned round, and glared at Ruth. He patted her down, and then thrust a hand into her pocket.

"Do you mind." She twisted away from him, but it was too late.

He held her phone up, ended the call, and threw it into the bushes. "We need to hurry. They're onto us."

The men shoved Ruth onto the back seat of the Jaguar, and a few seconds later the car was in motion. They sped down a lane, across a car park, and out onto a village high street.

Ruth looked about, but the roads were empty, plus she was sandwiched between the two goons, and there was no way to jump from the car. Besides, it didn't slow at the next junction and took a hard right, heading toward a motorway.

At least Greg is safe, Ruth told herself.

Half a mile up the road, the Jaguar turned onto a slip road but came to an abrupt halt. Ruth almost slammed into the seat in front of her.

A police car blocked the way ahead, lights flashing.

The driver threw the car into reverse and backed away,

only for another police vehicle to swing into the road behind them, blocking their retreat.

Up ahead, the car doors flew open, and two officers leapt out, barking orders.

Ruth looked back as several more police cars swung into the road, lights flashing, sirens blaring. From the front passenger seat of one of them Greg stared back at her.

She waved and slumped in the seat. "Good lad."

Ruth decided there and then to treat her grandson to a second, extra jumbo-sized bag of snacks, at their very earliest opportunity.

After all, he'd earned it.

23

After arresting Train Driver Alan and his helper goons, the police officers drove Ruth and Greg back to a hive of activity where the uncoupled train carriages had come to rest.

Several more police cars and vans, two ambulances, and a fire engine sat next to the track.

A female officer with dark hair opened the rear doors of the police car and escorted Ruth and Greg toward the mayhem.

Hugo rushed over. "Thank goodness you're okay." He hugged Ruth. "Princess Mary will be just fine." Hugo waved in the direction of one of the ambulances. "All thanks to you." He smiled at Greg. "Your grandmother saved the day."

Greg's eyebrows rose, as if he thought Hugo should've listened to his grandmother sooner, but he kept his mouth shut.

Ruth's gaze shifted to the ambulance. Sure enough, the princess sat propped up on a gurney inside, while paramedics tended to her. She appeared woozy, obviously disorientated, but otherwise healthy.

Her relieved-looking protection officers stood guard, flanking the doors. Ruth didn't envy them, as they'd have lengthy reports to write for their superiors.

"What about Daniel?" she asked as the other ambulance drove away. "He's in that one? Will he be all right?"

"Detective White has suffered a serious head trauma. We'll know the full outcome in the next couple of days."

Ruth balled her fists. "Time to unmask our death dealer."

"You know who orchestrated this?" Hugo asked.

"I do. And I should've figured it out a long time ago." Perhaps she might have avoided the princess's unnecessary trauma. Ruth looked to her police officer companion. "Can you escort us to the salon carriage, please?" She didn't think anyone would try to harm them with so many people about, but on the other hand, Ruth did not want to take any more chances.

Her risk-taking quota for the month was filled to bursting.

The officer opened her mouth but quickly closed it again.

Detective Inspector Kirby, scowl etched onto his face, marched toward them with other police officers in tow. "Ruth Morgan, you're under arrest."

"I say." Hugo stepped in front of her. "What is this?"

"Out of my way." Kirby shoved Hugo aside and gestured for one of his men to cuff Ruth. "You do not have to say anything unless you—"

"Are you insane?" Greg interrupted.

Kirby's lip curled. "She's the mastermind. The culprit was clearly close to Mr Finsbury. It all adds up."

"Everyone on that train was close to Hugo," Greg snapped. "So your adding skills need work."

Ruth waved him down before he got arrested too.

"Sir." The female officer stepped forward. "We have suspects in custody. Sergeant Billingham is securing the site, and we have also accessed the GPS in their car. A team are on their way to another site outside Glasgow. We believe that to be the main hideout."

Or their intended place to keep the princess captive until ransom demands were met, Ruth thought.

Kirby waved the officer away and glared at Ruth.

"My arrest is unnecessary," she said. "I'd be more than happy to explain everything. Tell you all I know." Ruth pointed to the salon carriage, where the guests were seated. "Shall we? It will put your mind at rest, save you a lot of paperwork, and bring this ugly affair to a swift conclusion."

"I want an official statement," Inspector Kirby growled. "Not games." He thrust a finger at a police car. "Back at the station."

"How about both?" Ruth kept her voice level. "I think everyone on board would like to hear why they've been put through this ordeal." She glanced at Hugo. "Besides, there's still a killer among them, and you have no clue who they are. What's your plan? Arrest everyone until you pick apart the events and uncover the culprit? Wouldn't you rather drastically reduce your time on this case?" Ruth held her breath as she awaited his response.

Kirby hesitated for a moment, then motioned to the carriage. "We have thirty minutes before the rail company comes to shift these out of the way." He then gestured for several of his officers to follow.

Ruth signalled for Greg to join her too, before Kirby changed his mind.

As they strode toward the carriage, Greg breathed in her ear, "You're enjoying this, aren't you?"

She beamed.

Someone had placed an upturned crate in front of the carriage step, so there was no need for Ruth to ask her grandson to hoist her this time.

When she entered the salon, silence and worried faces greeted her. Everyone was here: Jane and Robert Minchent, Lord and Lady Hamilton, Victoria, Waylon, Carlos and Boyd, plus Angus the night porter and the remaining staff members.

"Good afternoon, ladies and gentlemen," Ruth said in a loud, clear voice. She winked at Greg and murmured, "I've always wanted to say that."

He rolled his eyes and sat.

Inspector Kirby didn't look amused. He folded his arms and remained by the door.

Ruth cleared her throat. "As you all know, there was a tragic murder on board the Finsbury Flyer. And today, another one attempted." She clasped her hands behind her back and paced in front of her audience as she spoke. "Someone killed Miles, and at first it wasn't apparent who." She took a breath as the events slotted into place. "When I arrived in Edinburgh, Miles was angry because he felt Hugo was not listening to his safety concerns."

"That's not true," Hugo said. "The man was paranoid."

Ruth shook her head. "Maybe not." She continued her slow pace. "Someone made changes to his original designs. I now think Miles took pictures of the other first-class double-sleeper carriage surreptitiously. The one originally at Finsbury Village. As it was being constructed."

Hugo scowled. "Miles' involvement was supposed to be over. His work was done, and I told him so. He had no business being there."

Ruth stopped pacing and fixed him with a hard look.

"Good job he did continue, otherwise we wouldn't know what we do now."

"And what's that?" Lord Hamilton asked with a puzzled expression.

Ruth shifted from one foot to the other as she gathered her thoughts. "After Miles' death, the killer was free to set up a distraction in the form of a train robbery. They led me on a wild goose chase, which I fell for." She sighed. "All in an attempt to distract me from the killer's real objective."

"To abduct the princess," Waylon said.

Ruth nodded. "I suspect Daniel had got close to uncovering the plan, so the killer—"

"Bashed him over the head," Lord Hamilton finished.

Lady Hamilton winced.

Ruth resumed pacing. "Another unforeseen setback was the fact Miles left behind plenty of clues in the form of photographs and blueprints."

"Blueprints?" A puzzled expression swept across Lord Hamilton's face again. "For this train?" He looked over at Hugo. "What on earth is going on, old chap?"

"To be more precise," Ruth continued, "Miles focussed on a few key elements." She held up a finger. "First was his concern regarding the carriage couplers."

"What's a coupler?" Jane Minchent asked in a small voice, her gaze lowered.

"The mechanism that connects carriages." Robert rested a hand on her leg and kept his unwavering focus on Ruth.

"They passed inspection." Hugo eyed a bottle of whiskey on a nearby shelf. "Several times throughout the build, and the subsequent test runs."

"Someone modified at least two of the couplers to appear normal," Ruth said, "when in fact they could be released manually and while the train was in motion." She looked over at Inspector Kirby. "The blueprints and photographs are still in the original carriage and will back up what I'm saying."

"Surely Miles brought these concerns to your attention," Lord Hamilton said to Hugo with incredulity.

Hugo gave a solemn nod.

"Well, damn it all, man." Lord Hamilton glared at him. "Why didn't you act?"

"I did," Hugo said. "The engineers found nothing out of the ordinary." He slumped onto a stool at the bar, deflated.

Ruth nodded to Inspector Kirby as he pulled a notepad and pen from his pocket. "You'll find several of the engineers are also on the payroll."

"Whose payroll?" Angus asked with a look of confusion.

"The killer's, of course," Lady Hamilton said with an impatient wave. "Go on, Ruth."

"Also among the design modifications Miles highlighted was a secret compartment that could be used to smuggle the princess. It's a box built beneath the replacement first-class double sleeper, on extendable rails able to traverse the gap and slide under the royal carriage." Ruth scanned their faces. "A deliberate addition in order for someone to slip into it unseen and take the princess by surprise."

"Who?" Robert Minchent asked with impatience.

Ruth held up a hand and resumed pacing. "Prior to that, the killer knew a murder would force the first-class carriages to be swapped out at Finsbury Village." She pictured the moment the train driver had convinced Hugo to do so. "A normal carriage for a modified one that would not pass inspections under normal circumstances." Ruth took a breath. "That same modified carriage is the one Miles photographed during its construction."

"Hold on, hold on." Lord Hamilton cleared his throat. "If

Miles knew about these changes to the carriages, and he brought his concerns to Hugo, then why on earth didn't Hugo act?"

Hugo stared at the floor.

"Because Daniel Price, AKA Detective White, told him not to," Ruth said. "Is that correct?"

"Detective?" Lady Hamilton's eyebrows shot up.

"The police believed it was a smuggling operation." Hugo let out a long breath. "They wanted to catch the gang in the act."

"Back in Edinburgh," Ruth continued, "the killer overheard I used to be a police officer, and they chose to turn that in their favour, knowing I'd also likely investigate any strange happenings."

Greg cleared his throat and muttered something about being reckless and nosey.

Ruth scanned the gathered passengers.

Waylon avoided eye contact, and Victoria shifted in her seat.

"I don't believe Miles was murdered because someone had it in for him." Ruth took a breath and resumed pacing. "But because the killer already knew he'd been snooping about, so he became their target, and they sent him a message."

Hugo looked up. "What message?"

Ruth cleared her throat. "It said, 'Hugo is lying. Come to the station immediately.' A ploy to get Miles here."

Hugo's expression turned more downcast. "I invited him onboard."

"He would've insisted anyway," Ruth said. "The killer needed an excuse to swap out carriages, so they used the opportunity to murder Miles. Two birds with one stone."

Hugo buried his face in his hands.

"Zoey gave a false confession, though." Robert Minchent's gaze shifted to Victoria, and he gripped the arms of his chair. "Why on earth would she do that? She's in on it?"

Victoria held on to her cane and remained tight-lipped.

"Someone wanted me to know early on that Zoey wasn't the real killer." Ruth leaned down to Greg and whispered instructions in his ear.

He blinked up at her for a few seconds and then stood and hurried off.

Ruth continued, "Detective White knew something was afoot, and that's why he made up a reason to bang on Miles' door this morning."

"Hold on," Lady Hamilton said. "He accused Miles of stealing his watch."

"There never was a watch," Robert murmured.

"Daniel— I mean, the detective, was drunk," Jane said.

"The killer figured out a real detective was on board," Ruth said. "He wasn't drunk, but drugged."

"Drugged?" Lady Hamilton's eyebrows rose. "Who'd do that?"

"Zoey." When only confused silence greeted this proclamation, Ruth added, "Zoey slipped Daniel something last night, and when he came to in the early hours of the morning, he realised what had happened to him. Zoey used the same drugs on Miles, to make him an easy target. She only needed time for the pills to work." Ruth resumed her slow pace.

"And no better way to slip him those pills than during a game of poker," Robert Minchent murmured.

Jane stared at the floor, wringing her fingers.

"That's why Miles kept winning?" Lord Hamilton almost looked relieved it hadn't been down to his bad luck. "To keep him there, so Zoey could drug the poor man?"

"I believe Zoey tried on a previous occasion," Ruth said. "During our champagne toast before dinner. However, Miles wound up with the wrong glass." Her attention moved to Waylon.

His face dropped. "I was ill."

"You'll need a blood test to be sure," Ruth said. "Zoey failed the first time, got you instead, and then had to try again later during the improvised poker game. Her original target was Miles, but when she figured out Daniel was an undercover detective, she saw an opportunity to take them both out. Must have given them a lot more than you received."

Greg returned, set a black toiletry bag on a nearby table, and sat back down.

Lady Hamilton raised a hand. "Are you telling us Zoey drugged the men but didn't kill anyone? Then who did?"

"Precisely," Lord Hamilton said. "And why on earth did she confess?"

"She was either paid a lot of money to do so, or the killer may have blackmailed her in some way." Ruth's gaze shifted across the room. "Isn't that right, Victoria?"

All eyes moved to her, and silence fell over the carriage.

However, Lord Hamilton leapt to his feet. "You? You're behind this?"

Inspector Kirby waved him down.

Lord Hamilton hesitated and then lowered himself back to the chair. "I can't believe it."

"These are unfounded accusations," Victoria said with a disgusted expression. "Pure fantasy. You have no proof I'm involved in anything."

"I wouldn't be so sure." Ruth gathered her thoughts and

continued. "You made it so Zoey's door squeaked, knowing I'd hear." She looked at the others. "Zoey moved about several times last night so I'd notice." She refocussed on Victoria. "Thus, the lack of noise at the time of Miles' murder meant Zoey had a tenuous alibi, but an alibi nonetheless, and therefore her confession to the murder was void."

"I don't follow." Lord Hamilton's brow furrowed. "What's your point?"

Ruth was about to answer when something else clicked into place. "The CCTV." She looked at Hugo. "When I logged in to see how Merlin was doing, there was a date and timestamp in the corner. A similar one was on your CCTV app, meaning it hadn't stopped recording at the time of the murder, but someone had turned out the lights."

"They messed with the electrics," Greg said. "Turning out the lights meant Victoria could move about without the cameras seeing her."

Ruth then remembered the detective's photos of a train layout made from cardboard and wood. She murmured, "Of course." Her gaze shifted back to Victoria. "You had your goons build a mock layout so you could familiarise yourself." Ruth brought up the images of the wooden and cardboard train carriage interiors on her phone and handed them to Inspector Kirby. She then returned to Victoria. "You visited Miles in the small hours of the morning, taking advantage of his drugged state. You gave him cause to turn away, Victoria, perhaps to place money in the drawer or retrieve something, and that's when you struck." Ruth composed herself. "Using your cane to locate his head with your left, you hit him with the other." She pictured the red mark on Miles' cheek—a similar mark on Daniel's too, left by Victoria's cane as she located their heads in three-dimensional space so she could strike with accuracy.

Victoria now scowled. "It's all nonsense."

Ruth pulled on a set of gloves and picked up the toiletry bag. She unzipped it and took out a nail file with the tip missing. "This is what Victoria used to make the door squeak," she said to Inspector Kirby. Next, Ruth pulled out a deck of cards.

"I found those on the desk," Greg said.

Ruth had asked him to gather the items from Victoria's compartment. She held the cards up to the light, detecting raised dots in the middle. "As I suspected, these playing cards are marked." Last, Ruth lifted out a bottle. "Here we are. Pills used to drug our fellow passengers." She rattled them. "Definitive proof Victoria was involved."

"Zoey planted those," Victoria snapped. "They have nothing to do with me. You're grasping at straws."

Ruth returned them to the bag, knowing forensic evidence would suggest otherwise.

"What about the murder weapon?" Detective Kirby asked as Ruth placed the toiletry bag on a table next to him.

She pursed her lips. "Best guess is the table lamps from her compartments. They're secured in a few places, but I suspect you'll find evidence Victoria unbolted them somehow, then returned the lamps on both occasions to their original positions."

That was another job for forensics.

"Why did you attempt to murder Daniel?" Robert Minchent stared at Victoria. "Why take the risk and draw attention?"

Ruth took a deep breath. "The setback at the time was everyone insisting they return to their compartments. Victoria hadn't foreseen that issue." She walked back to her.

"Isn't that right? You wanted to be in the first-class double sleeper on your own, then unhitch the rest of the train with us all in the back section, including the princess's protection officers."

"You did this for a ransom?" Lord Hamilton asked. "I thought you had money."

"The jewels are likely fake," Ruth said. "A diversion to be left in the safe."

Victoria sneered. "You have no proof any of this happened. You're making it up. Nothing but a self-righteous busybody b—"

"You are under arrest." Inspector Kirby pulled a set of handcuffs from his jacket pocket and walked toward her.

"Don't you dare touch me." She swung with her cane, narrowly missing Ruth.

Two officers darted across the carriage and restrained Victoria.

She struggled in her seat. "Get off me. It's her. Don't you see that? She's playing you for fools. She's the killer."

As the officers helped Victoria to her feet, Kirby recited the police caution.

Ruth took Hugo aside and whispered, "You recorded your conversations? Why? Does it have something to do with inviting Victoria in the first place? She's part of the gang you mentioned?"

Hugo watched the police officers escort her from the carriage, plus the other passengers and crew filing out after them. "In order to claw back from the brink of bankruptcy, I needed to go all in and convince Princess Mary to come along on this inaugural trip."

Greg joined them. "But that meant building a royal carriage."

Hugo nodded slowly. "Victoria came as a recommendation from one of the mechanics. She agreed to add her own finances. Nowhere near as much as I'm sure Princess Mary's ransom would have fetched, but enough to get the job completed." He took a breath. "In exchange, Victoria employed some of her people to help speed up construction." Hugo looked imploringly at Ruth. "But had I known what she was really up to . . ."

She rested a hand on his shoulder. "You were desperate."

Hugo's expression darkened. "Victoria insisted she come along on this maiden voyage. At the time, I had no idea she'd made those modifications. I thought Miles was paranoid. I'll never forgive myself for not standing up for Miles. It's my fault he's dead."

Ruth released him. "You didn't kill him, Hugo."

"I have a lot to answer for." Head bowed, Hugo left.

Ruth stood there for a few moments, composing her thoughts, and then she motioned for Greg to follow her out.

As they walked from the carriage toward the gathered police cars, she went over the events in her mind, and where she'd gone wrong. She should have been more insistent with Hugo in the beginning, and not rushed into danger.

Next time, if there was a next time, Ruth would trust her instincts and take greater care before leaping headfirst.

She glanced at Greg sending a text. "That reminds me, I need a new phone."

"Another one?" Greg said. "Why? What happened to yours?"

Sheepish, Ruth smiled. "Bad guys threw it away."

Greg shook his head. "I told you to activate—"

"Yeah, yeah," Ruth said. "Activate the tracking thingy. Then I could find it." She sighed. "But you would not have had so much fun coming after me, would you?" Ruth stopped. "Wait. Let me check something." She circled the carriages and peered down the other side.

Greg followed her. "What are we looking at?"

Ruth pointed to several hockey-puck-sized devices fixed along the carriages at regular intervals. "Phone signal blockers."

"That train driver fitted them once we'd stopped inside the tunnel?" Greg's phone rang, making them both jump, and he answered. "Hey. Yeah, okay." He extended the phone to Ruth.

As she headed back toward the waiting police cars, she looked at the phone's display:

Mum
CALLING

Ruth cringed, cupped her hand over the microphone, and whispered to Greg, "What have you told her?"

He shrugged. "Only some of it. She was worried I hadn't replied to her texts. Couldn't avoid her all day. You know what she's like."

Sara, Ruth's daughter, Greg's mother, wasn't exactly renowned for being calm when it came to Greg or his sister's safety and well-being.

Shoulders hitched, Ruth pressed the phone to her ear. "Hey, sweetie, how are—?"

The next few minutes felt like hours.

When Sara had finally finished berating her, all Ruth could manage was a weak "Sorry," along with a promise to not be so reckless, especially with her grandson in tow.

By the time Ruth hung up, her ears were ringing. "Guess I deserved that." She handed the phone back to Greg. "Come on. We need to give our statements at the station and then collect Merlin. After that, we have a long drive ahead of us."

"Where are we going?"

"Back to Finsbury Village." Ruth marched toward the police cars. "If you think I'm leaving Mrs Beeton back there, you're sorely mistaken."

Thank you for reading! If you've not yet read the Ruth Morgan series prequel:
MURDER ON THE OCEAN ODYSSEY
OUT NOW

We would be incredibly grateful if you could leave a star rating or review. Your invaluable support is vital to the Ruth Morgan Mystery Series' success and can make all the difference.

To be notified of FUTURE RELEASES in the Ruth Morgan series, click on the author name "Peter Jay Black" at Amazon (on any of Peter's book pages), and then "Follow" in the top left. OR Visit peterjayblack.com and join the free VIP list.

Also grab a FREE copy of
DEATH IN BROOKLYN
A Short Story set in the Fast-Paced Emma & Nightshade Crime Thriller Series.

IMPORTANT
Please remember to check your spam folder for any emails. You must confirm your sign-up before being added to the email list.

PETER JAY BLACK
BIBLIOGRAPHY

DEATH IN LONDON
Book One in a Fast-Paced Crime Thriller Series
https://mybook.to/DeathinLondonKindle

Emma leads a quiet life, away from her divorced parents' business interests, but when her father's fiancée turns up dead in her mother's warehouse, she can't ignore the threat of a civil war.

Unable to call the police, Emma's parents ask her to assist an eccentric private detective with the investigation. She reluctantly agrees, on the condition that when she's done they allow her to have her own life in America, away from the turmoil.

The amateur sleuths investigate the murder, and piece together a series of cryptic clues left by the killer, who seems to know the families intimately, but a mistake leads to the slaying of another close relative.

Now dragged into a world she's fought hard to avoid, Emma must do everything she can to help catch the culprit and restore peace. However, with time running out, could her parents be the next victims?

"Pick up Death in London today and start book one in a gripping Crime Thriller Mystery series."

***

DEATH IN MANHATTAN
Book One in a Fast-Paced Crime Thriller Series
https://mybook.to/DeathinManhattanKindle

When someone murders New York's leading crime boss, despite him being surrounded by advanced security, the event throws the underworld into chaos. Before anyone can figure out how the killer did it, he dies under mysterious circumstances and takes his secret to the grave.

Emma's uncle asks her to check out the crime scene, but she's reluctant to get involved, especially after the traumatic events back in London. However, with Nightshade's unique brand of encouragement, they figure out how the killer reached one of the most protected men in the world. Their lives are then complicated further when another member of the Syndicate is murdered, seemingly by the hands of the same deceased perpetrator.

Emma and Nightshade now find themselves in way over their heads, caught up in a race against time, trying to solve clues and expose a web of deception, but will they be quick enough to stop a war?

URBAN OUTLAWS
A High-Octane Middle Grade Action Series
<u>mybook.to/UrbanOutlaws</u>

In a bunker hidden deep beneath London live five extraordinary kids: meet world-famous hacker Jack, gadget geek Charlie, free runner Slink, comms chief Obi, and decoy diva Wren. They're not just friends; they're URBAN OUTLAWS. They outsmart London's crime gangs and hand out their dirty money through Random Acts of Kindness (R.A.K.s).

Others in the series:
URBAN OUTLAWS: BLACKOUT
<u>mybook.to/UOBlackout</u>

Power is out. Security is down. Computers hacked. The world's most destructive computer virus is out of control and the pressure is on for the Urban Outlaws to destroy it. Jack knows that it's not just the world's secrets that could end up in the wrong hands. The secret location of their bunker is at the fingertips of many and the identities of the Urban Outlaws are up for grabs. But capturing the virus feels like an almost impossible mission until they meet Hector. The Urban Outlaws know they need his help, but they have made some dangerous enemies. They could take a risk and win – or lose everything ...

URBAN OUTLAWS: LOCKDOWN
mybook.to/UOLockdown

he Urban Outlaws have been betrayed – and defeated. Or so Hector thought when he stole the world's most advanced computer virus. But Hector will need to try much harder than just crossing the Atlantic if he wants to outsmart Jack and his team ...

URBAN OUTLAWS: COUNTERSTRIKE
mybook.to/UOCounterstrike

The Urban Outlaws face their biggest challenge yet. They have to break into the Facility and find the ultimate weapon – Medusa – before Hector does. But there are five levels of security to crack and a mystery room that has Jack sweating whenever he thinks about it.

URBAN OUTLAWS: SHOCKWAVE
mybook.to/UOShockwave

The Urban Outlaws have been infected! Hector Del Sarto used them to spread the deadly Medusa virus and now the whole of London is in lockdown. Only Hector and his father have the antidote. Can Jack, Charlie, Obi, Slink and Wren work together to bring down the Del Sartos once and for all? The whole city depends on them!

GAME SPACE
Kids' Space Adventure
Jumanji Meets The Last Starfighter
mybook.to/GameSpace

Trapped Inside Alien Game. SEND HELP!

When Leo moves to Colorado, he uncovers a crashed UFO with an alien game on board. Forty years ago his grandmother fell into the virtual world and vanished.

Now determined to solve the mystery, Leo goes inside, believing he'll captain a spaceship and bring her home, but he finds himself surrounded by a decimated fleet and in real danger.

To survive, Leo must adapt quickly, win over new friends, and blend in. That won't be easy because one of them is deeply suspicious of him. Leo faces impossible challenges where the smallest misstep could mean losing his family, and his life.

STAR QUEST
(Game Space Book Two)
Gone Back Inside Alien Game. NEED HELP!
mybook.to/GS2StarQuest

Leo finishes writing about his previous space adventure and is ready to return to the game world. Once there, he'll complete a secret mission and convince his grandmother to finally come home. However, Grandpa John goes inside alone, and when he doesn't return in an instant, Leo knows something has gone horribly wrong.

ARCADIA
A Game Space FastRead
Kids' Space Adventure
mybook.to/ArcadiA

When her brother falls into the secret world of an alien arcade game, mystery-obsessed Kira must go in and rescue him. However, a simple task turns complicated as she finds herself in a universe filled with aliens, diverse creatures, and puzzles to solve.

In order to save her brother and the people of ArcadiA, Kira must make new friends, face her fears, and confront enemies, but time is running out.

ArcadiA is set in the Game Space universe, with new characters and locations.

**Print Length is approximately 97 pages (23k words) + Game Space sample chapters.

peterjayblack.com

Printed in Great Britain
by Amazon